William James Dawson

The Threshold of Manhood

a young man's words to young men

William James Dawson

The Threshold of Manhood
a young man's words to young men

ISBN/EAN: 9783337369408

Printed in Europe, USA, Canada, Australia, Japan

Cover: Foto ©Andreas Hilbeck / pixelio.de

More available books at **www.hansebooks.com**

THE

THRESHOLD OF MANHOOD.

A YOUNG MAN'S WORDS TO YOUNG MEN.

BY

W. J. DAWSON,

AUTHOR OF "A VISION OF SOULS; WITH OTHER BALLADS AND POEMS,"
"QUEST AND VISION: ESSAYS IN LIFE AND LITERATURE," ETC.

NEW YORK:

A. C. ARMSTRONG AND SON,

714, BROADWAY.

PREFACE.

THE sermons in this volume, with one or two exceptions, have been especially addressed to young
men. For five years, while resident in London, and
particularly in the latter portion of that time, my
ministry gave me special contact with young men, and
my previous sympathies were greatly quickened by
the closer knowledge I then gained of the temptations,
struggles, and needs of city youth. I found that
wherever there was any honest attempt made to deal
with their intellectual difficulties, and wherever there
was manifested an understanding sympathy of their
social needs, there was a frank and even affectionate
response accorded. The life of a young man in a
great city is often one of the loneliest of lives. He
has comrades, but few friends ; many companions, but
scarcely one counsellor. He has left the safe anchor-
age of home, and is often half-intoxicated with the
sense of his unrestrained liberty. At the most critical
and susceptible period of life he is most solitary, most
left to himself, and least guarded against the seductions
of impure delight. This period of life is the Threshold
of Manhood.

The two things most needed at such a time are the friendly aid of a thoroughly honest and manly piety, and, if possible, the social rallying-point of Christian club or home life. It is a question which religious households in great cities should discuss, whether it is not their bounden duty to open their doors freely to this crowd of young strangers who surround them; for to be cut off from the society of good women in the early stage of manhood is an unspeakable misfortune. It is a yet more urgent question whether the Churches should not provide in every city social centres for young manhood. I do not mean one or two huge institutions such as we now possess. I mean numerous homes and clubs, where young men coming up in search of situations could find help, welcome, and accommodation, and where after business hours they could gather in genial social intercourse. Some social stimulant the young nature craves, and must have. If the Churches do not provide it, the music-hall will.

I make no apology for the nature of these addresses. They retain the form of spoken counsels and appeals. Except by the occasional alteration of a phrase I have not attempted to recast them into a more literary mould. I simply seek by their publication a yet larger congregation than any I have talked with face to face.

W. J. DAWSON.

GLASGOW, 1889.

CONTENTS.

I.

PAGE

DECISION I

II.

A YOUNG MAN'S DIFFICULTIES 20

III.

ON IMPULSE AND OPPORTUNITY 41

IV.

THE TESTIMONY OF FACT 62

V.

WHAT IT IS THAT ENDURES 83

VI.

PURITY 102

VII.

THE SIN OF ESAU 120

VIII.

PAGE

SINS OF SILENCE 141

IX.

THE CHARACTER OF JUDAS 160

X.

JOB ON PESSIMISM 182

XI.

NATHAN AND DAVID 198

XII.

THE IMPOTENCE OF REVOLT AGAINST THE TRUTH . 214

XIII.

THE FATHERHOOD OF GOD 236

XIV.

THE USE OF MYSTERY 256

I.

DECISION.

"How long halt ye between two opinions? If the Lord be God follow Him : but if Baal, then follow him. And the people answered him not a word."—I KINGS xviii. 21.

THIS scene is one of the most memorable and striking in history. It represents one of those great culminating points when life suddenly becomes dramatic, when, as it were, the confused groups of men and women on the stage of life suddenly shift themselves into place and position, and the curtain rises on the acts of great tragedy. Such culminations occur also in the individual life, when the still river of our days deepens, and rushes on in loud thunder, and all our scattered energies become concentrated in one vast struggle. In such moments life is felt to be infinitely significant, and we know that it fulfils itself in the open eye of the angel-crowded heavens. In such moments the character of coming centuries is determined, and individual destiny is sealed and fixed.

What, then, are the elements which constitute this great scene ? First of all, you look upon the vision of a whole nation gone astray, blinded by sensuality, swept into the swift hells of a privileged licentiousness.

I

The doctrine of philosophic historians to-day is that
certain nations have been raised up to perform certain
missions, and perhaps on no other hypothesis can the
mystery of the dispersal of the human family so well
find solution.   The mission of the Jewish nation was
to enforce belief in the one spiritual and invisible
Jehovah, King of kings and Lord of lords.   Amid the
vile and endless degradations of universal idolatry,
they kept the light of a pure theocracy burning; and
the Jew has done more for the world by his piety
than the Greek by his culture, or the Roman by his
civilisation.   But ever and again in Jewish history
there came times when a black mist of all but universal
apostasy fell upon the land, and quenched the light
upon its altars, and filled the temples with a desolating
gloom.   Such a time had now come.   A corrupt court
had produced a corrupt people; and every bond of
morality, of patriotism, of spirituality, was strained or
broken.   One man only, and he a wild man of the
desert, remained faithful, and set himself with magnificent valour against king, and court, and people.   Far
away from the false and fevered life of cities, he worshipped where the stars shone like the altar-lights of
heaven, where the free air blew, and the healing silence
taught serenity.   He knew that Jehovah was God, for
His voice had reached him in the thunder, and the
whirlwind, and the fire.   He knew that, gild an idol
how you will, it is an idol still, and has eyes that
cannot see and mouth that is a carven dumbness.
He knew another thing: that this invisible Jehovah

demanded truth to the innermost convictions at all costs; so he built upon the granite of his own individuality, and dared to be original when originality meant death. He was, in a word, a strong man, "in whom the light of hope burned when it had gone out in others;" and such men, the Elijahs and the Daniels, the Luthers and the Knoxes, though they be discarded prophets and derided martyrs, are the saviours of the people who spit upon and mock them, and the glory of the lands which spill their blood in sacrifice.

How the pulse quickens as we read the story! In his splendid isolation stands this one man against king, court, and nation. For three years he has been a hunted fugitive; for three years Jezebel has enjoyed her wicked triumph; but this one man is unsubdued and unsubduable. At last he comes forth from his desert, and he comes like a thunderbolt. He bars the way of the king's chariot with a gesture, and silences him with one stern accusation: "Thou and thy father's house have made Israel to sin!" Never was the fearlessness of right so splendidly illustrated, or the impotence of evil so conclusively exposed. The hunter is dumb before his prey; the tyrant quails before his victim. There is a royalty in righteousness before which all other royalty is but tinsel; there is a supremacy in goodness which strikes the wicked dumb. Are you armed with that supremacy? Dare you stand fearless in the right though the heavens fall? Only then is a man invulnerable. No one can defeat a man who is in the right. He may be a wild man of the desert and stand in tattered garb, but the chariots of wrong stop at his signal, and kings fear his face. When Elijah says, "Call all Israel together to Carmel," Ahab knows he must obey. So to Carmel Israel is gathered; there the broken altars are rebuilt, and there the pregnant question of my text is put to the vast multitude, who at last, when the fire of God descends, cry in fearful acquiescence not less than profound conviction, "The Lord, He is the God! The Lord, He is the God!"

Now, the question of my text is as modern as if it had only been uttered yesterday; and I propose to consider the abiding elements of this subject. The transient elements peculiar to the age and people we may dismiss. What is the modern Baal set up in contrast with God? What are the issues of choice which confront us to-day?

First of all, it is the contrast between the rectitude of a noble character and the impotence of characters in a state of moral disintegration; it is the contrast between *righteousness and unrighteousness.* Ask for a moment, What was Israel in its best and noblest days? It was a people permeated with the love of righteousness. The only King was God. His unalterable glory was symbolised in the awful splendour of the Shechinah, His presence in the pillar and the cloud, the famine and the fire. He watched His people and rewarded them; He punished and pursued; He blessed and He blasted; He sent them hornets and angels. Go where they would, God always confronted them, and could as little be escaped as the heavens which closed them round or the air from which they drew their life. What He demanded was " truth in the inward parts," righteousness as the soul of public life, the very pulse of daily conduct. Accordingly, every law of Israel was framed to this end. Its land-laws were equitable and just. Its laws for personal conduct crushed vice as with an iron foot, and built up the sanctity of the home and the chastity of the individual. The poor were covered as with the wing of God, and the orphaned and widowed became every man's care. Covetousness and avarice were penal offences, and the sense of God was made so supreme in the national conscience that every man felt God near him as the awful Witness of his life and the swift Avenger of his wrong-doing. Such a people in the hour of battle could not but be supreme ; they moved like the glittering sword of God among the demoralised heathen peoples ; they were the Ironsides of ancient times ; and before their faith, their enthusiasm, their moral energy, the greatest heathen peoples succumbed, and the fairest portions of the earth became their heritage.

Ask what Baal meant to such a people, and the angry voices of Hebrew saint and prophet answer you in many a grim page of history or burning chapter of denunciation. Baal meant the vice, the licentiousness, the moral corruption, which Israel had been raised up to destroy—an obscured vision of God, a debased moral sense, the utter loss of faith and spirituality. And Baal means just the same thing to-day. Look around, and see how far righteousness is the common law of human life. Think of the crowd of men who have no vision of God, because they have thrown down His altars, and follow the fatal feet of Mammon, men whose haste is to be rich, and not to walk in God's ways, whose fear is to be ill-fed, and not to do evil, whose hope is not to gain the imperishable inheritance of character, but some perishable spoil snatched from the sordid banquet of this world's pleasures. It matters little to them that once there was a Cross upon the earth, that still it gleams on city dome and spire, or that others have laid down their lives to win them liberty and faith ; they live only for themselves. They talk loudly of their duty to themselves, and ignore their responsibilities to others ; and for them the Cross is but a legend, and its sacrifice a sacred myth. They do not ask, "Is it right?" but "Will it pay?" and to the "*Thou God seest me,*" which has been the secret of a thousand noble lives, their insolent rejoinder is, "Does God indeed know? He sleeps, or He is journeying. Let us eat, drink, and be merry, for to-morrow we die!" And so, because the noblest of all thoughts has passed out of their lives, the whole function of thought is vitiated, and the moral nature emasculated. To "get on" and to get pleasure, to escape the rough places of life, to live out of reach of its miseries and out of hearing of its voices of lamentation and appeal, is their all-sufficing aim ; and in following it they forget the living God, and serve that Baal who is the prince of the power of the air, the evil spirit, the mocker and derider, who was a liar from the beginning, and the relentless murderer of every pure ambition and unselfish impulse which can animate and deify the life of man. Righteousness : it stands embodied in this man, pure, strong, valiant, mightier than kings, invincible because consecrated to the service of the most high God. Unrighteousness : that, too, is embodied in a weak king seduced by an evil woman, in a people who have thrown off the fear of God, who rise up to play and lie down to dream, dazzled by a golden idol and emasculated by its sensual rites. It is the spectacle which every century presents to the youth who stands upon its thresholds and prepares to use the gift of years which God has given him ; and from the slopes of Carmel the thunder of that valiant voice rolls across the wastes and voids of time, where the bones of nations which have forgotten God lie piled in tragic warning : " How long halt ye between two opinions ? "

It is, again, the contrast between *purity and sensuality.* It was the sensual pollutions of Baal which awoke the most terrible denunciations of the Hebrew prophets, and sensuality is one of the first results of a life which has lost righteousness of thought. Do not mistake me. I do not say that impurity is the certain or inevitable result of loss of faith ; but I do say that the man who loses righteousness of thought at least challenges the demon of sensuality to enter in and possess him. Shall I draw a modern sketch of what this aspect of Baalism means ? It is a task I would thankfully evade, but it is a duty from which the minister of Christ dare not be recreant. It is a story with which every student of modern life is only too familiar, and it is written on a thousand broken hearts and miserable lives. Here is a youth reared in the ordered quiet of some country home, familiar with its domestic sanctities, its household affections and pieties. At length he leaves the home where the fragrance of prayer and love has sweetened daily life, and enters the great city; and then the spell of Baal begins to fall on him. He hears in the office, the warehouse, the shop, stories at which he blushes, but which he will soon learn eagerly to devour without blushing. The moral sensitiveness becomes deadened, and the influence of comradeship begins to tell. Through the ear-gate the enemy enters in, and soon the citadel is captured. One by one his small habitual pieties disappear ; the Testament his mother gave him lies unused ; the habit of prayer is dropped, for perhaps he shares a room with one who does not pray, and how difficult it is to pray then I know full well, for I have had to do it. In a few weeks the work is done ; the boy's pure imagination is polluted, the boy's blood begins to riot with unholy impulses, and on the inward ear there falls more clearly and resistlessly every hour the delirious whispers and suggestions of impure seduction. He begins to think it manly to be cynical, and clever to talk of women in such a way that if his mother heard him she might wish that she had never borne him. And if the evil goes no further, can any say how great the havoc that is wrought ? Is it nothing to fill the memory with unclean suggestions? Have you not found that the memory holds such images with a strange tenacity? Would not some of you gladly give a year of life if you could rid yourselves of foul and leprous ideas eagerly and ignorantly imbibed in younger days? Oh, I could tell you of many a man who has come to me, men educated in great colleges, lovers of right, seekers after truth, but almost in despair because their memories seemed poisoned with impure jests which they could not forget, and which haunted them like whispers of the pit. And I need not add that such moral deterioration seldom stops with the thought : it is incarnated in the life. And if I fill in my sketch aright, I must speak of things scarcely lawful for a man to utter : I must track this youth to the chambers of iniquity; I must picture his first shamed plunge into vice; I must show the gradual hardening of the heart, and darkening of the mind, and maiming of the will, till unchastity becomes a law, and impurity an impious and despotic master. You have heard the story of Frankenstein : how a great chemist strives to make a man, and builds the physical frame up bone by bone, and sinew by sinew, and at last finds some occult means whereby he breathes into him the spirit of life, and the monster moves and lives. He is its creator ; and from that hour the thing which he has made haunts him, dogs him, will not let him rest, is a walking terror he cannot evade, a hideous presence from which he cannot flee. So he who raises the devil of impure delight raises a devil very difficult to lay. It enters in, and brings with it seven other devils worse than itself. It quenches conscience, it masters the will, it destroys too often intellectual pleasures, it robs the mind of peace, and visits the body with loathsome suffering, till of a man made in God's image it leaves something worse than a beast: and it makes the body, which should be the temple of the Holy Ghost, the mere agent and minister of infamous delights. Purity: it is embodied in an Elijah whose thoughts are full of God, whose

> "Strength is as the strength of ten,
> Because his heart is pure."

Sensuality: it is embodied in a Jezebel who has given her name to all bad women, and an Ahab who forgets the duties of kingship in her guilty fascinations. Purity is the badge of every good and great man ; impurity is the foul hoof-print, the leprous taint, of every Baal-worshipper. Who are these who are evermore the saviours of their age? They are the pure in heart, who see God and "live ever in the great Taskmaster's eye." Who are these whose life is a wasted treasure; whose days are lit with lurid light; whose old age, if such comes, is diseased and miserable; who taint the young; who defile the pure; who die with their own damnation visibly stamped upon their bloated bodies, corrupt, obscene, vile ; whom we gladly cover up with the grave's merciful oblivion ? These are the impure, and they shall not see God, but the wrath of God abideth upon them. And once more from the slopes of Carmel that stern voice of Elijah pierces to the present age, an age of great cities cursed by impurity, an age when in literature, in art, in life, impurity is continually flaunted before the public eyes : " How long halt ye between two opinions ? "

The contrast, again, is between the *popularity of custom and the noble isolation of the remnant.* In every age there is a remnant, a holy seed, who defy the custom of the world, and cleave to God. It is the remnant, the ten righteous men, the aristocracy of virtue who save a nation and redeem a time ; and th·y do so in defiance of the many, who cheerfully go to their damnation and refuse to be saved. It is here, again, this subject is so intensely modern, and teaches eternal truths. The priests of Baal are four hundred ; they have spread their toils so carefully that the people do not want to be redeemed ; the force of habit, the dignity of royal sanction, the spells of passion, all are with them : and when that great voice cries, " I, even I only, remain a prophet of Jehovah," the people answer not a word. Is not this true still ? Do not all the people bow down before the golden image ? Is not everybody witched by sackbut, and psaltery, and harp ? Will not everybody in the office laugh at you as a greenhorn if you are virtuous, and mock you as a milksop if you are pious ? Does not all the world seem to go one way—the way of the tide, the broad way, the primrose path that leads to everlasting burning ? Is that so ? Well, even then it is no reason why you should join them. You are a man, not a reed shaken with the wind. You are here as God's servant ;

and it is to Him, and not to them, you must give account. Ask yourselves where would the world have been if all men had reasoned thus. Where would liberty have been if no patriot had bearded the tyranny of despots, or truth if no scholar had braved the ignorant fury of the mob, or sainthood if no martyr had dared the lion and the fire ? Where would the English Bible have been if Wycliffe had not defied the anathema of Rome, or the right of popular government if Hampden had not died upon the field, or the right of human liberty if Wilberforce had not lived down the enmity of capitalists and the scornful laughter of a hundred drawing rooms ? There is no more Divine right in majorities than in kings ; though a thousand do evil, it is no reason why you should. Dare to stand alone, to think your own thoughts, and go your own way, and have your own convictions and to act upon them. Dare to stand on God's side, though no one else will ; front the priests of Baal in open battle, and dare them to the test, and you shall not be confounded. Look around again. Why is it all reform is so slow ? Why is it the poor go unfriended and the rich unrebuked ? Why is it men daily sacrifice their spiritual honesty, and dare not defy conventionalism, and will not live by the truth ? Take a hundred men man by man, and each will tell you privately he is convinced of the need of reform ; take them in the mass and publicly, and why is it every lip is dumb, and every hand unlifted ? Can you tell me why this is ? Can you tell me why it is that you, who acknowledge my arguments, do not crown them by consecrating yourselves to the Lord ? It is because you are afraid of the paltry verdicts of human opinion ; you are cowards, and you know that you are cowards. It is so easy to go with the tide, even though you hear the rapids ; it is so hard to breast it, even though it means life eternal. And there again Elijah stands forth as the embodiment of manly courage—a man who dares to be true, who can die but will not lie, who is willing to be slain by the priests of Baal rather than purchase life by apostasy to God. And there again Ahab and the people stand as the embodiment of the cowardice of custom, the poltroonery of false conventionalism ; and when that noble voice rings along the slope of Carmel, though a hundred hearts vibrate, and, sunk as they are in vice, know that the true prophet is come at last, there is the silence of cowardice : " The people answered not a word."

Here, then, are the three great characteristics of Baal ; and are we not all too familiar with them ? Who has not found the difficulty of righteousness, and has not been made conscious of that fatal vitiation of character which manifests itself in tolerance of evil ? Who has not caught some waft of that intoxicating perfume of impurity which fills the world, and has not felt that something has gone out of his life, a bloom, a fragrance, a chastity of desire, a blessed guileless- ness, and somet! ing has come into it which has spread a contaminating darkness through the soul ? Who has not felt the force of custom and of numbers, like a

secret tide, sweeping him away in spite of himself?
And what is the remedy? Do what Elijah did: be
true to conviction and true to God. Elijah presents
precisely the type of religious manliness we want to-
day: intense power of conviction and firm grasp upon
reality. We think in masses; we act on regulation
patterns; we accept the axioms and platitudes of society:
how few think for themselves, or act upon their true
convictions! How often under stress of temptation
we pare down the truth to suit our company! We are
not entirely false; we do not lie, but we prevaricate;
we rely on dexterity and adroitness rather than intensity of statement: and so our words have no fire,
no thunder, no grip, about them. The secret of Elijah
is fearless sincerity. Conviction breeds conviction,
and the man who is only half convinced himself never
convinces other people. The Church itself has grown
afraid of plain-speaking; it is only parenthetically
brave, and is habitually apologetic, and therefore is
heard with disguised contempt, and dismissed with
easy scorn. The only way to regain authority is to
regain sincerity; and that is true both of the collective
Church and of the individual. We want a more virile
type of piety—fearless, sincere, uncompromising. We
want not pious sentimentalists, but men. We want
men who will bring into politics the old spirit of belief
in God and love of righteousness which Cromwell had;
men who will bring into literature the living faith wh. in
shall heal the Marah waters of our troubled thought
such as Bunyan brought; men who shall apply to com-

merce the Sermon on the Mount, and who shall bring
into the Church the inspired audacity and Divine
aggressiveness of the first Apostles. It is with you,
the young men of to-day, that the shaping of the future
lies. You will be the statesmen, the magistrates, the
merchants, the leaders of thought, in that coming time
whose light will only shine upon the graves of those
to whom we look to-day. Let the dead past bury
its dead. Let the reign of compromise, with all its
bitter humiliations, end for you just now; and to
that fearless voice which speaks from Carmel let us
reply, " The Lord, He is the God; it is Jehovah
whom we serve and whose we are !"

So, then, I notice, lastly, that a vast class of men,
and especially young men, is indicated here ; viz., the
undecided. They halt between two opinions ; they are
lame, and crippled, and impotent for want of one sturdy
act of will which would change their life. Remember
that power of will is a matter of habit, and that he
who tampers with his will at last destroys it. Can
you tell me who are the most hopeless wrecks that
toss on the broken waters of society ? They are men
without power of will. One such man came to my
house only the other day. He was a man of brilliant
promise, who began life side by side with me. When
he came to me, he was a tramp, and had the tramp's
squalor and the tramp's limp. He had slept for weeks
in low lodging-houses. It was useless to help him ; he
had destroyed his power of will. His nature was like
a rotten wall in which no nail would hold. I could

weep over him, I could keep him from starvation, but I could not rouse in him the power of will to save himself. There are thousands such—brilliant wrecks, of whom much was expected, but from whom nothing came, of whom their friends said twenty years ago, " He will be a great man," and fifteen years ago, " He has a good deal in him," and ten years ago, somewhat more doubtfully, " He may succeed yet," but of whom now they never speak at all, because they know that he in whom they hoped is a tragic failure, and the failure has been indecision. For God's sake, be decided, even though it be in sin, for there is more hope in that, than in a life frittered in vain compromise between God and Baal, in futile drifting between right and wrong. Every good emotion stifled is a good emotion seared ; every true impulse defeated makes such an impulse more difficult of repetition. If God is the Lord, serve Him, if Baal, then serve him ; and, deplorable as such a decision may be, it is better than a lifetime of shilly-shally. Yes, and it has more ultimate hope in it, for the more energetic a servant of the devil a man is the sooner does he find out what a bad master he has got. But, oh, decide ! Do not drift into that most hopeless class of worshippers who are touched by every sermon, convinced in every service, thrilled by every hymn, but never changed, or converted, or redeemed by any. I appeal to young natures, the force of will unvitiated in many, and only partially weakened in any ; and in God's name I ask you, " How long halt ye between two opinions ? "

I know I have your verdict ; your conscience is my judge. Not more surely if now the last dread trumpet sounded, and out of the chasm of the rent heavens the great white throne of judgment flashed into view, would the moral issues of a theme like this be settled than they are settled now. You know what is right and what is wrong. You know where the balance of final victory will be ; and you may well dread the eternal comradeship of that polluted crowd of blinded eyes and wasted brows who cursed their age with Baal-worship, and have gone to their own place. It only remains, therefore, for me to press the question, *How long?* How long ? For as these words reach you memories of the old home have stirred in you ; the prayers of a long-dead mother have vibrated on the ear, and her dying voice has thrilled you ; and you have thought of the men whom you have known, the lost men, all whose brilliant promise has burned down into dead ash, and whose bright young lives have been blighted in an early grave. The way of transgressors is hard. How long halt ye between two opinions ? *How long?* For the time is short. Nearer than we know stands the cloaked shadow, the inexorable messenger ; and the year will soon dawn which will only shine upon our graves.

> "Our life is a dream,
> Our time as a stream
> Glides swiftly away,
> And the fugitive moment refuses to stay."

How long haltest thou between two opinions ? *How*

long?   For, behold, prophets pass away ; and the voice
which God has specially sent to thrill and call you
shall have performed its task, and no other be vouchsafed ; and the time comes when there will be no open
vision in the land for you, nor answering oracle, and
character will acquire its last mould of awful permanence : " He that is holy, let him be holy still ; and he
that is filthy, let him be filthy still." How long haltest
thou between two opinions ? *How long?* For life
and death hang on the decision.   Like a gay ship the
young life bounds over the bright waters, and the
silver voice of riot fills the sunlight, and " all goes
merry as a marriage bell."   But even now the tempest
lowers ; the sea shivers into foam as the wind
strikes it ; and the grey waves run in thunder, and
break no more in ripples.   Infirm of purpose, how
long haltest thou between two opinions ? Knowest
thou not that he who steers no course steers the
wrong course, that he who makes no decision has
made the wrong decision ?   Dost thou not see, far
away, yet ever nearer, that belt of white foam
spanned by the thunder-cloud, smitten by the lightning, that last harbour, the final shore of doom ?
There is no time for delay ; is Jesus with thee in
the little ship ?   The storm comes on apace, and
death is near ; is He who stills the waters with thee
now ?   Now is the time ; there is no other.   Claim
the hour ; the reversion of the morrow is assured to
none of us.   I warn you, I appeal to you, I beseech
you, but I cannot save you.   You **must choose** ; you

only can. Remember the words of a great writer recently in our midst, —

> " This passing moment is an edifice
> Which the Omnipotent cannot rebuild ; "

and now, while it is called to-day, choose whom you will serve. Who this day will consecrate himself unto the Lord ?

II.

A YOUNG MAN'S DIFFICULTIES.

' If any man will do his will, he shall know of the doctrine, whether it be of God."—JOHN vii. 17.

I HAVE selected this text, but I do not mean to stick to it. I shall use it later on as an illuminating principle for those in intellectual difficulties. Why I have been led to choose this subject is briefly this : I have recently received a remarkable letter from a young man entirely unknown to me, in which he details his intellectual difficulties. As his identity is not likely to be revealed by anything I may say, I think it will be no breach of confidence if I take the main points of his letter as difficulties common to-day among many thinking young men, and say what I can about them. Leaving out certain portions of this letter which I regard as sacred, the case presented is this : My unknown correspondent says that until three years ago he was quite orthodox, but that since that time he has read certain works which have utterly undermined his faith. He names Matthew Arnold, Rénan, Huxley's " Life of Hume," Spencer's " Sociology," and various articles on Biblical criticism, and books on Buddhism. He adds that he has also read the Bible, "The Imitation of Christ," Wordsworth, Tennyson,

Shakespeare, Kingsley, and Robertson. He finds he does not believe in a "God who thinks and loves," in Jesus Christ still living as God, or in the supernatural. He does still believe in a vague "First Cause," the Source of life and power, and that Jesus was a sublime Teacher, who lived an ideal life, taught noble truths, died gloriously, and whose memory he loves and venerates. Certain dogmas—*e.g.*, original sin and eternal punishment—he never could believe in. Then there is the difficulty of Buddhism ; if Christ was God incarnate, why not Buddha, and may not another man arise who shall live as perfect a life as either ? And there is the difficulty of the pain and sorrow of the world, which seem inconsistent with the existence of a God of love. Finally, he adds pathetically that he is not in despair, duty is his law of life, and if there is any help outside ourselves he wants to find it. This letter has deeply moved me, because it is obviously the sincere utterance of an honest soul in difficulties ; and because they are typical difficulties with young men, I will do what I can to help you to their solution.

DOUBTS AND DOUBTERS.

Now, doubt is sometimes the crotchet of a feeble mind, sometimes the disease of a developing mind. It may be the evidence of sincerity or the outcome of inconsistency, the grim Apollyon with whom the true soul must grapple before the green pastures are reached or the haunting fiend invoked by the repudiation of moral obligations. Many men reject Christianity because they have already rejected Christian morality; and, having thrown away the law of conduct, they find it necessary to invent a theory to justify their revolt. Polygamy existed in Mohammedanism before polygamy was justified by Mohammed, just as slavery existed in Christian lands before men ransacked the Bible for texts and arguments in its support. In other words, it is common among men first to live as though there was no God, and then to persuade themselves there is no God. The philosophy does not produce the life, but the life produces the philosophy.

But there is another class of doubters to whom these strictures do not apply, and my correspondent is among them. Like the young ruler who came to Christ, they seek eternal life, and seek it honestly; but they find the quest beset with difficulties. We live in an age when the very foundations of religion have been laid bare, and the reason of man has claimed supreme domination and right of decision in religious as in all other spheres. A great world of new facts, of which our fathers never dreamed, lies open to us; and new currents of thought and tendency stream round us, and touch the mind on every side. Science has literally annexed new heavens and a new earth; Biblical criticism has quarried deep into the débris of buried centuries, and has brought up from the depths facts of solemn and far-reaching importance; the study of other religions has revealed to us elements of nobleness in systems of thought which our fathers scarcely regarded as worthy of more than passing contempt,

and certainly as unworthy of serious refutation ; and
on all sides there heaves a great sea of intellectual
ferment and unrest. Even poetry and fiction have
caught the vibration of the new movement ; and the
poet no longer sings, but preaches ; and the novelist no
longer paints idyllic life, but life at fever-heat, life in
intellectual ferment, life as spiritual battle for the
truth. And so far I think the signs of the times are
with us. Anything, even the most hostile and searching criticism, is better than indifference. When sincere
men doubt, it is a sign that they have begun to think,
and that they feel the immense solemnity and importance of religion. It is not, then, to the flippant and
ignorant questioner of sacred things I speak, but to the
sincere doubter. It is to the youth who has come to a
point of crisis in his career when he feels the kingdom
of thought shaken, and the kingdom of truth which
remains is not yet set up. I speak as one who has
himself sat in the shadow of death, and journeyed
through the impenetrable gloom. I, too, have had to
fight my way out of the valley of Apollyon, as many a
better man has had to do before me ; and I have found

> "A power was with me in the night
> Which made the darkness and the light,
> And dwells not in the light alone."

And because I know how bitter the struggle is, and
know also that there is a way out of it to the solid
ground and heavenly sunlight, I speak to those in
whose ears the spirit that denies is whispering even
while the choral singing of the sanctuary rises from

their lips, and who question the very existence of Christ even while the shadow of Christ, like a luminous and spiritual presence, falls across the tired heart unnoticed.

Primal Difficulties.

First, then, there are certain *primal difficulties* of religion felt by my correspondent. He finds it hard to believe in a God who "thinks and loves," in a living Christ, and in the supernatural; but he cannot help believing in a First Cause, and in Christ as a sublime Teacher whose memory he loves and venerates. Let us look at these points.

In a First Cause all nations have believed; a nation of atheists has never yet existed. It is the fool who says in his heart, "There is no God;" and nobody but the fool says it. It is no mere poetic sentiment which perceives upon the everlasting hills the burning wheel-tracks of the chariots of God, or which says of the serene pomp and splendour of the midnight firmament, "The heavens declare the glory of God, and the firmament showeth His handiwork." It is the natural cry of man when he finds something mightier than himself, an inscrutable wisdom and majesty in the ordering of the world which he inhabits. One of the greatest of German philosophers has spoken of two great facts which confront man everywhere : "the starry heavens above, the moral law within." Nor is it difficult to mark the connection between these two facts. Man is conscious of law above him and law within him ; and he thinks the power which shaped a star and works within the soul is one. The existence of a First Cause is therefore the creed of reason ; and reason sees its proof in the heaving ocean and movements of the stars, in the colouring of the leaf and ripening of the fruit, in all that vast process of law which, with a thousand minute or majestic adjustments, holds the universe in place and order.

But we want something more than the God of the reason ; we want the God of the heart, the God who " thinks and loves." Mark, then, where the argument stands. Thought and love are human words for human functions ; if, then, they are not the creation of God, whence are they ? See what they have wrought in human life. Civilisation is nothing but embodied thought ; the human family is nothing but embodied love. When I go down the Clyde to see some vast vessel launched, it is no mere mass of inert steel and timber I look upon ; it is a visible thought which slides down the cradle at a sign, and floats off into the deep water like a thing of life. When I cross the Border, it is a thought that carries me, a winged and fiery thought, whose name is swiftness and whose glory is its strength. This church is thought translated into stone ; the picture is thought translated into colour ; music is thought translated into harmony; speech is thought translated into sound ; and books are thought translated into symbols. Are not the heavens also thought translated into splendour, and is not the earth thought translated into life and matter ? And of all this wealth of love which we find in human life, is not the same deduction just ? From whom has come the impulse of love ?

Who has made the heart which vibrates with ecstasy or thrills with agony in the joy or loss of another? It is love which is the golden barrier between man and the beast. The beast has passion and instinct; but man has the power of intelligent choice and spiritual devotion. How, then, can God be less than we? How can we conceive the Maker of the world creating faculties in man which He Himself does not possess? How can the picture be created without the sense of beauty in the artist, or the church without the sense of symmetry in the architect? No, we are not greater than God, but we are the shadows of God; and what we have in part, that He has in full. Our love is but the broken hint of His, our thought but the feeble echo of His wisdom, our noblest hope that hereafter we may know even as we are known; and so close and vital is this connection between man and God that the writer of Genesis says man was made in God's likeness, and Jesus urges us to be perfect, even as our Father in heaven is perfect. If there is a God at all, it is clear, then, that God must " think and love."

WHO WAS JESUS CHRIST?

But a further difficulty named is *belief in the living Christ.* Jesus Christ—who was He? That is the great question of the ages. In His own day the most brilliant scholars of the time asked, as in this very chapter, " How knoweth this man letters, having never learned?" And the most acute observers asked in something more than mere astonishment, " Whence hath this man these

things?" The reply of Jesus was simple and consistent. He said He was the Son of God. He said,
"My doctrine is not Mine, but His that sent Me." He
did not need human learning, because He had drunk at
the fountain-head of wisdom. He knew all things, not
by the laborious processes of acquisition and observation, but by Godlike intuition. Now, I will presently
refer to the difficulty of Buddhism stated by my correspondent ; but let me say now that no *human lips since
the world began ever uttered such a claim as this.*
Buddha repeatedly declared he was only a man ; he
refused Divine honours, and said that what he was
every man might become. Mohammed never swerved
from his honest declaration that there was one God,
and he was but His prophet. But Jesus never ranked
Himself even with the greatest of prophets and teachers.
He claimed to supersede them. He entered into the
firmament of human thought as the sun enters when
at the breath of dawn all the stars fade away, and are
visible no more. He had about Him none of the con-
ciliations and compromises of the mere human reformer;
He spoke with authority, and not as the scribes. He
held out to His followers superb promises which mere
genius could hardly have conceived, and which only
omnipotence could fulfil. In the last hours of His life
He solemnly asserted He was the Son of God ; He
described Himself as a King, and He died as a King
might die. What every man has, therefore, to face
about Jesus is this question : *Was He what He said
He was, or was He a fanatical impostor ?* His claim is

so great that you must concede all or nothing. I will
not press the question whether an impostor could have
uttered the sublime ethics of Jesus or have preached
the Sermon on the Mount; but I simply say every man
has to face this plain question : Was Jesus God, or was
He an impostor? It is useless to say we love and
venerate His memory if He was an impostor, because
we can do nothing of the kind. If Jesus was not what
He said He was, His life was not ideal, but infamous;
and He merited every stroke of the scourge and all the
anguish of the Cross for having deluded mankind with
vain hopes based upon a most blasphemous assumption.
Let us be honest in this matter. Let us be either Jews
or Christians. But for that species of reverence which
clings to the ethics of Jesus after denying the facts on
which the ethics are based there can be neither standing room nor respect. "Whence, then, has this man
these things ?"

The Heart of the World is with Christ.

But if we grant that Jesus was what He said He was,
then all difficulty about belief in the living Christ at
work among us to-day is gone. And what evidence
have we of Christ among us to-day? We have the
perpetual evidence of lives, not merely reformed, but
transfigured and regenerated by the power of Christ. I
point you the great phenomenon of human conversion.
Approach it honestly and examine it for yourselves.
Here are the facts. Christ is reported to have said just
before He disappeared from this world, " All power is

given unto Me, in heaven and in earth." He said that
after a given period of waiting a new, nameless, extraordinary spirit of power would change and animate His
disciples, and would spread throughout the world. In
the case of the Apostles it is clear that some such
extraordinary change did occur. The enemies of Jesus
were so confounded by the transformation effected in
Peter and John that, for want of a fuller explanation,
they said they "had been with Jesus." Paul gives a
circumstantial account of a miraculous change which
passed over him; and we know that his life was split
into two parts, as though an earthquake had torn it
asunder : and the parts differed as light and darkness
differ. Through all the early centuries similar records
abound. In the sixteenth century Luther tells the same
story, in the seventeenth Bunyan, in the eighteenth
Wesley, in the nineteenth an innumerable multitude.
The phenomenon is occurring to-day. It is variously
described, but essentially the accounts agree ; it is as
though a new life streamed into a dead heart, and a
transfiguring change passed over the entire character.
The drunkard then realises that he has a power which
snaps the bonds of habit, and the profligate feels within
him an impulse of purity which effectually lifts him out
of the rottenness in which he lay content. If you want
evidence, every minister in Great Britain can say, as
Wren's monument says in St. Paul's, "Circumspice ;"
and at a wave of the hand scores of thousands will spring
up and declare that Christ has saved them. And that
is conversion. That is what is meant by Christ living

to-day. Other men charm me, but this Man changes
me ; other men breathe into my brain the message of
their minds, this Man breathes into my soul the essence
of Himself. He passes like a live flame through my
nature, and leaves me glowing with spiritual vitality,
wonderful and glorious. No other man wields this
spell ; none has ever done so. I invite you, therefore,
to turn from the contentions of mere destructive criticism, the dreams of philosophic doubt, the wonders of
natural science, and face this extraordinary phenomenon
of human conversion. Surely it should be as inter-
esting as, and is far more important than, the age of a
Greek parchment or the dissection of a beetle's wing.
It is a Divine wonder ever new, and ever renewing
itself; and the only interpretation I can find for it is
that Jesus Christ spoke the truth when He said, "Lo,
I am with you alway, to the end of the world," for,
behold, " He is alive for evermore."

THE DIFFICULTY OF THE SUPERNATURAL.

As to the *difficulty of the supernatural,* that also disappears when we believe in a living God and a living
Christ. A live God can work wonders ; it is a dead
mechanism which is always uniform. Life means
freedom of action ; life means will and power ; and
power and will do not always obey conditions, but
create them. If I am not an animal, but a spirit ; if
this world is not my cradle and my grave ; if round
me lie unmeasured voids of mystery, worlds beyond
worlds of whose laws I know little or nothing ; then

it is not difficult for me to believe in the supernatural.
Not to believe in it is to apply my yard measure to
the infinite, and to make my narrow intelligence the
sole standard by which God is to be judged and the
universe adjusted. And who am I to say that God
never does the unusual—I, who think, but cannot
say what thought is; who live, but cannot find out
what life is; who feel and know I have a soul, yet
have never seen it, nor can describe what it is, or how
it came to be? To deny the supernatural is the last
imbecility of human ignorance and arrogance. And
who, after all, are these who so calmly write that
" miracles do not occur, and God cannot think or
love "? They are but a small and insignificant band
ranged against the giants of the world's past who
believed in God. The very names quoted by my
correspondent tell their own tale, for what sane man
would barter Shakespeare for Rénan, or Wordsworth
for Arnold, or Kingsley and Robertson for the innumerable smart writers of Biblical criticism who afflict us
in the magazines of to-day? And far as we have
gone in science, Kepler and Newton are not yet out-
shone ; and he would be a bold man who would venture
to throne either Spencer or Huxley beside Galileo and
Milton. No, sirs, depend upon it, the intellect as well
as the heart of the world is with Jesus Christ, nor
is it possible for me to believe that eighteen centuries,
crowned with the most illustrious names in history, have
all been wrong, that at last of living men Professor
Huxley alone should be right.

FAITH AND DOGMA.

I now come to certain *special difficulties* suggested by my correspondent. He says he never could believe in the dogmas of original sin or eternal punishment. I have but one observation to make here ; viz., that no man is bound to believe either in order to be converted and find the living God. Christ's question to all who sought His help was, "Believest thou that I am able to do this ?" He used no other catechism. All sorts of people came to Him : Roman soldiers, Jewish beggars, Greek exiles ; and each had different theological ideas. Christ said nothing about them ; He simply asked if they had faith in *Him*. Even when a man honestly replied that he had very little faith, and could only say, "I believe ; help Thou my unbelief," Christ did not hesitate to help him. And it is so still. If we postpone coming to Christ till we have assured ourselves of every dogma of Christianity we may wait for ever. The very fact that all the Churches disagree on dogma is sufficient to teach us that there is something of infinitely higher importance on which they agree, and that is the living Christ. The child does not need to understand all about the law of heredity before he can know his father loves him, nor need we gain any theological learning to prepare us for the healing and love of Christ. The fact is, men rake amid the dust of dogma when they should be coming to the Cross ; and while they fight over doctrines Jesus passes by, and their "eyes are holden," that they cannot see Him. Let us take the alphabet first ; we can leave the scholar-

ship till afterward.   Christianity is neither this dogma
nor that ; Christianity is Jesus Christ.

THE BUDDHIST SPECTRE.

And then as to this gigantic *brocken-spectre of
Buddhism,* which casts its chilling shadow over many
an inquiring mind.   What are we to say to that ?   Was
Christ better than Buddha ?   Is Christianity better
than Buddhism ? asks my correspondent.   We know
whence these ideas come.   During the last few years
Buddhism has become a study, and its noblest elements
have been again and again put before English readers.
The story of Buddha's great renunciation has been
told with matchless skill by Sir Edwin Arnold in " The
Light of Asia ;" the psalms of Buddha have been
translated into faultless cadence by Max Müller, and
other Oriental scholars.   And next to the story of
Jesus there is none nobler, and next to the Psalms of
David there are none more loftily devout.   Jesus said
of John, he was "a burning and a shining light ;" and
I find no difficulty in saying as much of Buddha.
The very spirit of Jesus breathes in such words as
these : " Never will I seek or receive private salvation ;
never will I enter into final peace alone, but for ever
and everywhere will I live and strive for the universal
redemption of every creature."   These are the words
of Buddha, and self-sacrifice as noble as that of the
Galilean inspired the life of Gautama.   The " light that
lighteth every man that cometh into the world " shone
in him ; and we can venerate and love him if we will,

3

but not with that species of faith which daily piles "forests of flowers on his stainless shrines," and daily moves "countless millions of lips to repeat the formula, 'I take refuge in Buddha.'" And why? Because we have known a greater, even Him who is the Light of the world. Buddhism preaches pessimism and extinction; Jesus brought life and immortality to light by the Gospel. Buddha claims no deity; he claims only to be an erring man, who tried, by the practice of noble virtues, to free himself from the tyranny of desire, and in return to gain, not the boon of life, but of death, to be extinguished and annihilated, as the bubble is extinguished in the ocean. The one point in which Buddhism touches Christianity is in its teaching of austere purity and self-sacrificing love. Buddha himself regarded his religion as elementary; he said it might last five thousand years, and then a new Buddha would appear. The Nirvana, or heaven, of Buddhism is simply painless annihilation, the complete destruction of identity and personality. Its promise is, Whoso followeth me shall die for evermore. The promise of Christ is, "Whoso believeth in Me shall never die." In Buddhism, strictly speaking, there is no God; in Christianity there is the ever-present sense of "our Father who art in heaven." Buddhism is one great truth, the truth of self-sacrifice, caught up and illuminated by a great example; it is the star hung upon the threshold of the day, and Christianity is that day in which it is swallowed up. Christ fulfils its hope; He completes the circle of which it is a segment. Buddhism, Mohammedanism, and Chris-

tianity are the three great historical religions; and, says
Max Müller, Christianity absorbs the best elements of
both, and adds the Diviner elements which they lack. As
for me, so far from Buddhism being a difficulty, I rejoice
in it as a glorious evidence that God has never forgotten His creatures, but in every age has nourished
the human heart with those instincts and impulses of
worship out of which all religion and virtue spring.

A little more patience, a little more insight, a little
more breadth of view, is what is needed for the dissipation of difficulties like these; and the same remark
applies to the philosophical difficulties suggested by
my correspondent in regard to the existence of pain
and suffering. Pain is the sentinel of life, the stern
guardian angel who shields us from destruction. If
pain did not teach us that fire burned, we should be
devoured by the cruel splendour; if the gash of the
knife caused no agony, there would be nothing to
remind us of our peril or save us from it. Every law
of nature is founded on some unalterable necessity,
and that which bears most hardly upon the individual
is often the most beneficial for the race. But, while
natural law cares for the race, spiritual law atones for
its defect by caring for the individual, and reminds us
that the very hairs of our head are all numbered.
Once let us grasp the great truth of a living God, of
God who is our Father, and in the light of that truth
all the others become clear; the impenetrable darkness
of the world lifts, and leaves us face to face with One
who loves, who pities, who saves.

" I say to thee, do thou repeat
    To the first man thou mayest meet
    In lane, highway, or open street,

" That he and we and all men move
    Under a canopy of love,
    As broad as the blue sky above ;

" That weary deserts we may tread,
    Dreary perplexities may thread,
    Through dark ways underground be led ;

" Yet, if we will our Guide obey
    The dreariest path, the darkest way,
    Shall issue out in heavenly day."

THE KEY OF KNOWLEDGE.

One last question remains then: *"How are we to find this knowledge?"* This text is the answer: "If any man willeth to do the will of the Father, he shall know of the doctrine." Man's mode of religion is to begin with the head; Christ's is to begin with the will and the heart. To the question, "What is truth?' man's reply is enlightenment; Christ's is surrender. Man says, " Prove me these things by a logic so keen that I cannot resist, and I submit;" Christ ignores the demand of the intellect, and addresses Himself to the spirit. And Christ is right, because mere enlightenment does not change the heart or transform the life. The drunkard and the profligate are well enough enlightened as to their folly, but the knowledge of the effects of alcohol on the body does not deter the drunkard from his vice, and the knowledge of the penalties of impurity does not convince the profligate of his fatal madness. The way of reform is not in mastering the theory of right, but in practising just as much of the right as we know. The doubter will never gain the light by analysing the qualities of darkness, but by resolutely following just such faint and feeble glimpses of the light as he may have. There are some things every man knows to be right and good; let him cleave to these, and the horizon will broaden to him. Into this Apollyon valley of doubt the truest and bravest spirits may come ; but it is never so dark but that the will of the Father can be discerned, like a Divinely luminous path, threading the gloom and leading upward. Says Robertson of this very experience in his own life, " But in all that struggle I am thankful to say the bewilderment never told upon my conduct." Mark that, young man. " In the thickest darkness I tried to keep my eye on nobleness and goodness, even when I suspected they were only will-o'-the-wisps." The question is, Are you ready to be taught ? Will you renounce your own will and do the will of the Father as far as you know it ? Will you act up to the frag- ment of conviction that is still yours, and if you have not the ten talents, be faithful to the solitary one ? The boy at school learns grammar without knowing its uses, and works out the tedious problems of Euclid without discerning their application. It is not till long after- wards the use is seen ; and in a sudden flush of triumph the youth realises that a language is unlocked to him, and a literature is his. So it is for you to learn what God wants to teach you *now.* Be true to that. Will with all your strength to do the will of God. If He hum- bles your intellect, submit ; and then when you inquire of the doctrine your obedience will be repaid, and the wisdom of God will make you wise unto salvation.

THE PROVINCE OF THE HEART.

And remember, finally, two things. First, we are not intellect only; the heart has to be reckoned with. "The heart has reasons which the reason does not know of," says Pascal. Faith in unseen things and things unproven to the perception is a daily necessity; we do not feel the earth move, but we believe it : we never saw the other side of the world, but we send our messages to its farthest boundary without misgiving. And every day, imprisoned as we are in a world of law, we triumph over law, just as every tree and flower defeats the law of gravitation when it forces its way upward to the light and seeks a wider world.

> "If e'er when faith had fallen asleep
> I heard a voice, 'Believe no more,'
> And heard an ever-breaking shore
> That tumbled in the godless deep,
>
> A warmth within the breast would melt
> The freezing reason's colder part,
> And, like a man in wrath, the heart
> Stood up, and answered, 'I have felt.'"

Yes, we have felt. When every fact has been against us, a Divine intuition in the heart has buoyed us up and given us hope. Beside the beds of the dying all the facts have seemed against us; but we have felt that all the virtue and the patience of that closing life could not be lost, but must survive somewhere, if only in obedience in that law of economy which permits no waste in nature. Beside the graves of great men we have felt that all those powers, sharpened to the finest uses, could not be utterly destroyed ; and it has been impossible for us to think of the putrefaction of the grave : we have perceived the entrance on immortality. And when the great earth has been dumb to our inquiry and the stars deaf to our prayer, we have still told ourselves our hopes should not be disinherited, nor our prayer be mocked. Do you remember that word of Paul's, " *With the heart a man believeth unto righteousness* " ? Oh, well do I remember how like a flash of light that verse illumined my soul one day when all was at its darkest for me. And then I saw what it all meant : that God did not ask me to believe with my intellect at all, but to trust Him with my heart. From that hour the world has brightened in me, for I know now that I have found God. Often and often now I cannot believe with the intellect, but I can with the heart. And so may you. Come, doubts and all, to the blessed Lord, and let your hearts go out to Him, and He shall give you rest unto your soul.

THE CROSS OF MYSTERY.

And the other thing I would ask you to remember is that Christ does not profess to have told us everything, or cleared up every human mystery. From vast tracts of thought He has not lifted the curtain ; they lie unilluminated, or revealed only by some vivid flash of light which makes the darkness visible. And when Jesus tells me to take up the cross and follow Him, He does not mean only the sacrifice of ease, or wealth, or

importunate desire; He means also that cross of un-
answered mystery which He lays upon my intellect,
and which is not the least heavy of the many crosses
He gives the children of men to bear. But He has told
me enough. He has revealed the infinite and com-
passionate Fatherhood of God. He has given me an
absolutely clear and infallible code of conduct. He has
shown me, not merely my duty, but how it may be done,
and has promised me a Divine influx of strength,
whereby I may accomplish it. He is alive for evermore, and stands even now close to each of us, as He
did to Thomas in the very moment when his heart was
sick with doubt. And what happened then? Thomas
had demanded proofs, and now he had them ; but he did
not use them. He thrust no hand into His side or finger
into the wound. He did not ask whether this solemn
Presence was the vision of hysteric ecstasy or hallucina-
tion. All he knew was that he saw his Master, and
the warmth of that living Presence streamed round
him, and his heart broke out in the rapturous cry:
"My Lord and my God!" Brother, Christ is now
breathing on thee the breath of life. Dismiss the voices
of the intellect, and let the heart speak. Believe with
all thine heart, and thou shalt enter into peace. O that
to any doubters who may read these words, and to my
unknown correspondent, there may come the dawn of
faith, heralded by that heart-piercing cry of Thomas
called Didymus, "My Lord and my God!"

III.

"And there followed Him a certain young man having a linen cloth cast about his naked body; and the young men laid hold on him: and he left the linen cloth, and fled from them naked."— MARK xiv. 51, 52.

THIS incident is related by St. Mark only, and is one of those undesigned touches of realism which gives dramatic completeness to the scene. Christ is in Gethsemane; it is the hour and power of darkness. He knows now that nothing but the Cross awaits Him, that He has spoken to a wicked and gainsaying people, and that the bitter cup of defeat must be drunk to the last dregs. He knows also—and that is the most poignant thought of all—that His own disciples have had no real or stable faith in Him, and that His own familiar friend has lifted up his heel against Him. When Christ stepped out of the supper-chamber and passed through the moonlit olive-gardens, singing a psalm with His disciples, it was in truth a requiem for great hopes, a dirge for ended faith and confidence.

Is there any bitterer trouble to a great soul that has toiled for others than to feel that its toil has been wasted, to know that its heroic love is answered by indifference, its self-sacrifice by hostility and contempt ? Can God

call any human spirit to a more tragic Gethsemane
than this ?   It was that and more—the crushing sense
of hum⁀n sin, the burden of the wrong of others—
which Christ felt in that hour when the torches of
His foes flashed through the shadows of the olive-
gardens and the trampling of innumerable feet fell
upon His ear. The whole city was aroused ; and in the
tumult and excitement, probably the youth mentioned
in this text sprang from his bed and ran toward the
garden. Who he was and what he knew of Christ it
is impossible to say ; but it is not unnatural to suppose
that he may often have seen Christ, and heard Him, and
may possibly have loved Him.   He may have been one
of those young men who had questioned Christ about
eternal life, and whom Jesus had loved for the integrity
and simplicity of his spirit.   That he was no stranger
to Christ we may infer from the fact that he follows
Him when others flee ; and that he must have felt for
Christ some passionate impulse of love or curiosity we
may judge from the fact that he leaps from his bed
and runs nearly naked to the garden at the first sound
of approaching danger.   Did he hope to defend Christ ?
Did he hope to warn Him or to save Him ?   We
cannot tell, but this at least is clear : here is a young
man moved by a generous and noble impulse toward
Jesus, who has a supreme chance of proving his love
and courage in the hour of Christ's deadliest peril, but
who loses the golden opportunity, and in the confusion
of the arrest forsakes Jesus, as did all the others.

  There, then, the history terminates ; and nothing

more can be conjectured or explained. But the incident is fruitful of suggestion, and is worthy of your
thought. Fix your eyes then upon the scene, the
sublime figure of Jesus standing calm and undefended
in the presence of His foes; the tumult, the terror,
the confusion, of the arrest; and somewhere in the
crowd, his eager face revealed to us by the broken
lights of the torches or the moon, this youth, with
who can say what a conflict of noble passion in his
heart? We are going to talk with this young man.
We are going to ask him the secret of his conduct, and
learn the secret of our own. Look at him well, then:
a young man seized by young men, struggling to get
at Christ, half throttled and wholly frightened in the
attempt; that is the scene which we must keep in view
while we talk together.

"There followed Him a certain young man." That
I take to be the statement of the *supreme attraction
there is in Jesus Christ for youth*. Have you ever
pondered the fact that Jesus Himself was a young
Man, and that all His marvellous life was lived out in a
brief period of years which never reached maturity?
Our adoration of Christ not infrequently obscures
a lesson like this, obvious as it is in studying
the life of the Man Christ Jesus. There is to me
something infinitely touching and impressive in this
youthfulness of Jesus Christ. We are accustomed
to-day to leaders of thought and society who are
grey with service, and it is rarely that a man leaps
into notice now till middle life is reached. And

therefore it is, I suppose, that we talk so wisely of the need there is for men to learn the world before they attempt to reform it; and the favourite way of silencing youth is to sneer at its lack of experience. It is a custom of long tradition to make arithmetical computations about the ignorance of youth, as if wisdom were the sole monopoly of age and folly the prerogative of youth. It was precisely in this way that grey-headed doctors of the law treated Jesus; they computed His birthday when they could not answer His arguments, and closed all controversy by remarking, " He is not fifty years old, and does he teach us ? " And as we see this young Carpenter, fresh from the homely rusticities of Nazareth, standing up before the elders of His people, teaching, rebuking, illumining them, what is the moral significance of the spectacle ? We see that Jesus represents the glory and supremacy of youth. He teaches us that intuition is Diviner than experience, and that the intuitions of youth are a nobler force than the experience of age. All this supernatural wisdom, from whose founts the ages have drunk, is the utterance of a young Man; all this Divine life, whose deeds have stirred the souls of millions, was the ·life of a young Man, who barely touched the threshold of mid-age, when the sudden darkness fell and covered all. And the lesson is neither new nor strange. The trumpet of God peals to every human soul, "What thou doest, do quickly." The greatest deeds of the world, the greatest poetry, the deepest and most fruitful influences, the most splendid conquests and achievements—these are all the work of young men. He who does not come upon the stage of action till mid-life finds half the audience gone, and hears the fingers of death busy with the pulleys that bring down the curtain. Life is too short for the postponement of great purposes; he who moves the world must bring to his task the courageous buoyancy of youth, not the procrastinating caution and timidity of age. There is always room for youth in the world. The world is always crying out in its weariness for the power of youth to come and do what the slow hands of age cannot accomplish. It is to a young Man the world owes the Sermon on the Mount; it is to a young Man we owe the redemption of the world: and what wonder is it, then, that Jesus Christ should be the centre of intense attraction for the young?

And you will notice, too, as you read the life of Christ, that He also felt a strong attraction to the young. He reciprocated their hopes, He loved them for the freshness of their impulses, and was very sorry when they turned away from Him. People have asked me sometimes, "Why do you so often preach to young men? Why not preach a special sermon to old men? Why this intense desire and effort to help and save young men?" I will tell you why it is. It is because I believe that if ever the kingdom of Jesus Christ is to be set up upon the earth, it must be young men who will lay the foundations' of its strength, and shape the pillars of its splendour, and be the master-architects of

its success. The kingdom of Christ is not something
we go to, but that comes to us; it means the complete
purification of human life, in all its offices, till the will
of God is done on earth even as it is done in heaven :
and if ever that stupendous battle is won, it is the
young men of the age, and of the ages, who must win
it. Ask yourselves how new thoughts infect society,
how a new theory of poetry, or philosophy, or science
becomes established; and the reply always is that you
must first infect the young with its message, and then
you can safely leave them to do the rest. Take for
instance, a great poet like Wordsworth, who writes
amid all but universal scorn for nearly forty years, and
whose name is received by every critic of his early
days with guffaws of brutal ridicule. Then there is a
change, and Oxford receives him with reverence, and
by common consent and acclamation he becomes the
Laureate of his country. How did this happen ? The
explanation is that those who jabbered idiotic abuse at
Wordsworth were old men, and those who believed in
him were young men. They were the leaven that
leavened the whole lump. They carried their evangel
with them, and they spread it. At length the hour
came when no man was left to contradict them, and
then the slow public believed their witness ; and a new
poetry of pure and simple sentiment, which taught the
dignity and sang the sanctity of the homeliest human
life, received its due reward in the praise of all the
world. It is so in all the great kingdom of human
thought : the young men are the crusaders who conquer

the centuries. The world belongs to its youth; and
what the youth of a nation is, that the future of the
nation must be. Is it then a contemptible, because a
merely sensational, impulse which urges me to speak
to this vanguard of the future which I see around me ?
No. If I speak specially to you, it is because I know
that if drunkenness and profligacy shall cease to curse
the twentieth century, it is because you will be pure
and sober; if juster views of God and human duty will
prevail, it is because you must first imbibe them; if
there shall rise a nobler and completer society of more
helpful human hands and more serviceable lives,—wealth
redeemed from selfishness and poverty from dishonour,
what is vile in human custom purged into purity, what
is false illumined with the truth, what is true strengthened into triumph—if, in a word, this world of weak and
struggling creatures shall indeed recognise Christ as the
Light of life and Leader of its thought, it is because you
will first find Him, and teach in yourselves the lessons
of this Diviner obedience, and be in yourselves the
forces of this Diviner victory. That work none but
you can do. Let the old man rest; his work is done,
and the time of his departure is at hand. But with
infinite love and expectation the great Captain of souls
looks on you, the young, the strong, the eager, whose
hearts are all athrob with forceful impulses and
passions, and cries, " Will ye also be My disciples ? "

" They all forsook Him and fled," but this young
man followed Jesus. That was a noble impulse, and
impulse is one of the finest qualities of youth. And

what is impulse ? It is an act of the heart rather than of the will, a spontaneous movement of the soul. It is impulse which makes us love, and justifies itself by creating love in others. By what law is it that the lark springs aloft at the first sign of day, and is already singing at heaven's gate when it is yet half dark below, and the everlasting doors have not opened for the entrance of the sun ? It is an impulse in its own nature which bids it sing and soar, and sends it up like winged music into the waste heavens, which it floods with invisible delight. By what law is it that the little child flushes when the father's footstep is heard, and leaps up to his lips to welcome him ? It is simply the impulse of love, not meditated nor pre-meditated, the swift, spontaneous action of the heart. Or what force is it which prompts the man who has never dreamed of doing anything heroic when he rose at morn, to suddenly leap into the running tide to rescue some poor soul he never saw before, and does not even know ? It is impulse, the strenuous impulse of courage and humanity. It was such an impulse which made this young man suddenly range himself on the side of Christ in the moment when all others had deserted Him. For one brief, glorious moment he was the only human soul in all this world of men who dared to stand with Jesus. Quicker than we can describe it the whole drama was over; there was no time for reason or debate. And who does not justify, and who will not applaud, the impulse ? Who does not perceive that it is in such Divine moments of intense feeling we see the narrow way to eternal life, and as we look back upon them we know that

> "Just this or that poor impulse,
> Which for once had play unstifled,
> Seems the whole work of a lifetime
> That away the rest has trifled"?

Oh, I know that it is easy enough and common enough to scorn impulse and talk of impulsive people as though they were foolish and hysterical people; but I say, Give me your impulse, and you may keep your caution. I never heard that caution ever did anything yet but put the drag upon the wheel of progress, but impulse is the flaming force which drives it. If the lark debated how it could well climb up the steep, invisible stairways of the heavens, or the child why it should kiss its parent, or the man whether he was justified in saving the drowning, there would be neither song, nor love, nor courage left us. And it is because love is an impulse, and because the relation between us and Christ, if there be any relation at all, is love, that I bid you now follow the impulse which impels you toward Christ. Do not fight against it; follow it. Let the heart act for you, and the brain will follow. You are not asked to explain Christ or understand Him; you are asked to love Him. Let your impulse leap up into the sky that is yet dark, and, like the lark, it will see the light while yet the song is on the lip. The great, startling, tragic, decisive acts of life are all sudden. They are the work of moments. Our act leaps from us like an immitigable fire, which

4

we can no longer restrain, because we feel, we think, we love, intensely. And in such an intense moment of sacred impulse we find Christ, we love Him, we side with Him, we adore Him, and follow Him. We surrender ourselves to the guidance of the heart; and in the surrender of ourselves we find the Son of God, and are vivified by His embrace.

But, you will say, is impulse a safe guide? May it not lead men to ruinous folly and punishment? Yes, a bad impulse may, but not a good one. There are impulses of the flesh and impulses of the spirit, impulses which we know to be from our baser selves and impulses which flash on us from all that is highest in us; and we can readily enough distinguish them, and know the good from the evil. It is because men follow the bad impulse—the tingling of the sensual nerve, the craving of the bestial appetite, the thousand hungry passions which consume us—that they lose the power of feeling noble impulses, and learn to think of all impulse as a ruinous and delusive thing. You must judge the source of an impulse by its quality and object, and it is by that rule I judge the impulse of this young man right and good. For what was its object? It was Christ. What was its quality? It was courageous. He felt the heroic fibre thrill in him; the forlorn majesty of Christ appealed to him; he longed to stand beside Jesus, and defend Him, and be His comrade to the death. Do you feel that? Do you recognise Jesus Christ as the Captain of salvation, not in any narrow and selfish sense, but literally of the

world's salvation ; that He is fighting for the redemption
of man from all sorrow and wrong into all purity and
glory ? Oh, why so many men, called or miscalled
Christians, do so little for the world, is because they
recognise Christ only in relation to themselves, and not
in His relation to the world at all. Christ is to them
personal safety, not personal service. With those immeasurable, Divine, unselfish aims which led Christ to
the Cross they have no sympathy, because they have
no understanding. They see the Christ who heals,
not the Christ who serves, who suffers, who rules, who
is against every wrong and tyranny, and is the courageous Champion of all the poor, and trampled, and
despised. They see the Christ who utters comfortable
words and kind, not the Christ of Gethsemane, drinking
the cup of bitterness He might have avoided, alone
because He dared to die for righteousness' sake,
deserted because none other dared so much as He.
And it is the Christ of Gethsemane we need to see.
We need to catch that glow of spiritual comradeship
with Him which makes us cry,—

> "O Thou pale form, so dimly seen, deep-eyed,
> Do I not
> Pant when I read of the consummate deeds ?
> Do I not shake to hear aught question Thee ?"

The sort of religion we want is the courageous religion
which is not afraid to face Gethsemane and Calvary,
and holds not its life dear unto it for the sake of the
Gospel. There is no night which darkens over the
wide world when the soldiers do not go out to seize

Christ, no morning which dawns when the world has not got its Calvary ready where Christ is crucified afresh. The mere sentimental impulse which makes you admire Christ we do not want; thousands in Jerusalem on the night of His arrest had that, who were not willing to lose an hour's rest on His behalf, or to lift a voice in His defence upon the fatal day which followed. We want the brave impulse which makes men range themselves on the side of Christ in the hour of His worst desolation, when He is despised in the office and jeered at in the workshop, when men forget Him in the avarice of trade and insult Him in the frivolity of pleasure, when the world marches all its forces on Gethsemane, and the hoarse cry of the people fills the air, "Away with Him! He is not fit to live!" When Wilberforce was in the thick of his great agitation against the slave trade, an old, gouty peer said to him, "So, young man, you intend to reform society, do you? Do you see *that?*" said he, pointing to a cross near by. "That is what those come to who attempt to reform society." And it is true still, and true for you, if you are bold enough to make it so. Dare you be Christ's disciple? Dare you follow the courageous impulse of the heart which makes you feel the world well lost for Christ? It is the very glory and quality of youth to be courageous. It is youth which climbs "the imminent deadly breach," and faces the deadly hail of battle; it is youth which defies the tyranny of custom and the hatred of the world. We have compassion for age that sees fears in the way, but

youth which is cowardly is contemptible. There is
not one of you who would not rather be exiled for ever
than be branded as a coward and know that you
deserved it. That is why Christ wants you. That is
why your place is at the side of Christ. When all
men forsake Him, it is the hour of youth to prove its
chivalry and rally to His side. Dare you do that?
Will you follow the impulse of the soul which draws
you to the Son of God? See, the torches flash upon a
hundred angry faces; spears are lifted; oaths are
uttered; blows are struck : but He, the supreme Master
of the world, stands calm, and turning His piercing
eyes on you, cries, "If any man will be My disciple,
let him take up his cross and follow Me."

Turn the subject round again : "*And the young men
laid hold on him : and he left his linen cloth, and fled from
them naked.*" It was a hard trial ; when Apostles fled,
one young man might well flee : yet he behaved so nobly
while the power of that self-forgetful impulse was on
him that we could weep tears of disappointment to see
him do this. To have been the only one of all mankind who went with Jesus to prison and to judgment,
the solitary soul faithful among the faithless found—
that was the part he might have played ; and, oh, what
a part to miss ! And see, they were not old men who
dismayed him and broke his purpose down. There are
young men against Jesus as well as old men, and there
is no limit of age in that crowd which mocks Christ
in Gethsemane. Perhaps these young men who laid
hands upon him knew him : old comrades of light and

jesting hours, who thought him mad ; cautious youths who intended risking nothing themselves, and objected to anybody else doing so ; youths roused from the midnight debauch by the riot in the street, who found a piquant jest in hustling this young man and cursing him for his folly, a folly far too wise for them to understand, a madness too Divine for them to dream of. Sooner than he guessed his courage was put to the test, and it broke down miserably beneath the strain.   He had no time to grasp Christ's hand or touch His garment ; in an instant the irrevocable deed was done.   Terror seized him ; and before he could ask what he had done, he had left his raiment in the hands of his foes, and had fled into the night.   Breathless and frantic, we see him plunge into the deep shadows of the olive trees ; and as he runs a burst of jeering laughter follows him ; and, worse than any taunt of man, there burns in his heart the bitter sense of his own defeat and cowardice.

" *And he fled naked.*"   Cannot we too well fill up the picture for ourselves ?   Here is a youth but lately come up to the university.   Far away in some quiet spot of north or west you had your home among the simple faiths and pieties of rustic life.   Your ears were familiar with the Bible from a child, and its words were woven into the very texture of your mind.   You knew what it was to hear a father's prayers, and to watch a mother's life of steadfast purity and self-denying toil. You heard prayer, and you prayed ; you read the Scripture, and loved it ; you were full of simple trust, and never doubted. But now what is your history? You have got into the wrong set, and your piety is shaken. You have learned to think lightly of religion and to jest at purity. You have sat in the seat of the scorner, or have at least listened to its cynicism; and wherever young men gather, the seat of the scorner is there: and the devil usually takes good care to fill it with a competent professor. If you ask me what has happened to you, I can tell you in a sentence: the young men have laid hands on you, and your faith in God is gone.

Here, again, is a youth who once had a fair ideal of what life ought to be, and strove to realise it. You valued purity and loved truth, and you were pure and truthful almost without conscious effort. Your days were sweet with health, and your sleep wholesome with peace; Nature breathed her joy into your soul, and God visited you in hopes and yearnings after goodness. I know what has happened to you. It takes no very penetrating eye to discern the marks of a great catastrophe upon you. The frankness of your smile is gone, and the impress of hateful knowledge is on your face. The young men have laid hold of you; the black sheep of the warehouse have infected you. Comradeship, which should have strengthened you, has slain you. You can listen to abominable things without shrinking, and say vile things without shame; and there is pollution in your presence and peril to the pure in your very touch. Once you were not far from the kingdom of God. Your impulse would have driven you to the side of Christ; but the young men laid their hands upon you, and you fled. The calamity which has befallen you is that your purity is gone.

There are those of you also who have not lost faith or purity, but you have lost the impulse toward religion. The spiritual force that once was in you has decayed, and mainly because you refused to yield to it. Religion has become to you a formal thing, and appeals fall dead upon you, because your heart is a vacuum. The vital air of religious life has been pumped out of you by trifling with holy things and resisting holy impulses. The word for you also is true that the young men, the cynic and the worldling, have laid hands on you; and you have fled. Oh, how solemn and far-reaching are these pregnant words! How many hungry, empty, naked souls crowd round us who have renounced Christ for fear of man, and who turn hither and thither, seeking rest and finding none, conscious of cowardice, and tortured by the knowledge of weakness, and ever fleeing through the darkness to that deeper darkness where character acquires eternal permanence, and he that is unholy is unholy still! Can I do you a better service then than warn you against the peril of evil comradeship? Do we not all know men, gay, brilliant, fascinating, with a natural quality of leadership, whose work it is to corrupt the purity and sap the faith of those around them? I will tell you what is the common curse of all places where young men gather together, whether in the school, the university, the barracks, the club, or the office. It is an inordinate worship of merely intellectual force or the qualities of personal fascination. The character of a man is the last thing you inquire about. You ask, Is he witty? Can he sing a good song? Is he clever? Can he tell a good story? You do not ask, Does he love God? Does he honour purity, and meet the great demands of truth and righteousness? You are attracted by the specious glitter of mere surface qualities; and you do not ask about the qualities of his heart, his life, his action. How many men have I known who have excelled in all these qualities of jovial comradeship without possessing one single element of noble character! And the influence of such men is utterly destructive, and their course in life is marked by the poisonous deposits they have left behind in other lives. And how many amiable and well-meaning youths have I known who were the victims of such men! Evil communications have corrupted good manners: purity has perished in the polluted atmosphere of the comradeship they chose, just as flowers cannot live in the reeking air of the bar-room; truth has died in them, because they have admired the brilliant liar, and the love of God, because they have followed the lead of a man in whose thoughts God had no place; and if I wrote their lives, I could do so in a single sentence: " The young men laid hold on them, and they fled." It is a sufficient biography; and all over these lands there are homes where joy is dead and parents weep in secret for the sons who have been taken in the toils of evil comradeship.

There are two questions, then, for you to determine;

and the first is, *What is your relation to Christ?* I do
not say to religion as a theological system or to the
Church as a religious organisation, but to Christ.
Here is One who claims to be the Son of God and the
Master of the world. You acknowledge that claim, in
part at least, when you join in His worship. If that
supreme claim is admitted, then you must define your
relation to this Christ, who is alive for evermore, and
by whom you will be judged. In all the closing scenes
of Christ's life, we see Him, not in His relation to the
multitude, but to individuals : to Caiaphas, to Herod,
to Peter, to Pilate ; and it is so here. In the intense
light which falls on this scene, we see Christ and this
young man alone ; and all other figures for the time are
lost in darkness. The tragedy of Gethsemane is sus-
pended until this personal incident is settled. And so
you stand in sharp, clear, unmistakable juxtaposition
with Christ ; and you must determine what your future
relation to Him shall be. Do you hate Him or love
Him ? Are you for or against Him ? Is His cause
your cause ? The Christ of Gethsemane stands before
you in the unhealed wrongs and sorrows of His
world; do you mean to help or perpetuate them ?
Do you elect to stand with the brutal and passionate
crowd that pushes Christ on to execution or with
this solitary human soul who dares to follow when
others flee and loves while others hate ? Sooner or
later that choice will be forced on you, for Christ
permits no compromise. It is a question of anta-
gonism or service, and ask yourself whether it is not

time that you boldly defined what your relation to
Jesus is.

The second question is, *Do you want religion?* If
you turn to the story of Pentecost, you will find that
those who received the Holy Ghost on that memorable
day were not the promiscuous multitude, but "devout
men," already impregnated with religious truth. They
were seekers after truth, who had followed the light
they had *close up*. Just as steel once polarised is
always susceptible to the magnetic force, so they were
polarised by previous devoutness; and when the Apostles
addressed them, the living current of the Divine magnetism flowed into them without a break. So you
may roughly divide the mass of men into those who
want religion and those who care nothing for it. The
young men who laid hold on this youth did not want
religion; they were the riffraff of the city, the midnight roysterers "flown with insolence and wine," to
whom the whole occasion was adventure. This young
man did want religion, and was conscious of the charm
of Christ. The youth whose weekday life is passed
in the bar-room and the billiard saloon, and who enters
the sanctuary on the seventh day in occasional obedience to troublesome custom, does not really want
religion. He has no real interest in it. But the youth
who loves truth and wants to find it has already
prepared himself for its reception. Have you done
this? Do not pretend an interest in religion you do
not feel; that is adding insincerity to callousness. Be
honest with yourself, and ask whether you do really

want religion or not, for that is the question you must first settle if you would go further and define your relation to the Christ of Gethsemane.

And, lastly, let me remind you that if you would settle these solemn questions, you must dismiss all solicitation of comradeship. They are your questions; you alone can settle them. We cannot help following in imagination this young man. What became of him? Think of all he had seen and felt that night, the turbulence and stress of passion which had shaken him. It is impossible for men to forget such hours. They make too deep and indelible an impression on their lives. The coward cannot forget that once he was almost heroic, or the cynic that he was once almost religious. The man who has been as near Christ as this young man was, and then forsaken Him, must bear the scar of his treachery, the mortifying memory of his infirmity of purpose, through all his life. Can you not picture this youth as he reaches home that night, breathless, sobbing, unstrung by the vehement excitement he had suffered? What a night for any man to pass through! How the face of Christ would haunt him, with its reproachful friendliness and forlorn pathos of appeal! Can we not distinguish this youth in the crowd around the judgment-hall of Pilate, or standing bowed in fruitless shame in the darkness of Calvary, with the loud dying cry of Jesus ringing in his ears? Whatever future life was his, of this at least we may be pretty sure: that night in Gethsemane would always stand out terribly clear and luminous as the one supreme event, the crowning moral opportunity, of his life. And he lost it. He lost that which never could be his again. For the great lesson of moral impulse is that it is so quick to come and go, that we must needs be alert to use it, and dare not trifle with it. " Kiss the Son, lest He be angry, and ye perish from the way," says the Psalmist, for all too soon the Son passes from our sight, and the impulse we restrained has no other opportunity of vindication. And once more, as the torchlight fades ·away, and silence once again possesses the garden where Jesus sorrowed, that Divine voice comes to us from the broadening distance, " Will ye also be My disciples?" "Will ye also go away?"

IV.

THE TESTIMONY OF FACT.

"Now when they saw the boldness of Peter and John, and perceived that they were unlearned and ignorant men, they marvelled ; and they took knowledge of them, that they had been with Jesus. And beholding the man that was healed standing with them, they could say nothing against it."—ACTS iv. 13, 14.

THE force of this passage is that it is the testimony of enemies to the effects of Christianity, and such testimony is the most valuable form of evidence. Through all the long line of Christian history this testimony has been repeated. It is hardly too much to say that it is beneath the dignity of Christianity to publish apologetics or subtle arguments why it should be permitted to exist ; it exists because it must, because it cannot help existing, and because it is justified by its results. From the moment when the darkness rolled away from Calvary an infinite light has filled the world, and it has been daybreak everywhere. Men have instinctively realised the presence of a new force in the world, and they have been forced to respect it. Like light, it has grown silently ; but, like light, it has also been invincible: it has come with a potent supremacy, subduing men as the light subdues the darkness when at the break of day it beats the darkness into flakes of crimson fire beneath its feet. The light asks no leave of men to shine, no permit of any human power to fill the world; but surely and pervasively it takes possession of the waking earth, and defies dislodgment or defeat. Its evidence is in itself. Its right to be is its power to cleanse and bless. To the blind man the light does not exist, indeed; but the blind man is not a fit judge of light, nor do we go to him to tell us what the light is like, or what it makes of the grey world when its sudden splendours fall out of the chambers of the east, and all lands are flooded with the vivifying radiance. When we want to know what the light is like, we ask our own eyes to tell us; when we want to know what Christianity is like, we ask those who have seen and felt it, and who have witnessed its work day by day upon man and human society. And the reply even of its enemies is, "A notable miracle hath been done, and we cannot deny it;" we fear, we wonder, we hate, but we can say "nothing against it."

Here, then, stand these two simple-minded men against the world, and challenge its utmost scrutiny. Who they were we know; what they were we are told in the famous phrase that they were "unlearned and ignorant men." In birth, in station, in manners, in intellectual calibre and knowledge, they are not to be mentioned in the same breath as their adversaries. They are men of the commonest social type, men who in the ordinary course of things would have lived and died in village industry and obscurity. What then is there remarkable about them? This: that they have been the chosen companions of the Man of Nazareth, the Son of God. They have broken bread with the visible God; they have heard the wisdom of the Eternal, and walked in daily intimacy with Jesus Christ. And the power of that supreme companionship has told upon them. The spiritual force of Jesus Christ has streamed through and through their nature, till it has changed them from glory into glory; and they have risen into a dignity of manhood strangely new and glorious. Do we not know how love can transfigure and renew men still? Have we not watched the subtle assimilations of love as it softens asperities, and cleanses the thoughts, and moulds the mind, till in those who have loved each other tenderly through long years so perfect an affinity is set up that thought answers to thought, and even feature to feature, and voice to voice in its sympathetic inflexions and reduplications? This process, but upon a Diviner scale and in a completer method than the world has ever known, has been accomplished here. The miraculous force of Jesus has not merely streamed through their nature, but it has left its power upon them. They too can work miracles; they too can touch the sick, and, behold, they are made whole. Jesus is living in them; they themselves are temples of the Holy Ghost, and agents of the miraculous power of Christ. In earthly culture they are ignorant still; in the wisdom of books they are still unlearned; of the mere accomplishments of oratory they are still destitute, and have the uncouth utterance of Nazareth, the provincial twang which the polished scholars of Jerusalem abhor and the temper of scholarship resents ; but they walk clothed with moral dignity, and speak, as their Master did, with authority, and not as the scribes. The limit of the change is accurately defined in them ; no miracle makes up to them the defects of early education, but the miracle is in the transfiguration of their character, the enlargement and consummation of their manhood. What does it all mean ? How do you explain it ? The explanation is given in the one pregnant sei tence that the rulers "took knowledge of them that they had been with Jesus."

Now let us study this group of men a moment. There, then, are the "rulers, and elders, and scribes." Their identification in modern life is not difficult. They are the aristocracy of their nation. They represent, so to speak, both Houses of Parliament and Convocation thrown in. They stand for all the political power and intellectual culture of their time. We can see them as they gather in grave confabulation, learned men, acute men, entirely respectable men, men of ligi t and leading, naturally contemptuous of the populace and indifferent to its praise or blame. And here also stands this poor abject cripple, one of the habitual beggars at the gate of the Temple, an unconsidered item of humanity, with no claim to notice save his physical misfortune. Life to him has been one slow tragedy ; he has been lame from his birth. We can see him also, excited and astonished, devoured with curiosity, hardly able to believe that his feet are his, watching the scene with a shrewd eye, and eager to see these great men who never gave him anything but their shadows as they passed in and out of the Beautiful Gate of the Temple, discomfited by these two miracle-men of Galilee.   And here are the two men, Peter and John, in whom the real interest of the scene is centred. One of them we know with something like intimacy. We know that Peter was a coward.   No one has yet forgotten the tale of Peter's boasting and the fact of Peter's denial.   We know that Peter was an uncouth fisherman, and we still hear the servant-girl in the hall of Caiaphas telling him that his speech bewrayeth him. We know that Peter had been bred up in all natural reverence for the priesthood, and ought, according to all natural anticipation, to have been very humble in the presence of his betters, and doubly humble with the memory of that ugly story of his broken boast clinging to him.   But see, he is nothing of the kind. He stands up before the elders of his people with an almost offensively aggressive manliness.   He speaks with a majesty and fire of phrase worthy of a great orator.   He accuses, he reproaches, he rebukes, the lords temporal and the lords spiritual of his nation.   He is bold even to rashness; he is vehement even to insult. And what is more, no one interrupts him ; no one gain-says or replies to him.   He is the uncontested master of the situation.   And as he speaks his voice grows more sonorous, the strength of his passion gives strange power and vehemence to his words, till at last, in one

great burst of defiant faith, he concludes thus : " This
is the stone which was set at nought of you builders,
which is become the head of the corner. Neither is
there salvation in any other: for there is none other
name under heaven given among men whereby we must
be saved." The only companion picture in history to
this is that memorable moment when a poor German
monk, facet o face with all the imperial and ecclesiastical
power of his time, and with the fire of martyrdom
almost lit beneath his feet, cri.·d at last to the Arch-
duke's splendid court and the great company of priests
and nobles who through the long day of controversy had
tried alternately to argue or frighten him down : " Here
I take my stand. God help me. I cannot retract ! "

Here, then, is a sample of what Christianity can
do ; and I submit it to your judgment. And the first
thing I ask you to notice is that Christ *emancipates
and enfranchises the intellect.* You perceive at once that
the intellectual stature of these men has been infinitely
increased by their comradeship with Jesus. I need
not delay on this point ; it needs neither argument nor
explanatory rhetoric. I state a fact, and an incon-
trovertible fact. And I do so for this reason : that
there is a flippant and foolish assumption abroad that
Christianity, so far from emancipating the intellect,
enslaves it. To believe—that is, to accept truth on any
other evidence than the evidence of the senses or the
reason—is, I am told, to put a fetter upon the intellect ;
to disbelieve is to enter into intellectual enfranchisement. Then when a young man has repudiated the

faith of his fathers and classified his Bible among the
romance books of history; when he has joined the
noble company of the doubters who are prouder of
their doubts than wise men are of their discoveries;
or when he has become an Agnostic, who does not
know and will not even take the trouble to doubt;
then, when the voice of Jesus Christ is silenced, and
instead the great babble of humai opinion is received
as a sufficing gospel, then come liberation and growth
of mind, then are experienced enlargement of faculty
and intellectual new birth! That is the assumption
which challenges the young men of to-day on every
side; and, I say, never was there a more entire and
mischievous blunder. Has the repudiation of Christianity ever led men to wider intellectual life? If those
who have repudiated Christianity have been great men,
is it not in spite of their infidelity, and not because
of it? When we have read the record of such lives,
has it not been easy to perceive that the absence
of religious faith produced defect and limitation of
intellect, and not enlargement? What is there in the
wisdom of Jesus Christ to stultify the most daring
mind, or repress the largest intellectual energy? Did
Christ fetter or emancipate the intellect of Paul? Did
He stifle or inspire the genius of Augustine? Michael
Angelo was no fool, and he adored Jesus Christ.
Milton was no dullard when he wrote his immortal
epic, nor Newton when he threaded the maze of natural
law, nor Kepler when he swept the heavens with his
scrutiny ànd made a pathway for his thoughts amid

the suns and constellations, nor Wordsworth when he sought the revelation of nature amid the silences of mountain tarn and solitude, nor Ruskin when he touches with illuminating magic the world of art; yet all these, and many others worthy to be ranked with them, have dwelt or dwell in the knowledge of the Lord Jesus Christ. It is not the faithful, but the faithless, who dwell in a contracted world, with half the intellectual faculties dead or torpid for the lack of use—it is they who put back the wheels of progress, not they who serve the world in the name that is above every name. Do not be deceived with the insolent pretensions of unbelief. Pause before you believe its promises of liberty, and recollect that the intolerance of heterodoxy is ten thousandfold stronger and more intense than the intolerance of orthodoxy. Do not take unbelief at its own price, nor accept its empty boasts as historic certainties. Think of Peter and John, and consider what Christianity did for them. Mark the new and intense intellectual life of these unlearned and ignorant men. See how they become orators, authors, historians, poets; see how vast an impulse and enlargement of intellect Christianity produces in them; and then remember that Christ is on the side of the intellect, and not against it. It is surely no common thing that fishermen and churls should suddenly become the organisers of a Church, the lucid exponents of a Divine and subtle system of thought and morals, the shapers of the world's future, and heroic workers in the world's progress; and the power that gave them this infinite expansion of faculty was no common power: it was the power of Jesus Christ working in them and through them to do His good pleasure.

And that this should be so is readily explained by the fact that nothing gives so deep an impulse to the intellect as the certainty of eternal things. Tell me, that I am only a creature curiously fashioned from the dust, that this world is all I have, that I am but an insignificant life struck out from the great whole, a spark of ethereal fire falling back into the night from which I came, a bead of foam tossed a moment on the sea of conscious being and lost again in the next roll of the dubious wave—tell me that, and you rob me of the very instinct of intellectual progress. What impulse have I then to expand powers which I know are doomed to speedy and complete annihilation? What is all this laborious structure of civilisation but a bitter mockery, the playing of ants upon an ant-hill, which the first heedless foot may kick away? Why should I strain my mind to know all mysteries and speak all tongues, if all this wealth of knowledge and experience is but the accumulation of the miser, which never can be used in any world beyond? Tell me I have no future beyond the grave, and the very impulse of intellectual progress is destroyed. But, oh, make me know, not by mere hearsay or the dull force of argument, but in myself and through my own spirit, that there is an invisible world close at hand to me, that what I am is but the promise of what I can be, that I can speak with that hidden world, that One is there who made me, loves me, wants me, and is waiting for me, and then the horizon of my thought broadens into infinity. Then I walk this little earth with a new sense of power, and dignity, and hope. Then I can rise above the maxims of the foolish and the customs of the cowardly, and talk to Sanhedrims boldly, in my own natural rights as a man. Then I am indeed renewed, emancipated with a glorious liberty, for I am filled unutterably full of glory and of God. Yea, I can even work miracles. My poor words take force and fire from the power of God which is in me, and are winged with a mastery which is not my own. I can do all things through Him that strengtheneth me, for I am ennobled with that vision of the world to come ; and others take knowledge of me that I have been with Jesus. My brother, this is no vain dream. I speak the words of truth and soberness. I point out to you plain, clear, indisputable facts. Again and again has Christ taken hold of illiterate men, and made them kings of thought and deed, the saviours of society, the emancipators of an age. The power of the world to come made John Bunyan a great writer, and John Hunt a great missionary. God found the one mending kettles and the other driving the plough ; and the work of one lives in an immortal book, of the other in a converted nation. And therefore I say you will never know what the fulness of intellectual life is till the mind that was in Christ is the mind that is in you. You will never even recognise the possibilities of

greatness which lie slumbering in your nature, waiting
for development, till you become a new creature in
Christ Jesus and know Him whom to know is life
eternal.

But the effect of contact with Christ is not only intellectual enfranchisement : *it is moral courage.* It was
the *boldness* of Peter and John which astonished every
one. There was a gigantic audacity about the men
which positively staggered the grave and potent fathers
of the Sanhedrim. What, could they believe their
ears ? This man, this fellow, this rude, illiterate
peasant, rebuking them ! Why, all Jerusalem knew
that but a few weeks ago he had sneaked away like a
pitiful cur in the hour of his Master's peril ; and now
look at him ! He plucks them by the beard, and flouts
them to their face. He positively has no respect whatever for dignitaries. He is as uncontrollable as a
whirlwind. He smites right and left, and has a sort
of diabolically inspired instinct for striking hardest on
the tenderest places. What does it mean ? What
are things coming to ? And the fellow cannot even
speak decently, and has probably never had a day's
education in his life ! You can overhear all the
whisper and the babble, for the world has often heard
it. And as I look upon the scene the lesson I learn
is that the firstfruit of Christianity is not meekness,
but *courage*, not the saintlike spirit of gentleness, but
the soldierly spirit of audacity.

Does that sound a strange gospel ? If so, it is because you have never read the Acts of the Apostles.

I know very well that the prevalent idea of Christianity
is something very different from this. Christianity is
supposed to be something to make men meek and
prudent, to draw the sap of manhood, and restrain
the too boisterous energies of youth. You must bend
all your energies to save your own soul. You must
be very careful not to offend anybody, for does not
St. Paul teach that we should live at peace with all
men ? You must be decorous to those who disagree
with you, and be content to politely differ with the
enemy, and must needs walk warily in this present
evil world and daily adorn the great doctrine of
Christian non-intervention ! Yes, that is a common
enough view of Christianity ; and its total effect has
been to reduce Christianity to a matter of hymn-singing,
and sermon-making, and pew-letting ! Behold the
magnificent result : meekness translated into pliability,
gentleness sunk into cowardice, and prudence transformed into the most hideous selfishness and egotism !
But as I read the Acts of the Apostles a new and
altogether different conception of Christianity dawns
upon me. I find that it was the boldness of the
Apostles which astonished everybody. They spake
as though joy did make them speak. They faced
death with the sublime innocence of children who had
never even thought of it. They did right with a perfectly heroic self-forgetfulness, never asking for a
moment where right would lead them. Elders, scribes,
priests, Sanhedrims, and mobs were all one to them ;
they had a work to do, and, like their Master, were

straitened till it was accomplished. They were swept on by an overmastering impulse; they acted as men inspired; they manifested a superb fearlessness which filled even their enemies with admiration. What was this impulse? How did they do this? The explanation is given in the words of one of that immortal brotherhood, who wrote, "The love of Christ constraineth me." "I count all things but loss for the excellency of the knowledge of Christ Jesus my Lord." "For to me to live is Christ; and to die is gain."

And moral courage is based on two things: first the *certainty of right*, and second *carelessness of self*; that is, conviction and unselfishness. To be right is to be strong. To be certain of your facts is to be invincible in argument. To know that Jesus Christ has risen from the dead because we have felt the risen presence with us, and to feel hourly the life of that Christ who is born again in the heart, thrilling and throbbing through every thought and act of life— that is the secret of Christian boldness. Who cares for man then? Does not the voice of Jesus reach us: "Fear not them that kill the body, and *after that* have no more that they can do"? Who fears the enmity of the world? Does not He say, "Be of good cheer; I have overcome the world"? Who walks in the terror of death then? Death is for us extinct, annihilated, deposed; and we say, with Richard Baxter,—

> "If life be long, I will be glad
> That I may still obey;
> If short, yet why should I be sad
> To soar to endless day?"

And not fearing death, the fear of lesser evils is removed; a sublime carelessness about self is ours.
The praise or blame of men is nothing to us. Wealth
has no lure, pleasure no bribe, ease no paradise, poverty
no terror. And again I say this is not rhapsody, but
historic fact. This is the temper which Christianity
has produced in the lives of tens of thousands, who
lived not to be ministered unto, but to minister. Oh,
when shall we all share it? When shall we shake
ourselves free of the fear of each other, and dare to
be fools for Christ's sake, that His wisdom may be
revealed in us? When shall we dare to do what He
did—make ourselves of "no reputation"—be outcast
from men, that we may be found in Him? When
will that boldness of rebuke which characterised Christ
characterise us, in the face of the lies, and tyrannies,
and evils, and impurities of our day? Oh, when shall
we cease to be cowards, and rise into the boldness of the
first Christians? And the answer is, When we *live with
Christ as they did;* and then, when Christ is all and in
all, and our words become the just reflection of our lives,
and our life is hid with Christ in God, then, and not
before, will others wonder at our moral boldness, and
take knowledge of us that we have been with Jesus.

The last thing to be noticed is, then, that Christianity
bases itself upon *concrete fact.* "And beholding the man
that was healed standing with them, they could say
nothing against it." There is the triumphant and in-
controvertible evidence—the man healed. Internal and
external evidence, arguments *a priori* and arguments

a posteriori, subtle deductions for the historic authenticity of Christianity drawn from idiom and mannerism, pleas, treatises, systems, apologetics—let them all go; here is the supreme evidence: " And beholding the man who was healed standing with them." Christianity does not arrest your attention as a system of thought, but as a fact; not as a philosophy, but as a life. It addresses itself to the common-sense of mankind. It holds no traffic in intellectual casuistries, which are the riddles of the learned; it puts its proof so plainly that the wayfaring man, though a fool, cannot err therein. There are more fools than wise men in the world, and Christianity takes count of the fools. For one who can follow a profound argument, there are a million incapable of sustained thought; and Christianity addresses itself to the incapacities of the common people. Common people have a healthy hunger for facts; and for that matter, even learned people have a wholesome respect for them. Fact is indeed the highest argument. It is the invincible granite on which the wave of intellectual subtlety is always broken. It cannot be put down, or got rid of, or ignored. When you have quite done your profound harangue, it says, " I am still here. You have not explained me. Please to reckon with me, for you have got to do so sooner or later." You want fact, then, do you? You ask, not for sermons, but for facts, do you? You shall have them. Here is a fact which has been standing in the world's highway this eighteen hundred years, and no one has yet been able to get rid of it: " And beholding the man

who was healed standing with them." It was no hal-
lucination. It could not be got rid of by rubbing the
eyes and trying a fresh argument. Here was a man
who yesterday could not walk, who had never walked
in his life, and here he stood whole, firm-footed, virile,
able to walk or race with the strongest of them. Peter
might be insolent, but the man was healed, and that
was enough to give vehemence to a less turbulent
tongue than Peter's. Christianity may be exploded by
a hundred treatises, and indeed its total overthrow has
been so often announced that we have ceased to be
troubled by the news; but here is the fact, men are
healed, millions of them, and are being healed every
day. What have you to say to that? When the
Sanhedrim looked upon that very lively and obvious
fact of the healed cripple, they did the only thing
sensible men could do: they admitted they could say
nothing against it.

And it is on that fact I take my stand. Will the
eyes of some youth who is already half atheist and
altogether infidel read these pages? I hope they may.
You repudiate Christianity because it presents serious
difficulties to a philosophic mind. The iron system
of necessitarianism which you have built up is logically
consistent and complete. It may seem to you right
that the world should be emancipated from the follies
of supernaturalism and the credulities of creeds. You
may even believe that you would confer an inestimable
benefit upon mankind in destroying its faith in Jesus.
Shelley thought so once; Rénan thinks so to-day: I will

take it for granted that you honestly think so too. But now can you tell me what actual benefit atheism has yet conferred upon mankind, or on yourself? Has atheism proved itself beneficent or philanthropic? Has it given men the victory over selfishness? Has it wiped away the tears of the mourner, or comforted the bruised heart of the orphan, or given crushed and struggling men a new impulse to heroic endeavour? Has it ever yet built an orphanage, an almshouse, a refuge for the outcast? Can it show me the man that it has healed? I have never heard of him. I have heard of the men it has destroyed, but never of the men whom it has healed. I do not remember to have seen an infidel orphanage, an iconoclasts' hospital, or even an almshouse for atheist widows. You can destroy, but you cannot construct. You can slay, but you cannot make alive. You can deform and defile, and make a man's life so bitter to him that suicide wears a new enchantment; but you cannot heal. I show you the men whom Christianity has healed. I show you the drunkard who is sober, the hopeless who have learned to look up again and become victors, the profligates who have received a new impulse of purity which has lifted them into newness of life, the children of darkness who have become the children of the light. Can you say anything against it?

Or does the Socialist read these words? You too have honest aims. You are filled with the spirit of righteous indignation against the artificial inequalities of life and man's inhumanity to man. In so far I

agree with you. But you preach the gospel of spolia-
tion, the crusade of universal anarchy, as the prelude
to the age of universal happiness ; and in that I disagree with you. You had your chance just a hundred
years ago in France ; did you heal mankind with that
fiery medicine of class-hatred and revenge ? Is the
man who was healed found in France to-day ? Did
that tremendous cautery of revolution after all extir-
pate the disease it aimed to cure ? I point you to the
one true Socialist, Jesus Christ of Nazareth. Take
His teachings as the code of individual conduct,
and you will soon find the world leavened with a
new spirit. Every force that to-day purifies and
sweetens the life of nations is the direct fruit of His
influence in the world. Wherever Christianity has
been honestly applied, there the working socialism of
love and charity has been set up ; and the difference
between us is simply this : what you seek in vain to
do by force, Jesus Christ accomplishes by kindness.
Can you say anything against it ?

And, lastly, I turn, in like manner, to the numerous
modern Sanhedrims of philosophers and pedants, statesmen who construct ideal republics, writers who are
eloquent for untried remedies, Church dignitaries who
have lost the spirit of Christ in the pomp and comfort
of the world's rewards. Spin the bright weft of your
philosophic doubts, construct your ideal society—on
paper, pour out your volumes of learned speculation
and poetic foreshadowings of the ideal future, but is
the man who is healed standing in your midst ? Have

you ever really helped any human spirit to a nobler style of living ? Call your congresses, good Churchmen, if you will ; appear in all the pomp of ecclesiastical state : but is the man healed in the midst ? It is to that test all our schemes of human regeneration must come. And as I ask the question old scenes seem to kindle into life before me. I see John Bunyan dragged before your fathers, and sent home to prison for preaching the Gospel. I see John Wesley reviled or ignored by your elders in the hour when he was saving England frcm the curse your lethargy had brought upon her. I see poor Salvation Army captains brought before you to-day, much as the Galilean fishermen were brought before your relatives a long time ago in Jerusalem, to be handed round, and discussed, and criticised with envious magnanimity or wondering contempt. Well, Bunyan, and Wesley, and the Salvation Army can at least give a good account of the notable miracle which has been wrought through them in the healing of multitudes. You can say nothing against it, for the facts are with them. Wherever Christ is, there the old miracle of salvation is still wrought. And therefore I hail any man, any Church, any system, any institution, that can show me the man healed with them. I care not how it may shock my prejudices, how it may insult my dignified prcconceptions ; if men are saved, Christ is there. That is the one infallible token of His presence. That is the one unalterable sign of the true Church, for there is " none other name under heaven given among men whereby we must be saved."

The cripple still lies in the Beautiful Gate of the Temple, and the problem we have to solve to-day is how he is to be healed. It is the problem of statesmanship not less than of the Church. Sabbath by Sabbath, as we come up to the ordered and decorous worship of the Church, there in our very pathway lies the loathsome and leprous form of the unhealed sorrow and misery of the world. The dumb beggar at the gate rebukes us for our pride, and pierces our comfortable formality with the poignant glance of his appeal. He is the living, shuddering, breathing agony of the world laid at our gate; the sorrows of centuries look out from his dim eyes, and are written on his wasted cheeks. And we are told to-day that, whatever power there was once in Christianity to heal this disfigured form, that force is now exhausted, and the time has come to formulate a religion of humanity which shall supersede the religion of Jesus Christ. Do you remember Tennyson's poem "In the Children's Hospital"? A little child lies white and patient waiting for the surgeon's knife, and prays to Jesus to help her bear the unknown pain. But the surgeon smiles with grim scepticism at her prayer; and the nurse who tells the story says,—

"Then he muttered half to himself; but I know that I heard him say,
'All very well, but the good Lord Jesus has had His day.'
Had? Has it come? It has only dawned. It will come by-and-bye.
Oh, how could I serve in the wards if the hope of the world was a lie?
How could I bear with the sights and the loathsome smells of disease
But that He said, 'Ye do it to Me when ye do it to these'?"

That puts the whole contention in a nutshell. If the

6

good Lord Jesus has had His day, then farewell to the charities and sacrifices which have made life easier to millions ! The truest love of humanity is kindled at the Cross. It is all very well to argue on paper that the moral effects of Christianity can go on without any necessary belief in Christ, but the fact remains that when Christ passes out of Christianity, Christianity is gone. It was in His name and by His power alone that the Apostles spoke healing to this man. In the living love of Christ alone is there the force that can arm men to be the true servants of humanity. In this at least the ages have altered nothing. And this day of His perfect victory has not yet come. But slowly as we pray and toil there rises on the eyes of the spirit the vision that aged poet saw, when he sat down at the end of a long life to write his last poem in the solemn shadows of approaching death. It was a noble farewell to the world ; it is a noble creed for those also who stand upon the threshold of its struggle :—

> "Out of the shadow of night
> The world rolls into light;
> It is daybreak everywhere."

V.

"For all that is in the world, the lust of the flesh, and the lust of the eyes, and the pride of life, is not of the Father, but is of the world. And the world passeth away, and the lust thereof: but he that doeth the will of God abideth for ever."—I JOHN ii. 16, 17.

A NY one who reads the Epistles must be struck with the constant recurrence of such phrases as "the world," "this world," occasionally "this evil world." In what sense is the word used? Do the Apostles speak of "the world" in our use of the term, as the physical universe, with its glorious vesture of living bloom and beauty, or is "this world" put in contrast with the other worlds of the stellar universe with which astronomy has made us familiar? We know that the latter supposition is impossible, for the veil of mystery which covers the firmament was not removed for the eyes of John and Paul; and of that star-sown heaven, with its rings of light and array of planets moving in their ordered courses, they knew nothing. We know that the other interpretation of the phrase would be almost as unfamiliar to them, for it is a curious thing to note that not once in the Acts of the Apostles, not once in the familiar diaries and letters of the Apostles, is there a solitary reference to what we know as natural beauty. The Apostles travelled through the noblest scenery of Europe, but there is not a single phrase which has reached us which might lead us to suppose that they felt its inspiration or were impressed with its charm and glory. It is quite admissible, indeed, to suppose that when they spoke of the world passing away they did include the physical universe, which to them was an unsubstantial pageant. They believed and taught that, firm and stable as the globe looked, yet it was a mere bright illusion, and would vanish in a moment when the elements melted with fervent heat. But in their common use of the phrase "the world" this is scarcely included. In their mouths the word acquired a new and original significance. What was that significance? The Apostle tells you in these phrases which are my text.

"The world" to John meant the great fabric of human civilisation, the pomp and splendour, the glory and desire, the lust and ambition, of that creature called man who was its lord and master. It was man who gave significance to the world. It was man who was vastly more than the globe he lived upon. And to John that globe was a place of infinite trial and temptation, and its supreme temptation was to blind men by its shows and splendours to the spiritual significance of life. It was the Vanity Fair, where the pilgrims of eternity forgot their noblest purposes and were allured from their Divine quest. Its gaiety and glory, its glittering baubles and visions of beauty, bewitched the sense and made man forget the greatness of his origin and the greatness of his destiny; in its booths of pleasure and chambers of delight, its novelty and fascination, and airy laughter, men were allured to destruction and forgot that they were pilgrims and sojourners as all their fathers were. And what, after all, was the world but a mere series of shows and vanities, like a village fair, all alive at night with light and music, and in the morning nothing left but the trodden grass and a broken pole or two to mark where it had been. It was passing away like a stage picture upon which the curtain would soon fall. It would pass, and "leave not a wrack behind;" but he that did the will of God, he that pushed on in his quest towards the house of God beyond, would abide for ever.

One can readily construct a very noble picture of the influence which these thoughts had upon the lives of the Apostles. One can follow Paul or John as they pass on their many pilgrimages, with their faces lighted with this rapt and silent flame and their hearts full of this great and simple thought. We see them enter great cities—cities like Athens, and Ephesus, and Corinth. There, on every side, rise vast temples, theatres, academies. There the chariots, with silver axles, go flashing down the streets; and the soldiers, with glittering banners, are massed in mimic war; and the air is everywhere perfumed with pleasure, and alive with the quick, eager, throbbing vitality of a great and sensuous people. We follow these men as they walk in their tattered raiment among the happy throngs, and we notice that that still flame upon their faces seems to burn brighter as they go. The flower-decked throngs, the crowded theatre, the music of the viol and lute—the spectacle of all that various, busy, brilliant life, seems to have no fascination for them. They pass on to the city's poorest quarter, and there, entering some low doorway, they look upon a very different scene. And what is that? It is a little group of simple, humble, hard-working men and women who have come together to learn the lessons of the Crucified. But on their faces, too, there burns this same flame, and their faces are marked by this same upward wistfulness, for these men are united by a common thought and are animated by a common purpose. And what is that? The thought is this: that, after all, that great world outside is passing away. Time, the great scene-shifter, already touches it; and soon silence will have fallen on theatre and stadium, and it will have vanished like a dream. But this little group of men have discovered something which will never fade or wither; they have found the great secret after which the East had always yearned, the futile dream of science and of philosophy for ages. They have found immortal life. Ephesus will pass; Corinth will be sown with dust; the chariot-wheels of time will roll over all these great cities of Asia Minor, and level and obliterate them so that one stone will not be left upon another. The great world itself will be rolled up like a garment, and put away like a worn-out vesture. But these men and women will stand unhurt amid the wreck of empire, and stand victorious over time and death. They are heirs of God and joint-heirs with Christ. "The world passeth away, but he that doeth the will of God abides for ever."

Now, let us ask, was this the mere morbid dream of an ascetic, or was it true ? And if it be true, in what way is it true ? What is it that is passing away ? What is it that abides ? Why does it abide ? Let us try for a few moments to answer these questions.

"The world." "*This* world." By implication, then, there is another world. I need not dwell long upon that primary fact. I only dwell upon it that I may say this much : that if there are any people who more than others are apt to forget the existence of another and a spiritual world, unseen, but real and close to them day and night, it is the people who live in cities. The very housetops shut out the visible heavens from view. The contiguity of human life seems to lessen the sense of Divine mystery. Men who spend many solitary hours with nature—men whose calling is in the great waters or the open fields—cannot help feeling something of the ghostly side of nature. For them there are presences on the solitary hills ; there are voices in the wind ; and there is the sense of unseen life touching them on all sides, to which the imagination is sensitive and conscious. But when men come to live in cities, they are like little children who crowd round the bright fire in a little room, and do their best to forget the illimitable mystery of the wide night that

reigns without.   There is no solitude; there is no time
for silent communing; there is no chance for nature to
find us.   The veil between us and the angel-world
seemed very thin in the days when the rushing of the
wind over the wide moor at night seemed like the
passing of many wings, and when the shimmering of
the moonlight in the shadow of the trees was like the
white gliding of heavenly presences.   But here it is a
thick and stifling curtain, and the sense of wonder
slowly perishes within us.   We have no sense that
we are passing away.   We are like men on board ship
who fulfil their duty hour after hour as though they
were upon the land, and forget that every moment the
screw turns and the wake of foam flies behind, and
league after league of wave is passed; and busy as
they are, still they are being borne on unconsciously
beneath the wind-swept vault of heaven to the distant
harbour.   Everything with us seems so fixed and so
stable—the bank, the 'change, the office, the order and
routine of life and duty—that the natural instinct
of another world, real and near, gradually decays, and
we are apt to become men of this world, who have
their portion in this life.

But John specifies in these phrases precisely what he
means when he says that the world is passing away.
First of all, he says that " the lust of the flesh " passes
away.   By that I understand the animal needs and
appetites, the physical strength and vigour.   If you
take it in the narrowest sense, how true it is.   " Lust,
when it has conceived, bringeth forth death."   Lust

stings itself to death. There is a period in life when
the desires of the flesh exercise immense influence and
subtle power over the imagination. They seem to
promise illimitable delight and inexhaustible p'easure.
They sting the flesh with their violence, and send the
blood boiling through the veins like a tide of fire.
The imagination runs through the world and sees
everywhere alluring forms which point to intoxicating
joys. That is not an unusual experience. It is
common to all of us in the heyday of youth and
strength; and I only allude to it to ask this question: Have you considered that this is passing away?
Do you know that the gamut of appetite and passion
is very limited after all? You can soon reach
up and strike the topmost note, and downward and
strike the lowest. Do you know that these violent
delights have violent ends? They are soon exhausted,
and the hungry passion is satiated, and the promise
which it made is found a cheat. It is so. It is so if
for no other reason than this: because physical life
itself fails. Youth is soon gone; manhood is soon
passed; old age is soon reached. You are not what
you were. Already the keen edge and zest of earthly
appetite is blunted. You dislike, perhaps, to admit it;
and yet you know in your hearts that the best cup of
wine which life has to give you is already drunk, and
that life will never prepare again for you the like.
You say, perhaps, as Shelley said—and some of you
say it at the age at which Shelley said it: you say it at
thirty; you say it with a heart embittered; you say

it with a life shattered; you say it standing amid
ruined hopes—

> " O world, O life, O time,
>   On whose last steps I climb,
>   Trembling at that where I stood firm before,
>   When shall return the glory of my prime ?
>   No more, ah nevermore !

> "Out of the day and the night
>   A joy has taken flight ;
>   Fresh spring, summer, and winter hoar
>   Shall fill my heart with grief,
>   But with delight
>   No more, ah nevermore !"

In other words, the lust of the flesh is passing away.
Your desires, and passions, and appetites are already
weakened by drudgery, by sickness, by use, by years ;
and they smoulder like a fire which is almost spent.
You fan it for a moment into feverish activity, but that
is all.   The flame spurts up to die down again into
deeper darkness.

Have you lived, then, for the lust of the flesh ?   Are
you, young man, living for the lust of the flesh ?   Are
the chief uses and joys of your life mere animal uses
and joys ?   Then you will soon be bankrupt.   They
are passing away ; and you will soon realise the bitter
epigram, "Youth is folly ; manhood is struggle ; old
age is regret."

Then, again, John uses another phrase : "the lust
of the eyes."   The eye is the portal of innumerable
delights.   It is "the meeting-place of many worlds."
Through it there stream in upon the mind the vision
of beauty, the revelation of science, the pomp and

pageantry of earthly power, all the bright, shifting splendour of human glory. Have you ever considered that riches appeal mainly to the eye ? It is the eye which interprets to a man the stateliness of the house which he has built, the beauty of the gardens which he has laid out, the picture's charm, the statue's grace, the horse's symmetry—in a word, all those costly embellishments with which wealth can adorn life. To the blind man they are nothing. To be blind is to lose almost everything that riches can bestow. Yet, says John, the lust of the eyes, too, is a fading passion which is soon satiated. The first house a man buys looks better and bigger to him than any house he owns afterwards. The first picture a man owns brings him more genuine pleasure than all the others put together. And, after all, a man can only sleep in one bed at a time, and can only live in one house at a time ; and that lust of the eye which desires to add house to house and land to land has a lessening pleasure in its acquisitions. Like the lust of the flesh, after all it is a life of sensation ; and all sensation is limited and soon exhausted. You, perhaps, have set your hope in some such direction as this. You desire to be rich ; your eye lusts for the luxurious abodes of wealth and the circumstance and state of social greatness. When the lust of the flesh fails, the lust of the eye often develops ; and the man who has lost the one frantically tries to recoup himself by flying to the other. But it is vain. The miseries of the idle rich, their *ennui*, their listlessness, their discontent, their imbecile thirst for new sensations, their perpetual invention of new and artificial joys, remind us how true are the words of John that the lust of the eyes, too, passes away.

And the third aspect of the world John characterises as "the pride of life." That may signify either the pride of power or the pride of knowledge. Take it, for instance, as the pride of power. Take it in regard to that great and splendid empire with which the Apostles were familiar. It seemed built to last for ever. It was just; it was powerful; it was imposing. To be a Roman was to be armed with an invincible defence. It was a proud boast which clothed the meanest man with dignity. The tramp of the legions of Rome echoed in every city; the silver eagles were borne in triumph through all the world; its laws had imposed civilisation upon the most barbarous peoples; and its power had crushed nation after nation like green withs in the hand of a giant. There was no sign in John's day of any overthrow. Its colossal fabric rose without seam or fissure, and it seemed as stable as the everlasting hills. Yet this solitary man told the truth when he said, not merely that it would pass away, but that it was passing away. He recognised a deeper law than man's—that mysterious law of God which seems to take nation after nation, and give to nations their chance, and strengthen them with universal victory, and then depose them, lest one good custom should corrupt the world. Egypt, Chaldea, Babylon, Greece, all had had their day, and ceased to be. And so it would be with Rome. This

solitary man stood before its impregnable walls, and
saw the doom already written on them, and in his
vision saw them sink in the great abyss, and time close
up above the wreck, as the waters close up above some
stupendous shipwreck. He said that it would pass
away and was passing away. We to-day know that
it has passed away.

And it is true of the pride of knowledge. The justest
and noblest pride of life, because the highest, is the
pride of knowledge. Yet that, too, is transient.
Nothing shifts its boundaries so often. Nothing is so
illusive. Nothing passes through such strange and
rapid transformations. The knowledge of Galileo
would be the ignorance of to-day ; and if Isaac Newton
were alive now, he would have to go to school again.
A century, a half-century, a single decade, is often
sufficient to thrust the most brilliant discoveries into
oblivion, and to number them with the memories of an
obsolete past. The steam engine has supplanted the
coach ; but the steam engine is already passing away,
and in fifty years' time will be supplanted by some
greater and more serviceable power. The telegraph
has bound nations, together, and has made all nations
neighbours; but the telephone is becoming its rival: and
in another century and less, perhaps, men will hear each
other's whispers round the globe. Gas has played its
part, but few can doubt that years will efface it with a
nobler light ; and our children will wonder at our gas
jets, just as we wonder at and pity our ancestors with
their farthing candles. A thousand illustrations might

be given of how knowledge perpetually effaces its past, and the discoveries of which we are so proud perish even while we praise them. You cannot rest in science, for science knows no rest. It knows no finality. It is like Jonah's gourd: it doubles itself while he sleeps. It does not abide ; it cannot abide. It is merely another great object lesson which the Great Master puts upon His black-board, as it were ; and then He rubs the diagram out and begins a higher and nobler one. If, then, you enthrone yourself on the confident edicts of the latest science, if you should oppose to the simplicity of the Divine teaching the intellectual pride of a mind secure in what it calls " scientific certainty," I reply that there is no certainty in science ; it is passing away. It affords no place for the sole of the foot. The knowledge of to-day will be the ignorance of to-morrow, and the abstrusest calculations of time will be the mere rudiments and alphabet of eternity.

Nor is this a mournful truth. It is rather a glorious and hopeful one. It is no tolling bell which announces that the world is passing away. It is rather the pealing of a triumphant trumpet. It means that God's law is progress ; and that is a glorious truth for those who can understand it. But there is a mournful side to progress, and it is that many men resent it, and cling to their old habitations long after the doom of decay has been written over them. School is an admirable thing, but we do not always want to be at school. We catch visions of a larger life beyond. We are waiting for the moment when the Master will say that school is ended, and the door is opened ; and we shall leave this little schoolhouse to find a world larger than we dreamt of, and nobler and more various in its employments than we have ever conceived. That is the true view of life ; and therefore we cannot regret, but rather rejoice, that one by one our lessons are ending, our classes are being passed : we are graduating in the discipline of life, and are passing to the life of eternity.

Well, then, what is it that abides ? In a word it is character. It is what a man is, not what a man knows, or what a man acquires, or what a man achieves. Character outlives the centuries. Moses, Paul, John, stand before the world to-day untouched by the defacement of time. What they were they are, and what they are they will be through all the unmeasured and immeasurable spaces of eternity. The lust of the flesh perishes. Of all those gay multitudes who filled the streets of Ephesus, and paced with busy feet across the squares of Corinth, not a footprint remains ; and their passion, their pride, and their lust have perished with them. The lust of the eyes perishes; and Babylon is marked by a heap of rubbish, and ancient Rome by a crumbling arch, a weather-beaten pillar, a ruined Coliseum.

> "Where the domed and daring palace
> Shot its spires
> Up like fires ;
> Where a tower in ancient time
> Sprang sublime,
> And a burning ring all round
> The chariots traced
> As they raced ;

> Where the multitude of men
> Breathed joy and woe
> Long ago,
> Now the country does not even
> Boast a tree,
> As you see."

And the pride of life, the curious speculations of the world's greatest philosophers, become the ˌpastime of the learned ; and their names become thin shadows in a vanished past.   But there is something that abides ; it is character.   "He that does the will of God abides for ever."

And that is true in its mere altruistic and earthly sense.   Character abides.   We all of us know the beautiful verse of George Eliot,—

> "Oh, may I join the choir invisible
> Of those immortal dead who live again
> In lives made better by their presence."

It expresses a noble truth ; such lives do live again. Such lives do not know death.   The trampling and confusion of victorious armies die away ; the pomp and glory of throne and court perish ; the very conquests of knowledge are forgotten.   But lives that are lived for others, lives that are lived in doing the will of God, lives that sow the seed of goodness and of noble impulse in the hearts of others—those lives go on living, and defy the centuries.   The thoughts of Paul are more to us to-day than all the triumphs of Rome.   The life of Jesus is infinitely more to us than the lives of all the Cæsars put together.   And when the glory of empire is forgotten, and when all

the brilliant achievements of a man's life are blotted
out by the obliterating hand of death, Jesus tells us
there is one thing which will be remembered—one
thing which, perhaps, the man himself has forgotten,
but it is remembered in the heart of God : inasmuch
as this man "gave a cup of water" to one of these
little ones, it is remembered at the judgment day,
when he stands before his Master. Goodness, mercy,
love, all that constitutes character—the life lived in
the service of others, the life poured out in self-forgetful toil, the life of the saint, and the hero, and
the martyr—we see that these do abide for ever in
the memory of mankind ; and still more do they abide
in the records of heaven.

But John goes deeper than that, he shows us how
character is to be gained. It is by doing the will
of God. In each man's heart there is the revelation
of that will. There is no life that God does not
touch. There is no man who can escape the scrutiny
or who can escape the voice of God ; and to do that
will of God as that will is revealed, to do it when
it is difficult, to do it simply, and humbly, and obe-
diently—that is the way towards character, towards
character which outlives death.

Notice, it is personal life which John speaks of when
he says that such a man will abide for ever. It is not
the immortality of memory and influence. It is not
that impersonal immortality which simply means that
our lives will be a mere bright tradition living among
men and blessing them when we are gone. Oh, no :

7

it is personal life. The man who does the will of
God passes through a stage of moral evolution. He
enters upon immortal life. He has broken the barrier
of the earthly, and has inherited the heavenly. He
has touched a higher life, and has already begun to
live with an everlasting and Divine vitality. Doing
the will of God, he has put himself, as it were, in
line and in touch with the living power of the universe;
and he shares its life. He has broken the walls of
this sluggish life as the chrysalis breaks its cerements
when the silken wings are given to it, and it flutters
away into the spring air, "a thing of beauty and
a joy for ever." So the man who does the will
of God has passed out of a lower condition into a
higher condition. He has passed through a moral
evolution which enables him to lay hold of a larger
and of a higher life. He is joined to God, and God
is immortal. He is grafted on a living tree; and,
poor as the graft may be, the life of that Divine
tree soon fills its veins : and it, too, lives for ever.

O, young men! there is the secret of immortality.
Do the will of God; love the love of God; live the
life of God : and "this is life eternal, to know the
only true God, and Jesus Christ, whom He has sent."

And, blessed be God, there are men all over the
world who have consciously entered upon this eternal
life. Just as we see Paul or John turning aside from
the crowded ways of some great city, leaving the wide
streets, with their brilliant throngs and their vivid and
various life; just as we catch sight of them as they

enter some low doorway and find a little group of
men and women who have received this message
of immortality, so we turn aside from the streets of
our great cities, and every here and there we find
gathered little groups and congregations of men and
women who have consciously entered on eternal
life. Not many great, not many mighty, but many
poor and many humble there are, whose life is filled
with this daily consciousness of life in God. They
feel in themselves the power of an endless life. They
know that Christ is born in them, the hope of glory.
They know in whom they have believed, and are
persuaded that He will keep that which they have committed to Him against the eternal day. Their poor
homes are lit with the splendour of the true Shechinah.
Their feet move to the sound of heavenly music. Their
homes are filled with the whisperings of voices sweeter
than any earthly. They are daily trying to live as
Christ lived. They are seeking to be gentle, meek,
and humble, to comfort the broken-hearted sister, to
nurse the sick child, to lift the stumbling feet. London
will pass away; its cathedral, its Parliament-house,
its palaces, its Bank, its Exchange, its mighty streets,
its noble monuments, will all crumble before the breath
of the ages; and some day, perhaps, the sea will
roll over the spot where now St. Paul's lifts its
golden cross, and the wild fowl will cry over the
place where once St. Stephen's sheltered those who
held the world in awe: but these, the poorest and
the humblest of them, will live long after London

has vanished like a distempered dream—for, having done the will of God on earth, they will have fitted themselves to do the will of God in heaven, and will abide for ever. The greatness of England herself will one day pass away. The bonds of her mighty empire will be loosened. The story of her long supremacy will become a tale of reverend antiquity, and other fleets than ours will sail the seas, and another flag than ours will be carried round the world in triumph. But the victory of these, who did the will of God, will still abide, and they will share the glory of a kingdom which is everlasting and of whose power there is no end.

And at last the world itself will toil onward to its close, and its central fires will cool and its infinite life and glory will perish; but in that hour

"When the stars grow cold,
And the world grows old,
And the leaves of the judgment book unfold,"

those who have done the will of the Father will still abide in a world where there is no night, no sorrow or sighing, no decay or death. Oh, it is no dream, it is no poet's vision, it is no vain utterance. It is the message of Christ, uttered, perhaps, to rebellious hearts and to sceptical ears, that we may come unto Him and have life, and have it more abundantly.

And we may do another thing: we may become men of this world, and have our portion in this life. We may be dazzled and deceived by its splendours; we may deny free play to the nobler instincts that are

within us; we may quench the Holy Spirit which
kindles in us Divine yearnings. You may narrow
your life down till you become contented with it in
its narrowness, just as the prisoner, long imprisoned,
forgets the green, bright world outside and the singing
of the lark, and at last is content with his cell, and even
comforts himself that his cell is better than another
next to him; and so because there is a lower depth
still opening which he has not yet reached, he is happy
in his narrow world, and congratulates himself on his
imprisonment. And so you will have your portion in
this life. You will have it as Dives had it, of whom
it is said: "He died and was buried." There was
nothing else to say. But that treasure in the heaven,
that secure habitation, that Divine life of purity and
duty, you will have lost. You will have gained that
which brings with it sorrow in the getting. You will
have lost that which alone was worth the gaining;
and what shall it profit a man if he gain the whole
world and lose his own life—his life of lives, his
own soul?

VI.

PURITY.

"Keep thyself pure."—1 TIM. v. 22.

THIS is a counsel to a young man, spoken by an
aged man. The young are the strength of the
present and the inheritors of the future ; theirs is the
accumulated wisdom of the ages which are ended and
the endless hopes of the ages which are to come.
They bring the vigour of undiminished energy into
the struggle where older men are weary, and are the
perpetual reserve-force which nature marches up to re-
inforce the baffled armies of to-day. That which aged
hearts have longed in vain to see they will behold ; the
broken promises of the past it will be theirs to possess
and redeem. The old man catches at his few remaining
years of life as a miser at his lessening gold, but the
young man has a sense of infinite wealth in the un-
squandered future which is his. To be young is to
be a millionaire in hope, to feel young is very bliss. A
nation's future is with her young men, for what the man
of twenty thinks the nation will soon think. I address
you, then, as the only truly wealthy people in the world
—rich in strength, in resolve, in ambition, in time, in
opportunity ; you, who stand in the golden gateways

of the dawn, and see the years before you like a fruitful country at your feet ripe for conquest; and with
no nobler word can I salute you, as you go down to
your battle and your inheritance, than this w rd of
Paul's to Timothy: 'Keep thyself pure."

Now, if I were to ask you, *What is the greatest force
in human life?* I wonder what reply you would give me.
There are many men, and among them those with the
keenest knowledge of the world, who would perhaps
answer, *Money.* See, they would say, what money can do!
It can dictate war or peace for nations, it binds together
the most distant lands with invisible cords, it can lift
the beggar into honour and the pauper into the proud-
est vantage-ground of luxury, it can shake the markets
of the world with one whisper of its golden lips, it
can infect whole peoples with the frenzy of avarice at
the rattling of its burnished coin. Money, like a mighty
sorceress, mesmerises the world into obedience; and to
possess it the patriot will sell his country, the man of
genius his brains, the woman her chastity, the merchant
his conscience. Money harnesses the lightning to run
its errands, and plucks the heart of the earth out to swell
its gains. It is the life-blood of commerce and the
defence of nations. For lack of it the charities of noble
hearts are unexpressed, and the inventor's skill is para-
lysed upon the brink of victory. Great is money, cries
the youth who stands amid the whirl of life in a great
city, for is it not what all the city seeks, the secret pivot
round which all the vast circles of the roaring, restless
maelström perpetually revolve and race?

Or, says another, *Power*, force of intellect, foresight, will—these things are the mightiest forces in human life. The faculty of governing makes one man the lord of millions, and one nation the dictator of the world. Money without brains is a weapon without hands to wield it; money is the end of little men, but the means of great ones. But this strenuous faculty, which we call greatness in a man, is the real master, gathering into its mighty hands the threads of opportunity, and weaving from them the purple robe of fame, defying circumstance, and making it the ladder of ambition.

Or, cries yet another, *Love* is the real master of the universe. Men are governed by their passions, and the heart is the rudder which turns the ship of man- hood whither it will upon the roaring time-floods. The heart prompts the intellect, and the intellect rules the will, and the will shapes the world. Love, in the blindness of its passion, has wrecked empires, ruined statesmen, and sapped the pillars of the most ancient thrones and temples. It is, in fact, the vital heat of life, and the hearts of men are the real seats of govern- ment, the centres from which the world is ruled.

Money, Power, Love—is there no mightier force in the world than these? Money, which takes to itself wings and flies away; power, which covers the world with empire and perishes in the impotence of exile; love, which drops its magic wand at the vision of the open grave? Think again; is there nothing higher, mightier, diviner? There is. Character is the grandest force the world possesses. It is that which determines the use and direction of money, and love, and ambition. It is that which is the secret force working behind and through all human life. It is character which shapes the centuries, and leaves its indelible mark on the records of the world. Character never dies; the tomb is its enfranchisement, the indefinite enlargement of its area of influence. The words of Shakespeare are but the beautiful vesture spun to clothe his character, and his character is the living form which moves within his works. Character is that solitary and inalienable possession which time and death cannot destroy, which survives vicissitudes and sorrows, which rises triumphant over the brief infamy of slander, and pierces the frail defence of lying praise; character is that which shapes life and determines destiny, and which death itself is impotent to annihilate or overthrow.

Now, push the question a step further, and ask, what is the greatest force in determining character? There, again, you might reply, Energy, perseverance, purpose; but these are the results rather than the causes of character. There is a diviner quality, and that is Purity. Purity is life; purity is the true vital element which supplies energy to character. Glance over the crowded field of human action, and see how true this is. There are men we meet who seem prodigally gifted in many ways, but there is some mysterious lack about them, of which we are painfully conscious. Their words are eloquent and beautiful enough, yet they do not impress us; their presence is fascinating, yet it has no potency really to affect others. Somehow we do

not trust them; there is an instinct which warns us
they are laths painted to look like iron, that their
brilliance springs from no true interior light, but is
merely outward, like the deceptive glimmer of phos-
phorescent paint, which makes a clothes-prop shine
like a pillar of fire; that, in fact, the real man is very
different to the apparent man. There are other men
we meet whose intellectual gifts are perhaps very
limited, but yet they are clothed with a mysterious
power, and make us sensible of a prevailing personality.
There is something accompanying the word they speak,
a breath of divinest music which pierces to the heart's
core. Men say when they leave such a man, " He's a
good man," although he has never said a word about
religion. Bad and worldly men seem to feel a strange
and subtle fragrance falling on their world-hardened
hearts while they talk with them, like the faint gust of
sweet perfume blown by spring winds from distant
violet-beds and yellow meadows, which sometimes
penetrates the London smoke, and meets us unaware,
and suddenly makes us yearn for the country. What
is this power? It is purity. Like the light which
shone on the face of Moses after he had talked with
God, so a mysterious splendour seems to clothe the
man whose heart is pure. But the impure heart
vitiates everything. It leers like a satyr out of the
eyes which gleam with intellect; it runs like a mocking
discord through the voice which thrills with eloquence.
The impure man carries with him a force which per-
meates and spoils everything, and which discounts all

his gifts of intellect. It was purity which robed Christ as with a garment of power, and was an invisible armour shielding Him from the shafts of enmity. It was the secret of a majesty men could not comprehend, of a spell men yielded to even while they hated Him. It fell upon them like a great and searching light ; silent as the light it wrought its magic, mighty as the light it miraculously prevailed, beautiful as the light it shamed the darkness and drove it back discomfited. Unquenched by infamy and death, it broke out anew upon a cross at whose foot the very executioner cried, " This is a just man ;" and it has since flooded the world with a splendour which has pierced all ages and drawn the wondering regard of all. Christ was the Light of the world, and the light that dwelt in Him was the Divine Light of a perfect purity.

That absolute sinless purity of Christ stands alone ; but I have now to ask you to remember that there are two great inheritances which every man starts the world with—viz., *Human Innocence and Purity.* Christ presupposed that when He looked round upon that great crowd at the Mount, and said, " Blessed are the pure in heart, for they shall see God." He seemed to have recognised there some of those flower-like human faces which are full of innocence. Paul also urges Timothy to maintain unimpaired that which he already possesses : " Keep thyself pure." Christ makes the type of Christian character a little child ; and to have a child's heart—fresh, loving, docile, innocent—is to enter the kingdom of God. Do you say, Has the

child no evil tendencies ? There are tendencies, tem-
pers, passions which are full of peril, but the child's
heart is pure, his mind is untainted. He comes to us
clothed in the celestial raiment of innocence, and purity
is the crown and secret of his beauty. O blessed little
children, we are sometimes tempted to cry, would that
we could keep you from the evil sights and sounds of
this sad world ! Would that we might shut you up in
some garden of lilies and roses, far from the ways of
men, that you might grow as sweetly as the flowers,
and be clothed with as fair a beauty, and distil as rich
a fragrance ! Would that the tender bloom upon the
mind might never be rubbed off, that the pathetic
ignorance of evil might never be bartered for polluting
knowledge ! But for whom is that possible ? And if
it were possible, would it be desirable ? Have not men
and women often fled the world to escape the evil of
the world, and has not the result been that the pollutions of the monastery have outweighed its pieties ?
I should be a poor counsellor of young men if I taught
you that purity is only possible by isolation from the
world. We do not want that sort of holiness which
can only thrive in seclusion ; we want that virile,
manly purity which keeps itself unspotted from the
world, even amid its worst debasements, just as the
lily lifts its slender chalice of white and gold to heaven,
untainted by the soil in which it grows, though that
soil be the reservoir of death and putrefaction. You
may make your bed in hell, and yet be clothed with
the raiment of heaven ; you may touch the impure,

and know the secrets of impurity, and yet keep the untainted thought and uncorrupted life. Innocence perishes, but purity may survive. One has the fragile beauty of the flower, the other of the block of crystal, drawn out of the darkness, but still white; or of the diamond, lying in its bed of clay, but with the fiery sunlight still stored up in its heart, and flashed forth undimmed upon the comradeship of dust in which it lies. Innocent we scarce can be; pure we all may be.

I ask you then to notice, *Purity is possible; it is a possession; it may be kept.* "Keep thyself:" that teaches individual responsibility. Get that fact clear and distinct to the mind; grasp it, and live by it. And why do I emphasise this very trite and commonplace observation? Because we live in a world of bottomless cant, and the first duty of a true man is to free his mind from cant. Men pray "lead us not into temptation," and then hang round a drinking-bar; they say "deliver us from evil," and then sit down to read a scrofulous French novel. Men pray God to keep them, and then open their ears to the foul story or indecent jest; they look to God's grace to save them, but they take no pains to save themselves. But God's grace is useless to the man who will not use it. It is like the sunlight; we can have it for the asking, but we must draw up our blinds to let it in. It is like water—everywhere—but God does not cause it to spring up exactly under our dining-room tables to save us the trouble of drawing it; if we want it, we must fetch it. How can God keep a man pure who has eyes full of adultery, and who lets his imagination feed upon the secret suggestions of unchaste passion ? A ·man might as well pray to escape fever, and yet persist in sleeping with a fever corpse ; to escape fever you must guard against it. Young men plead the strength of their passions and the ardency of their imaginations, but strong passions are simply an indication of weak will. The world is full of bright and holy things for the imagination to feed upon ; but if you feed it with offal, what wonder that the thought is coarse ? A man's will is the king of his body ; let the will rule then. But remember you cannot take fire into the bosom and not be burned ; you cannot listen to impure jests and be unpolluted ; you cannot read vile stories and remain clean ; the seat of the scorner is a bad place to sing God's praises in, and he who stands in the way of the ungodly soon is hustled onward by the crowd, and must needs walk and run in the way too. If thou wouldst be pure, "Keep thyself pure."

Further, it must be noted *Purity is not Outward, but Inward.* How can a man keep himself pure ? Read Leviticus, and you will see how men once attempted it. The Mosaic law is one great treatise on purity ; there were certain meats impure, certain acts and conditions of health impure, and certain washings and ceremonies were needed to restore the forfeited purity. It was all outward and physical, and for a degraded people, learning the alphabet of morality, it was no doubt a good and wise discipline. Nations walk before they run; they learn the elements of physical purity before the greater lesson of spiritual purity, and perhaps a clean body has more to do with a clean mind than some of us suppose. But because this Mosaic purity was all physical and outward, it broke down ultimately. Men found out that purity began within and worked outward, not without and worked inward. And so, what did David say? He had no doubt scrupulously observed every law of physical purity, and yet in one wild hour of passion he became an adulterer and a murderer. And then what did he say? "Create in me a clean heart, O God, and renew a right spirit within me!" The fifty-first Psalm is the most pathetic cry which ever came up to God from the depths of a man's sore heart and sinful spirit! It is the acknowledgment that sin begins inside a man, and that there can be no change of act till there is a change of heart; that to be pure the spirit must be pure; to act righteously we must think righteously; to live well before men we must live well before God. "Oh," cries the poor, soiled, broken-spirited man in his hour of shame, "create *in me* a clean heart, and renew a right spirit within me!"

Perhaps this lesson also, that Purity is inward and not outward, seems a very trite and commonplace one; but see how much it implies. Are not men perpetually blaming *circumstance* instead of self? There is a youth listening to my words who is fresh from the country. The first effect the multitudinous life of a great city has had on your mind is to loosen your sense of

responsibility.   Your individuality seems blotted out
in this great mass of men.   At home every one knew
you, and this sense of their scrutiny was a restraint
upon you.   Here no one knows you, and you are in
the perilous position of one who can do wrong without
loss of reputation.   And then, too, there is another
influence of a great city which you have already felt.
A great city seems to give publicity to things only
hinted at in the country.   Life is on a magnificent
scale, and the cracks scarcely discerned on the small
picture yawn wide and plain on the vaster canvas.
You see things you only dreamt, and hear things you
only thought, and touch things you only imagined.
And then you begin to delude yourself that if you had
only remained in the village you could have been pure,
but that purity is scarcely possible in a " Sodom of
covetousness and fornication," whose smoke ascends
day and night, and blots out the healing vision and
blue serenity of heaven.   Is that what you say ?   It
is all false, sir, and you know it !   The village has its
vice as well as the city ; morally the city is only the
village writ large.   If you are not pure in thought
here, neither would you be there.   Such excuses
simply amount to this : you were virtuous when you
could not sin, but you are ready to sin as soon as
opportunity shall connive with your desire.   You blame
the situation, but the man makes the situation, not the
situation the man.   I have no faith in hot-house virtue
which can only thrive in peculiar soils, and at given
temperatures ; **true virtue is virtue anywhere.**   The

true gentleman behaves as finely before paupers as
before kings ; the truly honest man is as honest standing up to his knees in another man's gold as in keeping
a bag of coppers safe; and true purity is purity anywhere, just as light is light everywhere, whether it
stream into the lazar-house of vice, or fall on the
sumptuous embroideries which are in kings' chambers.
And why is it so ? Because it is inward and not outward ; it is independent of circumstances and triumphs
over them. If you have the pure heart, it will be as
pure amid the smoke of London as in the clear atmosphere of your native village ; and so far from speaking
in scornful anger of great cities, you will recognise
that great cities are the great battle-grounds of Christ,
where the harder conditions of the strife only make
the warfare doubly glorious.

See, too, how men deceive themselves by practising
an outward purity when there is none within. You
have never done an unchaste deed, you resent the
imputation with an angry blush. And, O my brother,
it is much to be able to say that! There are thousands
who would give a year of life to be able to say it,
thousands who to-day are plagued with the hideous
memory of one vile act, and who cry in vain, as Lady
Macbeth did, "Out, damned spot !" But examine
your own heart, and tell me what thoughts are yours ?
What shapes are these which inhabit the secret
chambers of the soul ? Have you made your memory
the haunt of unclean stories ? Do you not often set
the imagination on fire with evil suggestions, till

8

through the unguarded doorways of the heart troop the satyrs, and your inward eye gazes unabashed on the riot of corruption ? You have not done the act but you have thought it ; you have not broken the command, but you have desired to; outwardly you are without spot, but you are a leper within. O, let me plead with you, " Keep thyself pure." " Every man is tempted when he is led away of his own lust and enticed." You are the tempter of yourself. Sin is a thing of desire before it can be incarnated in the deed. Dismiss the alluring shape; shake off the vile spell ; fall to your knees and pray mightily to the God who gives us the power we lack, for you stand in slippery places. The foulest monsters of humanity once stood where you are standing. They drank in eagerly the suggestions of iniquity; they acted out the drama of wrong a thousand times in the empty theatre of the heart. Then the divine shyness of modesty began to die away; they went a little and a little nearer to the dance of death, till its poisonous wind swept their faces, and the odour of its intoxicating pollution smote upon their senses, and the fringe of its flying raiment touched them as it passed, till insensibly their feet too began to tremble with the passion of the dance, and at last they were drawn into its hideous circle, and swept on and on till, fallen, broken, maimed, ruined, there was given unto them the heart of a beast and not the heart of a man ! By the fiery anguish and the shame, the lazar-house and the early grave, the ruin of great gifts and downfall of brilliant hopes and purposes, I adjure you, young man, " Keep thyself pure."

I put purity before you, then, as the *badge of the noblest manhood*. A man is never so contemptible as when he imagines there is anything clever in wickedness. Yet men do imagine it, and say it too. Innocence is ridiculed, and vice is half admired. To be a man of the world, to see life, to know its shameful by-paths, and be familiar with its mysteries of wickedness—this is often the ambition of very young and very foolish men. There are those who must know these things, because their duty lies among the shadows of human life. The magistrate, the physician, the minister must know many things which are sad and tragical and bad to know. For the great majority the veil which covers those darker secrets of life need not be lifted ; and let them thank God for it. But mark, that is nevertheless not purity which can only exist by ignorance of evil. Who is purer, the country youth who cannot imagine the dreadful indecencies of a London slum, or the man who knows every nook of their secret foulness, because he is daily there to help, and purify, and heal ? Is the country maiden, with her sweet and innocent thoughts, any purer than an Elizabeth Fry, standing as Carlyle described having seen her stand, like a fair white lily among the nameless abominations of old Newgate ? No ; it is the purity of such natures which is the secret of their sympathy, and their sympathy is the fountain of their service. Prudishness shuns the vicious as an infected

population ; purity pities them, and goes among them
to redeem them. Prudishness shudders at evil where
no evil is meant ; purity touches evil, but is undefiled.
Prudishness affects a virtue, though it has it not ; but
the strength of true virtue is not to shun vice, but to
vanquish it. Prudishness is the outcome of a diseased
pruriency ; but to the pure all things are pure, and the
knowledge of ill falls from true purity as the mud-clots
from the white raiment of Faithful at the fair. To be
pure in heart is to be strong for the service of man ;
and the purer a man is the more pitiful, self-sacrificing,
and effective will be his service. ' Blessed are the
pure in heart, for they shall see God." With them
the vision of God perpetually tarries, and they know
Him whom to know is life eternal. These are the
men we want to-day ; men who see God, who live
ever in the clear light of God, who know Him as a
Father and serve Him as a Master, who touch Him
and are strong. These are the men we want to-day—
men unstained by impurity, but pitiful to the impure,
to whom no depth is too low or heart too vile for the
healing touch of their wise and tender sympathy. We
want pure men in the Press, the Senate, and the office,
who shall shame vice into silence by their lives, and
raise men into manly virtue by their deeds. We want
pure men and pure women in the drawing-rooms of
society, who shall make the profligate conscious of his
moral leprosy by their example, and visit him with
that rebuke which society is ever so loath to give to
the titled and the wealthy. When such men attack

wrong their "strength is as the strength of ten, because their hearts are pure." They bring to the battle of the right no maimed and halting will, but the undiminished vigour of a clean heart and right spirit. And it is because the battle of the future is with the young men of any given age, these words of an old veteran to a young man gather such solemn emphasis and force, " Keep thyself pure."

There are those to whom I speak who have lost not only innocence, but purity. Your memory is full of the unquiet ghosts of long-dead deeds of wrong; your record is one of strong passions and weak will. There is nothing which sears the conscience like impurity ; there is nothing so fatal to the finest instincts and so debasing to the nobler impulses. Of that you yourselves are only too bitter witnesses; you do the sin, and hate it ; you fly the sin, and are drawn back by a lure stronger than your will ; you resolve to break the bond, but the chain of habit seems rusted into the very flesh ; and often, O how often ! you think of the bright days of young innocence, and wish with what a passion of wild regret you were a boy again. That cannot be. But you may be born again. You may be forgiven, and receive into yourself the principle of a new life which is stronger than sin. " His name shall be called Jesus, for He shall save His people from their sins." Was ever music half so sweet as that ? It *is* music : the music of a Divine hope. Christ claims your manhood ; He waits to restore you to a nobler freedom, to instil the habit of love which shall be stronger than the habit of sin ; and you may know the truth, and the truth will make you free!

There are others who, like Timothy, owe much to heredity. Timothy had a godly mother and a godly grandmother, and came of pure and noble stock. The best inheritance God can give a man to start life with is a pious ancestry and a good home, and this many of you have had. But the purest ancestry, the godliest home, the cleanest blood, will not prevent temptation, and you are face to face with the great transgression of the world. Seek strength from God then, that you may keep your inheritance unimpaired. Beware the idle thought, the gleam of satanic entrancement shot on you from wicked eyes, the impure jest, the book which calls itself realistic, but whose realism is the literature of the sewer, the naked, shameless study of those secrets of putrefaction which God and nature hasten to hide in merciful oblivion—beware these things. To see God is better than to " see life," and " Blessed are the pure in heart, for they shall see God." There is no cleverness in vice ; it is mere brutality and shame, and to know nothing is better than to know evil. In virtue only is strength, in purity only is the secret of peaceful thoughts and manly energy, and wise and temperate life ripening into good old age. Take not the Sodom's apple though the very bloom of heaven seem to clothe it ; it will but turn to dust and bitterness between the teeth. Covet not the bad man's knowledge ; it is a poison working anguish and desolation in the life. Calm and undramatic as your life may appear beside the delirious

whirl and passion of lives swept into the dreadful maelström of evil, yet remember yours is safe life, yours is
true life, yours is noble life, yours is abiding life too. I
remind you of the last words of Gough, uttered in that
very instant when death laid his finger on his lips—
words in which the whole teaching of that eloquent
tongue seemed compressed : " Young man, keep your
record clean !" I remind you, also, of older words than
his, in which the wisdom of many buried ages lingers :
" Therefore, keep innocence "—or we will say purity—
" and do the thing which is right : so shalt thou be
brought at the last to thine end in peace."

VII.

THE SIN OF ESAU.

"Lest there be any fornicator or profane person, as Esau, who for one morsel of meat sold his birthright. For ye know how that afterward, when he would have inherited the blessing, he was rejected: for he found no place of repentance, though he sought it carefully with tears."—HEB. xii. 16, 17.

THE Bible is the story of the moral evolution of the human race, and it is this truth which gives such emphasis and value to the individual histories which are recorded in the Old Testament Scriptures. Sceptics say—nay, honest and perplexed doubters say, "Look at the frightful record of brutal and relentless wars which the Hebrew Scriptures contain; the fierce and cruel spirit which sometimes turns even the Psalms of David into curses, and strikes every string of that clear harp into discord; the records of individual violence, meanness, cupidity, craft, and lust, in which the historical books of Israel abound—and is this your Bible?" Yes, this is our Bible, and its very honesty is the pledge of its authenticity and the seal of its value. No other book takes so solemn a view of life, or is marked by so terrible a fidelity in its delineations of life. But throughout the Bible we see moral evolution going on. As the race of men march onward the light grows clearer, and the conception of God is nobler. Evolution begins its work in the dark voids of the uncreated world, and among the first blind struggles of a primeval race; it ends it in the city of which the Lamb is the light, where all nations and peoples and tongues swell the vast unison of the final song of triumph before the face of God. So rudimentary were Jacob's ideas of God that he thought when he fled from Esau that he had left God behind him in the tents of Luz, and it was with amazement he cried, when he woke from his dream of the staircase of fire on which the angels moved in tender ministrations, "God is here too! God was in this place and I knew it not!" And this truth, which dawned upon the mind of a fugitive suffering the rewards of sin, goes on expanding and completing itself until Christ says, "Lo, I am with you always," and Paul says, "God is not far from every one of us." The Bible is thus the priceless chronicle of the evolution of moral ideas, and this truth is the key to the right understanding of the Old Testament Scriptures. Man begins with rudimentary and imperfect conceptions of God; he ends with the universal prayer, "Our Father, which art in heaven!"

Another thing we need to be reminded of in studying the individual histories of the Old Testament is that human nature is essentially the same in all ages. Go deep down through the crust of the earth, the mere filament of soil and verdure with which nature covers her abysses, and what do we find? We find

immense and definite strata, which run under the soil
of many nations, now dipping deep, now breaking
through the surface, but uniting the antipodes themselves with a gigantic chain of stone. A hundred
differing races live and toil above; here the earth is
green with spring, and there white with snow and
swept by icy winds; but underneath all, this back-
bone of the world runs, and is unchanged. Even so,
beneath all differences of nationality and environment,
the primordial elements of human nature remain
unchanged. Beneath the dim gulfs of vanished time
runs an invisible network of communication, along
which the most distant age discharges the electric
current of its sympathy and influence to the most
modern. The rich man has the same prime elements
of character as the poor man, and "one touch of
nature makes the whole world kin." Beneath the
delicate veneer of the highest European civilisation
lurk the passions of the savage, and it only needs the
fierce call of war to awaken the murderous instincts
which have slumbered, and fill the world with a
sudden access of brutality and fury. The centuries
may lie thick as fallen leaves beneath Esau and Paul,
but there are underlying strata which unite them.
There are Esaus in modern life menaced by precisely
the same temptations before which the ancient Esau
fell, and therefore Paul's illustration is never obsolete
when he says, " Looking diligently, lest there be any
fornicator or profane person, as Esau." Esau's was a
beacon-life, casting a glare of lurid warning over

human history, like the light flashed down an iron
coast, gleaming fitfully over fatal waters, and pro-
claiming the sunken shoals and foaming wells of the
sea which wait to swallow the unwary. History is
full of such warning lights. Such a life was Byron's
—a great beacon-fire, lit with the wreck of high
hopes and splendid gifts. Such a life was Wolsey's,
"floating many a day upon a sea of glory," only to
sink at last in vast ruin and heart-brokenness. And
Esau teaches us how the best instincts of life may be
sacrificed to appetite, how life may be wasted, how
its natural nobility may be debased, how the bitter
"afterward" of old age may close amid vain regrets
and impotent repentance : " For we know how afterward, when he would have inherited the blessing, he
was rejected."

Let us look for a moment at the actors and the scene.
The narrative is singularly exact and vivid, and is
full of dramatic intensity. In the first scene we have
the hungry hunter coming in from a hard day's chase
upon the mountains, almost dying with exhaustion,
and the crafty supplanter, quick to see his opportunity, and unscrupulous to press it home to the
utmost. The fragrance of the pottage is a maddening
incitement to the sensual appetite of Esau, and Esau's
weakness is Jacob's opportunity. "And Jacob said,
Sell me this day thy birthright. And Esau said,
Behold I am at the point to die, and what profit
shall this birthright do to me?" Can we not read
the process of thought in Esau's mind ? "The birth-

right, what good was it ? It means no more money, or cattle, or land. It means only the barren honour of being priest, chaplain to the family. Jacob would make a better chaplain than I. What I want is pottage, not priesthood. Tangible food is better to a hungry man than the invisible possessions of honour." So he ate the pottage, wondering in his heart what Jacob could see in the birthright that was worth so much envious diplomacy, and how any man could stoop to so mean a trick to gain his ambitious ends. He felt something of the clumsy man's impotence in the presence of a subtler intellect, and something of the strong man's brusque contempt for intellectual motives he could not understand. He felt also the strong man's healthy scorn for meanness ; he was outwitted, and, says the record, " he despised Jacob." So do we. Our sympathy goes inevitably with the wronged man, and if we censure the man who so flippantly bartered his birthright, it is clear we cannot admire the man who practically stole it.

To compare the characters of Jacob and Esau in a sentence is difficult, but the contrast is instantly apparent. Let me use an illustration. You have seen a morning of pure and perfect radiance, passing at noon into a black turbulence of wind or tempest, or a haze of dull and heavy gloom. This is a transcript of the life of Esau. You have also seen the troubled day breaking through thick mists, and you have watched, with almost eager interest, the sun battling his way through heavy masses of clouds, shining feebly

at first in faint victory, but at last going down in full
and peaceful glory. Such is the life of Jacob. Jacob
was a man full of faults, and among them were con-
spicuous those least easily forgiven, namely, faults
of meanness. We most of us feel we would rather
receive a sound blow than an underhand thrust, and
Jacob was expert in underhand tricks. For this
chapter of his history there is neither defence nor
excuse, and do not let us suppose God approved it.
On the contrary, God measured out upon him instant
and terrible retribution. He became a fugitive and
an outlaw, for twenty years he toiled in weary exile,
he never saw his mother's face again, and when he
came back purified and pardoned, the shadow of his
old sin met him on the threshold of the land he loved,
and turned his triumph into terror, and his joy into
bitterness. But the great thing we notice about Jacob
is that his character grew in strength and dignity : he
learned the bitter wisdom which is taught by error,
and rose on stepping-stones of his dead self to higher
things.

Esau's, on the other hand, is the very character most
men impulsively admire. He was free, frank, and
generous, and we feel there was about him a certain
nobility and sturdy grace. He brings the free air of
the mountains with him, a wholesome atmosphere of
honesty and manliness. But he was essentially an *unspiritual* man, in whom the finer instincts are gradually
dulled and obliterated. He despises the religious faith
which alone could give him the one element of true

stability, the note of noble character which he lacked, and so gradually he degenerates into the free wild man, the strong hunter, the trained athlete, the splendid savage. There are many such men in our midst to-day, men for whom the culture of the body is everything, and the culture of the intellect and spirit nothing. There is a sort of sensuous pagan delight in bodily strength and prowess still alive and active in the world, and the natural man despises the spiritual man. But with Esau what happens? At length the body and its appetites become supreme with him, and so the sun passes into thick gloom, and the character otherwise so admirable is wrecked. In Esau we watch the slow debasement of character, in Jacob its gradual purification and redemption.

The second scene of the dying Isaac, half-incredulous before the deceit of Jacob, the triple lie of the supplanter, "I am Esau, thy first-born," and then the exceeding bitter cry of Esau, " Bless me, even me also, O my father," when the blessing has gone from him beyond retrieval, is one of the most pathetic in the literature of the world. That exceeding bitter cry of Esau rings along the centuries, and still sets the heart vibrating with genuine pity, and that pity deepens into scorn and loathing of the mother and son who could conspire in such a plot. It is true that having bought the birthright, the blessing had become Jacob's, but there was a manly way of claiming it, and a treacherous way of stealing it, and Jacob, always physically a coward, naturally preferred adroitness to straightforwardness. But the first thing to remember is that no adroitness of temptation on Jacob's part can be accepted as any sufficient excuse for the irreverence and weakness of Esau. When Esau sold the birthright he was undoubtedly the victim of a strong temptation. It came upon him unawares, his great hunger pleaded with him, every languid pulse turned devil's advocate; but, nevertheless, only a morally weak man could have acted as Esau did. There was plenty of food in the world, and a noble man would rather have starved than have purchased food at such a price. But we are all clever at shifting responsibility, and are readily persuaded that we are to be pitied rather than blamed. We can always find a convenient Jacob upon whom the real fault of our wrong-doing should be visited: It was the serpent tempted us, it was the occasion, it was some horrible concatenation of unfortunate circumstances. The public-house had a fatal contiguity to our craving. The wine was on the table; we were pressed to drink; it was a birthday, a bridal, a holiday; ordinarily we are sober men, honest men, truthful men —so the excuses run, and can be multiplied with facile ingenuity. But think you those excuses will be accepted at the Judgment Day? Nay, are they accepted now? Do they even impose upon ourselves? Do they pass current at the bar of our own conscience? Brethren, the blame of all wrong-doing rests alone with the wrong-doer. I would say no harsh word against the man who is overtaken in a fault. I know well how true are those lines of Burns :—

"Who made the heart, 'tis He alone
Decidedly can try us;
He knows each chord, each different tone,
Each spring, each various bias.

"And at the balance we are mute,
We never can adjust it;
What's done we partly may compute;
We know not what's resisted."

But we are the architects of circumstance, not the victims of it; we may defy it, we may subdue it, we may "breast the blows of circumstance and grapple with our evil star." Admirable opportunities of theft do not excuse the thief, nor fatal glibness of speech the liar. Christ saw all the glory of the world pass before Him, and yet uttered no little, half-whispered word of hesitating allegiance to evil. No; a man is not the creature of circumstance, but the master of it; and if a man be a drunkard, a glutton, a profligate, it is not his opportunities of doing evil which will absolve him, for a thousand have walked the same path, and have walked it unseduced. "Esau despised Jacob:" a man with a more sensitive conscience would have despised himself.

"*A fornicator or profane person:*" the words sound unnecessarily hard and bitter, do they not? " Fornicator"—terrible, damning word, burning like a drop of corrosive acid into the fair page of history, and leaving its indelible stigma on name and character! "A profane person,' a godless and God-forgetting man, literally a man outside the temple, cast out from holiness, excommunicated from the sweetest and tenderest sanctities of life! What has this man done to deserve such an

overwhelming verdict of reproach? He had preferred
appetite to God's favour, the sensual to the spiritual;
that was the sin of Esau. He did what every drunkard
does who sells himself to the bewitchment and exhilara-
tion of the winecup, who parts with name and honour,
fair fame and friends, for the frenzy of an hour, who
sinks at last into the cunning maniac, who will cheat
the sentries of the most vigilant love, and in one fierce
bid will sell body and soul together for the gratification
of the horrible appetite which has mastered him. He
did what every man does who gives the rein to his passions, and finds his highest pleasures in the sensations
and desires of the flesh. He did what every man does
who derides or neglects the spiritual verities which
environ human life, who appraises religion with cheap
scorn, and, refusing to see the miracle and mercy of
God, tacitly agrees to dismiss religion as a dream of
fools and women. He did what every man does who
makes it his supreme ambition to secure the savoury
messes of wealth and position which the world can
offer him, and whose enjoyments are the pleasures of
the man who is little better than a splendid human
animal. It is thus that the sin of Esau must be measured. To be the firstborn, according to the standards
of his time, was a man's highest inheritance, and Esau
flung it from him in contemptuous indifference. To
represent his family, and to do it nobly, is an ambition
we can share and understand; but Esau had no interest in anything beyond the passing moment. What
was better than that a man should rejoice in his

9

strength, and have pleasure in the full passion and
vigour of his days ? To take up the sacred burden of
chieftainship when Isaac was gone, and to bear it
nobly, was an honourable ambition ; but Esau was
essentially an unspiritual man, and could scoff at
honours other men and better men estimated at a
priceless worth. The rejection of the birthright looks
a small thing ; but it was not so ; it was casting God's
gift back in His teeth ; and, hard as the words of Paul
are, yet they are true. It is as though a ray of white
light out of eternity lit up the scene and revealed it in
its true significance ; it is as though the heavens opened
above these two men, and in their depths we saw all
the elder brothers of the race gazing down with sorrow-
ful resentment and amazement on this despiser of his
birthright, who is a fornicator and a profane person.
For profanity is not swearing only ; it is an attitude of
mind, and there is an irreverence of the heart as well
as of the lip. Fornication is not one form of sin
merely ; it is the type of all those gross lusts of the
flesh which obscure and finally choke the spirit. *You*
a fornicator ! You shrink from the foul word as from a
blow. Ay, but you eat, drink, and are merry, and
appetite is the law of life, and the pleasures of appetite
your supreme passion. *You* profane ! Not in spoken
blasphemy it may be, but you live only for the seen, and
Christ calls you from the Cross, yet you will not even
turn your head to listen. You have not struck the
Christ, nor spat upon Him, nor wagged the head against
Him ; but this is your profanity, that you have cruci-

fied Him afresh by your neglect, and put Him to an
open shame by your contempt.

" *Who for one morsel of meat sold his birthright.*"
Oh, what horrible disproportion is there here ! What
Divine scorn breathes in the words ! How they scathe
the fool, and reveal the vastness of his folly ! How
they show the blind idiocy with which men who sin
forget the just proportion between the means and the
end ! *For a morsel of meat !* Yet have we not known
that fatal bargain struck ? We smile at the mediæval
legends of men selling their souls to the devil, but
morally they are true. I have seen men sell their
reverence to win the laughter of fools—the imbecile
applause of men whose only idea of wit is profanity or
indecency. I have seen men sell their ease of conscience
to secure a moment's immunity from duty, or their purity
for the fierce devouring pleasure, or worse, for the cold
and calculated licence of a moment's guilty passion.
Every police-court illustrates for how paltry and uncer-
tain a reward men will risk their liberties and lives.
There are thousands on the pavement of this wicked
city, thousands in the offices and behind the counters,
some even in the pulpit, w..o for one morsel of meat have
sold their birthright. They have sold their best aspirations, their spiritual honesty, their intellectual freedom ;
they have pawned the heavenly raiment of the spirit,
and cast away the wealth of noble feelings and divine
desires, and have hardened themselves into a routine
of avarice, or empty pleasure, or cowardly time-serving.
And for what ? Ask that when the lights of life burn

dim and the feast is over, and the clear white light of
the last dawn breaks in upon the disordered life. Ask
that when you sit—which may God forbid—a grey-
haired man whose mind is but a charnel-house of evil
memories, where bad thoughts stir and writhe like
serpents in the dark, and remorse utters its perpetual
wail. Ask that when the first chill drop of the death-
water laps the feet, and rises higher and higher to
the lip! For what? A morsel of meat, a sop thrown to
the insatiable wolves of passion, a brief joy long since
turned to the dust and bitterness of sad remembrance;
and that is the devil's wages! Truly, the words of
Christ touch us here again: "What shall it profit a man
if he gain the whole world and lose his own soul?"

So then, the root of Esau's sin was *his scorn for the
spiritual side of life;* and is not that precisely the
crying sin of our modern life? It is not that you
dislike religion; you have not sufficient interest to
be hostile, and you are, therefore, simply indifferent.
It is not that you disbelieve religion; you quietly
dismiss the whole subject, so that God is not found
in your thoughts. There are so many things to do;
the campaign of daily business absorbs you as the
eagerness of the chase absorbed Esau, you hold fast
to the tangible realities of life, you desire the vivid
and actual pleasures of the present, and so the soul is
starved out of you, and the vision of God withdraws
itself because the surface of your life has become too
obscure to reflect it, and there is developed only the
animal man, in whom the spiritual sense, the large

hopes, the diviner aspirations, are shrunken into pitiable infirmity and impotence. Oh, how true is this of thousands, how true of some of us ! At first heedlessly, in mere lightheartedness ; at first almost unconsciously, but at last positively, you have dismissed God from your knowledge and turned your back on the spiritual side of things. But that spiritual side of life is still there ; the grave is there with its mystery, and the future with its recompense ; and the time will come—it may come soon—when those disregarded spiritual forces in life will reveal themselves in appalling omnipotence as they did to Esau, and the cry with which you will meet them will only be an exceeding bitter cry of infinite regret, of late but irremediable remorse.

It seems to me that the sin of Esau was essentially a *young man's sin.* It was the thoughtless repudiation of spiritual opportunities by a nature which had never tasted the bitter waters of suffering, a nature whose mere animal vigour had blunted the edge of its finer sympathies. To many a young man the home, unhappily, becomes irksome, and the restraint of its pieties and traditions unbearable. In his insolence of strength he has small patience with the slower feet of age ; in his buoyancy of spirit he has little care for the sadder thoughts of parents ; in the eagerness of his keen zest for the pleasures of life he forgets the sacredness of the ties which bind him to the home of his birth. Like a callow bird, no sooner is the wing strong than he is eager to leave the nest, and try his strength in the boundless blue of the free heavens, and his own selfish joy in life blinds him to the more sacred instincts which attach an eternal reverence to the mother who bore him, and the father who trained his life when it was feeble and sheltered it when it was weak.   He " hears the days before him, and the tumult of his life." He longs for freedom, and the sense of being his own master is an intoxicating joy. He will claim his portion, and go into a far country where the reproving eye can never follow him, and the burden of family responsibility be never reimposed. So the very buoyancy of youth becomes a snare, the very energy of manhood a means of ill, and not till the hour come when the strong man is called back to the home of his childhood by the sudden advent of death does he see his error, and pour out his heart in the bitterness of the cry, " Hast thou no blessing for me ?   Bless me, even me also, O my father ! "

You will notice, once more, *how the discovery of his loss* came finally to Esau.   " Ye know how that afterward, when he would have inherited the blessing, he was rejected ; for he found no place for repentance "— literally *no way to change his mind*—" though he sought it carefully with tears " His desire changed, but his environment was fixed ; he changed his mind, in our sense of the phrase, but he could not change his condition.

That discovery of loss did not come all at once. The great, strong hunter went forth, and hunted, and slept, and waked with the serene pulse of health, and what had he lost? The skies spread as fair above him, the mountains rose in the silence of their beauty as majestically around him, the blood leapt with all the old blissful magic in his veins as he hasted after the chase, his life went on as of yore, and what had he lost? If any higher quality had passed out of his life, he had not noticed it; it had passed like an unregarded shadow, and the sunlight seemed undimmed. And then at last there came that awful day, when his heart was broken in him, and the great judgment fell upon him, and the exceeding bitter cry rang out, praying for that which he had cast away, wailing in fruitless agony for opportunities for ever squandered, " Bless me, even me also, O my father." *Afterward.* It is the saddest word in human life. The irrevocable and irretrievable sob through its pathetic chords. It is a cry after the scorned angel who vanishes, the lost good we threw away, the better part we did not choose. O young man! you did not mean to break your mother's heart; you did not mean to fill her faded eyes with tears, and make her last thoughts of you sad and anxious thoughts : you only forgot to be regardful of her, you only spoke lightly and flippantly of the things she loved most, and we know how that *afterward*, when the fatal telegram found you in your folly, and you rushed home only to find the ears for ever closed to your late words of tenderness, oh, we know how you would have given worlds then to have said the things you never said, and to have unsaid what you said ! Oh, older man, you never meant to throw the chances of life away ; you were only vain and reckless you only chose doubtful companionships and let the years go by in emptiness of purpose and carelessness of good, and we know how to-day you would give all you have to be a youth again, and start life as you once meant to start, when you left home a bright lad to seek your fortune in a great city ! It is *afterward*—when the slight chain of habit, once a mere thread of gossamer, has hardened into links of adamant ; when the evil that once wore so fair a face has dropped the mask, and risen up a foul and hideous creature to subdue and slay us ; wh n we become conscious for the first time that we have thrown away that which was best worth having, and have done that which cannot be undone—it is then that the sense of infinite consequences following trivial deflections from the right, or what we foolishly thought trivial deflections, weighs upon us, and the exceeding bitter cry sobs like a restless ghost through every chamber of our life. There are shining doors of opportunity daily opened on us ; there are fair and noble chances which meet us with each day's new dawning ; and because we use them not, at last the bitter weeping waits us in the years which have no light. We create not only difficulties for ourselves, but impossibilities, not merely entanglements, but reversions of unspeakable remorse ; and then when the knowledge of our folly rushes on us, we cry, "Oh, if I only had ; if I only had not ;" but the great doors of opportunity are barred and bolted, and it is too late. *It might have been!* Words of ineffable mournfulness, but daily uttered! Words that sweep across the bright fields of life like a bitter wind, or like a low sigh pregnant with the agony of a million dying lips! How many men and women, in those brief but terrible moments when the mistakes of life reveal themselves in all the significance of their meaning and result, have uttered that low cry with streaming eyes and breaking heart, "It might have been!" All the ruined possibilities of the past reveal themselves, all the blooms of nobleness that had no fruitage, all the diviner desires that reached no achievement, and they see them with piercing clearness for one moment, as Esau saw them when he bowed over his father's dying lips; and then

> "They take up the burden of life again,
> Saying only, It might have been!
> God pity them, and pity us all
> Who vainly the dreams of youth recall.
> For of all sad words of tongue or pen,
> The saddest are these, It might have been!"

Brethren, ye know how that afterward when Esau would have changed his mind, he could not change his environment, and when he would have inherited the blessing he was rejected.

But is it true that a man may repent and find no place for repentance? Only in this sense, that he may change his mind but cannot escape the consequences of his folly: that there are things lost which can never be recalled.

But all was not lost for Esau : all is not lost for you.
The birthright, and the elder brother's blessing, these
were indeed gone, and gone beyond recalling.   But
there was the lesser blessing left, there was the promise
that after long years of servitude Esau should break
the yoke and have dominion— and was this nothing ?
A "sorrow's crown of sorrow is remembering happier
things," but hope turns from the desolated past, and
discerns the bright shapes that advance towards us
from the future.   Much is lost, my brother, but much
is left also.   You cannot get the past back, but you
have the present and the future.   You cannot know
again the child's bright innocence of heart, but the
blood of Jesus cleanseth from all sin.   You cannot
be as though the fire had never scarred you, but you
may come out of the searching flame purified.   You
are not what you might have been, but you may be
so much more than you are.

    "'O that it were possible, after long grief and pain,'

to recover our lost happiness," cries one of the sad
voices of our time, and that cannot be.   But there
is a deeper and a truer happiness that may yet be
won ; the long storm may roll away and leave the
heavens bright ; the thick darkness may lift, and a
better than youth's morning glory fall upon you, and
out of our very follies themselves we may build those
sharp stairs of expiation on which we shall climb
slowly to the skies.   It is the lost Christ came to save,
it is out of the life that seems ruined He builds the

new and nobler nature. Do you remember that touching story Gough tells of himself—how once he lay
brutalised and insensible with drink in the gutter,
with the full sun of summer pouring down on his
unsheltered face ? Many persons passed him in the
public way, and doubtless turned with shuddering
contempt from so foul a sight. If ever any man
looked helplessly lost and ruined it must have been
Gough, as he lay like a hog in the gutter that day.
But at length there drew near him a woman with a
Christlike heart in her, and she pitied him. She could
not lift him to his feet, it was useless to address him,
so what did she do ? She noted how the sun beat
perilously on the bloated face, and taking out her
handkerchief she gently laid it on that face, and went
away. Presently Gough woke. He felt the handkerchief, and began to ask how it got there. At last it
dawned upon him that some true heart had pitied
him, and he said to himself—" I am deep enough down,
God knows ; but some one has thought me worth
pitying, and if I am worth pitying I am worth saving !"
It was the turning-point of Gough's life ; he began to
hope, he began to think all was not lost. I bid you
hope, my brother. All is not lost, and never can be,
while Christ remains. And this is Christ's gospel of
good news.

And this is also Christ's consistent view of humanity.
Harlots, publicans, usurers, taxgatherers, the poor,
soiled, sinful masses of men and women who have
failed—so weak, so cursed with shameful follies, dwell-

ing some of them in the very scorch of hell, and with
the smell of fire upon them—yet they are not beyond
retrieving, they are not outcast from the Divine love,
Oh, no! How can that be, so long as we know that
Christ came to seek and save the lost, so long as His
words remain—"Him that cometh unto Me I will in
nowise cast out!'

VIII.

SINS OF SILENCE.

"And if a soul sin and hear the voice of swearing, and is a witness whether he hath seen or known of it : if he do not utter it, then he shall bear his iniquity."—LEV. v 1.

VERY probably the casual reader of the Scriptures has often asked, What is the true significance of this Book of Leviticus ? It seems dry, effete, obsolete. The minuteness of its details appears tedious and even offensive ; its unfaltering inquisition over the most secret realms of human life strikes upon our modern sense as something painful and repulsive. There is nothing which escapes the searching scrutiny of the Mosaic law ; it legislates for the lips and for the eye, for the appetites and for the senses, for the raiment and for the body, for wives and children, for masters and servants, for the sowing of the grain and the reaping of the harvest, for disease and health, for life and death. Its "Thou shalt not" peals like the thunder of Sinai, or the voice of the trumpet which waxed exceeding loud, everywhere over the crowded plains of human life ; its iron hand strikes heavily at all points on the slightest disobedience. It is rigid, exact, inflexible ; it demands absolute obedience in every jot and tittle. Well, what does it all mean ? Why do

we read it in the Christian sanctuaries of the nineteenth century ? Has not the world moved onward
into a larger liberty in the three thousand years since
it was written ? Have the books of the Mosaic law
in fact any real significance for the men of to-day ?

They have, and a most profound significance too.
The spiritual truth underlying the Mosaic law is that
man is under the direct eye of God, and his life is,
therefore, lifted into direct responsibility to God. God
sees us, and God sees everything about us and within
us. Sins of silence and secrecy, sins of public error
and notoriety, which go before a man to judgment, are
alike open and naked to Him with whom we have to
do. Space cannot shelter us ; if we take the wings of
the morning and fly to the uttermost parts of the earth,
He is there. Immensity cannot shield us ; if we could
sink into the depths of the sea, behold the beams of
His chambers are laid in the water-floods, and on the
uttermost verges of creation He still confronts us.
Darkness cannot cover us, for behold the darkness
and the light are both alike to Him. Moses taught that
the life of the meanest man fulfilled itself under the
open eye of heaven, and that God knew his downsitting
and his uprising, the words whispered in the ear of
solitude, and the secret vibrations of the impulse, which
was scarcely registered even on the dial of the will.
He was no mere atom in the human ant-hill, no
insignificant unit of humanity lost in the vast ebb and
flow of universal life, for insignificance is impossible
to man, and obscurity is denied him. He was a person,

active, powerful, working woe or weal to others; and just as the calling of a man's voice, or the footfall of a child's step, stir the waves of sound which travel onward and ever onward, till they may be said to break upon the shores of the furthest stars, so the influences of a man's life were boundless. His little part was acted out before God and all the angels, his whispers travelled through eternity, his footsteps echoed through the chambers of the Most High. That was the view of human life which Moses took, and he lived as "seeing Him who is invisible." That was the view of life which he taught in all the ramifications of his law,—that all human life, in its every department, lies under tribute to God, and that the motto for all true dignity and purity of life is, " Thou God seest me."

This passage which we are about to consider is a striking illustration of these principles. It recognises that sin may lie in silence as in speech, that to hear the word of swearing and not rebuke it is to share the guilt of it; that men are responsible to each other because they are responsible to God. There can be no lesson of greater service to the young men of our day than this. And why? Because it seems to me that the tendency of modern civilisation is on the one hand to exaggerate the *liberty of individuality*, and on the other hand to lessen the *duty of responsibility*. Man has become the great study of man, and is to-day the centre of art, of science, of literature. Art no longer paints Christ, but man; literature probes the mystery of his motives, and clothes with glowing phrase the

story of his love, his passion, and his heroism. Science
asks perpetually, Whence is he ? and all its profound
curiosities and patient researches travel upwards to
the culminating curiosity of that great inquiry, What
is man ? It may be said that even Nature has been
obscured by the immense shadow projected across her
by the personality of man. Man has dominated her,
and she is made to vibrate to his moods, and is interpreted by lyric rapture or sombre imaginings as he is
sad or happy. And what is the moral tendency of this
modern movement of thought ? It is upon the whole
to exalt man and obscure God, to leave every man to
become a law unto himself, and to snap effectually
those delicate but Divine fibres of moral responsibility
which bind man to man and hold society together.
One fruit of its influence is found, for instance, in the
morbid charity which the world extends to the faults
of men of genius, minifying their vices into mistakes,
their wickedness into frailty, and their most hideous
immoralities into mere errors of judgment. But the
law of Moses knew no such distinctions, and neither
does the law of Christ. There God is first, God is
supreme, God is Master. High and low, genius and
fool, king and beggar, owe common allegiance to Him,
and He is no respecter of persons. And you will find
that the noblest periods of history are the periods when
this belief was most vigorously held. It was the secret
of their moral dignity and victorious valour. It made
Israel the visible sword of God among the corrupt
heathen peoples they attacked. It filled the men of the

Reformation with the same gigantic energy; it made the words of Luther "half-battles;" it clothed Knox with that mysterious power before which a court quailed and a kingdom bowed obedient. It was the fiery force which throbbed in the heart of Puritan England; and the true secret of all this moral energy which has again and again overturned kingdoms, and driven back the powers of darkness in overwhelming defeat, while the sun of setting liberty was stayed above the nations— the secret is that these men felt and realised their direct relation to God, and acted on it. They lived their life with the keen consciousness that the inspecting eye of God was always on them: they "lived ever in the great Taskmaster's eye," to quote Milton's noble phrase. The secret of fidelity is this consciousness of the nearness of the Master: Lo, God is in this place: Thou God seest me.

There are three forces in human life, the action of which is illustrated by this passage. The first is *Influence*. What is influence? It is that intangible personal atmosphere which clothes every man, an invisible belt of magnetism, as it were, which he carries with him. Every human being seems to possess a moral atmosphere quite peculiar to himself, which invests and interprets him, and the presence of which others readily detect. For instance, a pure woman carries a moral and ennobling atmosphere with her. She enters a room where bad men, or light and foolish women are, where the talk has been perilous if not vicious, low-minded and mean-spirited, or

10

saturated with that underlying double-meaning which is the first symptom of corruption ; and it is as though a garden of lilies suddenly bloomed in the room. A sort of spiritual fragrance seems to pierce the heated air ; her very looks and garments exhale the odour of purity. She brings the beauty of holiness with her, and her face seems to wear a fresh light, like the light upon the faces of the young angels in the pictures of the old masters. There is an ineffable dignity of goodness and sweetness about her ; and pure and quiet thoughts make an invisible music round her as she comes. The atmosphere which clothes her seems to flood the room, and the coarse weeds of vicious thought and talk cannot thrive in it. How magically that loud, bad laugh is stilled ! How instantly the current of conversation is changed ! She has brought light, sweetness, fragrance with her ; she has made all that crowd of light, foolish, worldly people suddenly think of their dead mothers, their little children, of the flowers that filled the woods when they were young, of the angels they seemed to see in the bright day-dreams of childhood, of all sorts of tender and pathetic passages in past life ; yet she has not said a word ! Her influence has interpreted her.

Or look on the other side of the illustration. Picture a type of man but too common—the fast man of society. There is an exhalation of evil which goes before him and spreads around him. His smile is fascinating, his speech is bright and witty, there is no outward sign of the corrupting foulness within ; yet the pure feel

instinctively that an evil presence has drawn near
them, and good women say, "We don't like that
man!" We perhaps smile with a sense of superior
sagacity at what seems to us the absurdity of a woman's
reason, but intuition is a fine weapon, which pierces.
where the blunter edge of mere sagacity is useless.
The fastidious instinct of a true purity has instantly
detected such a man. There are subtle currents which
interpret him, a magnetic power of evil which sends
its shock out silently to the clean-hearted; and from
the pure-hearted there are delicate tentacles of feeling
which stretch out invisibly and touch him, and shrink
back dismayed with a sense of wrong. He says nothing,
but yet he interprets himself, and the atmosphere he
brings with him is felt by all sensitive souls at once
to be vile and dangerous. That is Influence : something subtle, indefinable, yet real; without lips, yet
speaking; without visible shape, yet acting with
tremendous potency, like the magnetic forces which
throb and travel unseen around us, hidden in the dew-
drop and uttered in the thunder; Influence, which
streams out from every human being, and shapes
others, and moulds and makes them ; Influence, which
is stronger than action, more eloquent than speech,
more enduring than life, which being holy sows the
centuries with the seeds of holy life, and being evil
multiplies, indeed, transgressors in the earth !

The second force is *Example*. That is something
more tangible, because it is· mainly a matter of words
and deeds. Every man sets a copy for his neighbour.

and his neighbour is quick to reproduce it. Wordsworth speaks of the little child from whom the remembered light of other worlds is slowly wasting into the
light of common day, as learning all he knows of the
world through the faculty of imitation :

> " The little actor cons another part,
>   As though his whole vocation
>   Were endless imitation."

But it is not only true of children ; all men are born
actors. We often find it ludicrously true, do we not ?
We catch the trick of another man's thought, we echo
the intonation of his voice, we reproduce the idiosyn-
crasy of his manner, we copy the very peculiarity of
his gait; yet it is all done with perfect unconscious-
ness on our part. What is called fashion is built upon
example : when a poet discards collars society goes
bare-necked, and when a princess limps society becomes
lame. If these were the only illustrations of the operation of this law of imitation we might content ourselves
with a tolerant amusement at human folly ; but when
imitation enters the world of morals it becomes a
solemn and a tragic thing. Then we find that no
man lives to himself; he could not if he would. The
covetous man has a miser for his son, the light woman
has a daughter hastening towards the ways of shame,
the unclean man poisons a workshop with his lecherous
imagination, the drunkard infects a whole neighbour-
hood with his vices, the swearer finds his little child,
scarce out of babyhood, uttering bestial oaths, and
shaping his tiny lips in the blasphemies which are the

common speech of the house in which he lives. Who knows how far a word may travel ? When it leaves us it is gone for ever. It has floated away into the blue heaven on wings of its own, and we cannot recall it if we would. It has set new thoughts stirring already in a score of hearts, and will travel on in multiplying influence till the ears of men are full of it. Each man lives in a huge whispering gallery, and his whispers travel round the world, growing louder as they go, till they fall back upon him like the reverberations of distant thunder. The word spoken in the ear is trumpeted upon the housetop ; forgotten by us, it is remembered by others ; dismissed by us, it has leapt into life elsewhere ; and on the threshold of another world, where every idle word is known, the speech of a lifetime rolls back upon the spiritual ear. Just as the phonograph treasures up the most delicate inflexions of the human voice, and can reproduce them at the will of the operator, so a thousand minds have already received the impression of our words, and, if they were evil, share the iniquity of them with us.

And then, from influence and example there results *Responsibility.* Do you say, " Am I my brother's keeper ? " You are. You cannot help yourself. You can as easily evade the law of gravitation as the law of human responsibility. If you cease to speak, that will not rid you of the burden ; you must cease to *be* to do that. Nay, even death itself is powerless to destroy influence. Often it multiplies it a thousand-fold. Death can enthrone a man upon a coign of vantage from which he speaks to all the ages. The poison of a bad life goes on infecting uncounted generations, just as good men from their graves touch the remotest ages, and inspire the youth of the most distant centuries to faith and heroism. Has John Bunyan ceased to be a living force in English life? He speaks to-day from such a pulpit as he never dreamed of in his life, and the walls of the cathedral where he preaches are the immeasurable horizons of the universe, and his congregation is as a multitude whom no man can number. Is the life of the heroes, the patriots, the martyrs really closed? They were never so much alive as now; the fire that slew them freed them, and the steps of their scaffolds were the staircase of immortality. They shaped the lives of others on a mighty scale, but you also do so, and not so insignificantly as you think. You speak, you think, you act; and every hour other lives take colour and purpose from yours. Thus influence and example bring with them responsibility to God and responsibility to man. Every man is your brother, all have claims upon you; and if you sin, and another witness it, behold he shares your iniquity.

Let us mark further the precise way in which these forces work. First it is clear that *personal sin always involves others.* " If a man hear the voice of swearing," if he even knows of it, he shares the complicity of the sin. There is always some one who hears, who witnesses, who shares. Steal forth, O youth, in the deep stillness of the night, wrap the darkness round yourself as a mantle, let your feet be shod with silence and your face covered with secrecy; go, glide stealthily as a shadow, and hide at the footfall of the traveller, and enter the chambers of sin like a thief, and shut the door without sound behind you—still some one sees, some one hears, some one notes the fact on the indelible tablets of his memory! There is always a witness where we least expect it; tread we never so softly, some one wakes, and hears, and guesses all about our errand. And that single human eye has in an instant seen everything, and that solitary human ear has vibrated to our speech and flashed the message up to that invisible scribe we call memory, who sits in the centre of the brain and writes down everything! What telegraph is there half so swift and wonderful as that rapid magic of the eye and ear, which instantly registers our minutest actions on another human creature's consciousness? The word half-withdrawn in its very utterance, the act for which we thought we had secured the most vigilant secrecy —they will be known, they will be pondered and acted on; or, if they be not acted on, yet have we passed on our guilty secret to others, and they share the iniquity of concealing it. Oh, brother, here is the most tragic and awful aspect of sin—we share our sins! We have involved others in our guilt, and if we forget they will go remembering. It is well that thou shouldest cleanse thy lips and sing to day the holy Sabbath song; but that wicked story thou didst tell has already been told and retold, and is working its foul wizardry of temptation in a hundred lives

already! It is well that thou shouldest stand in
God's house to-day, clothed with decorous reverence,
unsuspected, and with no scar of fire upon thee ; but
what of the poor soiled body of that other one, the
sharer of thy sin and shame ? For there is a dreadful
comradeship in guilt—often intentional, for men love
company in their sins, but often unintentional, for
others share what they concealed and know what they
did secretly. It is the most apalling aspect sin assumes ;
it is never sterile, it is always multiplying and prolific,
passing like a fever-taint from man to man ; till from
one sin a world is infected and corrupt.

Notice again, that he who sees a sin *and does not
rebuke it* shares the sin and bears its iniquity. The
only way to purge oneself of the contaminating con-
plicity of another man's guilt is instantly to rebuke it
or witness against it. There is no other course open
to a spiritual honesty.

Look, for instance, at this truth *personally*. No one
need go very far for an illustration. You are a youth
employed in a warehouse or office where religion is at
a discount. Wherever men and women assemble in
numbers—in the barrack, the warehouse, or the school,
there are always to be found the missionaries of the
evil one. In the warehouse there is sure to be a fast
set, a group of youths whose habitual talk is seasoned
with profanity or impurity, and who are always eager
to get an audience for their shameful recitals. Their
boasts are pretty generally mere brazen lies ; they
themselves are contemptible to every manly intelli-

gence; but they have influence; and they know it, and love to use it for evil. It is with them a malicious and exquisite amusement to say their most outrageous things when a comrade who professes piety is listening. You have heard their speech; what did you do? You were silent, you blushed, you felt ashamed, you were indignant, you turned aside full of abhorrence for the sin and contempt for the sinner, and no doubt you flattered yourself you must be very virtuous and good to feel such virtuous anger, and there you were content to rest. But this text puts an entirely new meaning on your conduct; because you did not witness against that sin you shared it. Blushing is one thing, confessing Christ quite another. Your silence made you the accomplice of the sin you hated; you are the yoke-fellow with the sinner, and "bear his iniquity." Oh, who is guiltless? Who has not allowed himself to become the confidant of bad secrets? Weakly, carelessly, unconsciously almost, for mere lack of robust fibre and quick honesty, you have drifted into a false position. The cynical confession has been made, the impure incident has been duly recited, and, having thus been a dumb auditor of a shameful story, you have felt you could not afterwards say what you wanted to say, and so have been silent, and have become the accomplice of the sin. The text speaks particularly of oaths, and certainly profane swearing is the most entirely stupid form of sin over invented. It is usually a meaningless habit. M n seldom think of what they are saying, and if a man must translate his irritation

into speech it would relieve his feelings quite as effectually to use a few mathematical terms, carefully
selected with a view to expressiveness and effect.
But I have ventured to enlarge the scope of this
passage, so that it covers the whole area of sins of
speech and example; and I say there is nothing more
perilous than to allow yourself to become the confidant
of bad men. You must witness against them if you
would be honest. Do not hesitate. Do it at once.
It will be easier to do it on the first impulse than ever
afterwards, and once done it will be always easy.
Failing to do it, the unmistakable verdict of this text—
and surely it is not an unreasonable deduction—is that
we share sin by not rebuking it, and bear its iniquities
by conspiring to cover it.

Look at this matter *nationally.* Look at what is
going on at the present time in India, Hong Kong,
the Barbadoes, wherever the flag of Britain is flying.
What is going on, do you ask? This, that wherever
that flag goes the shame of British vice follows. Your
police officers are being paid not to maintain order and
suppress vice, but to decoy, to deceive, and ruin native
women by every art possible to the ingenuity of infamy.
What the Government dare not do here it is doing
there, because there the native is weak and the
Englishman strong, and the public opinion of England
appears to be too distant a force to be feared or
reckoned with. When a Governor of Hong Kong
comes home, horrified by what he has seen and
known, and shows unmistakable signs of indignation,

he is forbidden by the Colonial Secretary to speak publicly on this question, and so the facts are stifled at the birth. Here is a case vouched for by no less competent an authority than Mrs. Josephine Butler, in which a poor Chinese woman, in fleeing from these British police whom we have made the sleuth-hounds to hunt down innocence, falls from a •housetop, and is taken up dead. The case of this outraged and murdered woman does not stand alone. It is typical. With one hand we build the church, and with the other the house of infamy ; with one hand we offer the Bible and with the other the certificate of shame ; and the bodyguard we provide for the missionary is the *police des mœurs !* And now, mark, who is responsible for all this ? According to my text, all who know the facts, and therefore from this hour all who hear these words are responsible for the existence of this licensed infamy. You are responsible, young man, in whose hands the future of England lies, and therefore I bid you witness with vehement anger against this great wrong done against God and womanhood. You do well to be angry, for the honour of your country is being stained, the dignity of womanhood is being outraged, the helplessness of weakness is being mocked ! By all that is chivalrous and pure, by all that is manly and righteous, it is your duty and mine to protest against this abominable wrong, everywhere, at all times, in season and out of season, till the rising tide of public indignation shall sweep it away ; and if you do not witness against it you connive at it, if you do not utter your protest against it your silence is a conspiracy to shelter it, if you do not rebuke it you share its present shame and the sure and overwhelming retribution which will follow !

This passage particularly rebukes, then, *sins of silence.* Sins of speech we can easily identify. The power of language is the distinguishing glory of man, and in proportion to the splendour of the power is the mischief of its perversion. · The tongue which is touched of God, the tongue of a Wesley or a Whitefield, the tongue of flame, whose utterance is the Spirit-call of heaven, an inspiration which sets the brain throbbing with new and noble thoughts, and the heart with the strong influx of spiritual motion—oh ! how vast a power it is. Its

> " Echoes roll from soul to soul,
> And grow for ever and for ever."

It speaks across the centuries, it makes the lips of death its trumpet to reach the unborn ages. Like the sweet and solemn reverberations of the Alpine horn in mountain solitudes, long after the authentic voice has ceased, the music of such voices falls upon the inward ear, and time and distance reduplicate and invigorate the magical purity of the effect. But the tongue which is set on fire of hell, impure, rancorous, bitter, glozing over vice with honeyed words, hiding poison in its soft speeches, the tongue that runs through the world and is a liar from the beginning, and finds its congenial task in slaying innocence and undermining character, how vast a curse is it ! But there are sins of silence too. To be silent when you should speak is as evil as to speak when you should be silent. To be tongue-tied by cowardice when wrong discovers its hideous nakedness to us, is as vile a thing as to praise wrong and sing the coronation song of wickedness. There are many men prodigally gifted with mere animal courage—the iron nerve, the steady hand—men who could ride with an unwhitened lip against a flaming battery, and stand amid the murderous rain of bullets on a battlefield as calm as on a parade-day, who in the higher tests of courage must be dismissed as cowards. They are the men of whom Bunyan spoke in his quaint verse—

> "Though you could crack a coward's crown,
> Or quarrel for a pin,
> You dare not on the wicked frown,
> Or speak against his sin."

It *is* harder to face ridicule than bullets, to witness against wrong than to lead forlorn hopes on the battlefield. But if we are Christ's freedmen we shall do it. We shall have the higher courage, we shall know the truth, and the truth will make us free of the fear of men. We shall see God, and, seeing Him, we shall see no fears in the way when His signal waves us forward ; and so we shall confess our Master before men, and He will confess us at the last in the presence of the holy angels.

The great need of the religious world at this hour is *manly men.* We want no goody-goody piety : we have too much of it, and could very well afford to export a

little.   We want none of the knock-kneed, nerveless,
sentimental piety, which grows ecstatic in singing hymns
on Sunday, and is conveniently blind to the injustices of
earth and the inhumanities of man to man on Monday.
The sort of religion which is put away with the Sunday
coat usually resembles the Sunday coat in fitting ill, and
looking like a genteel encumbrance ; the religion we
want is one that will stand the rough wear and tear of
daily life.   We want men who will do right though the
heavens fall, who believe in God and nothing else, and
who will confess Him though all men forsake them
and despitefully entreat them.   A new age is fast coming
on us, and a better one, I think.   That species of
Puritanism which believes in justice, righteousness, and
reality is rapidly passing into the ascendant, and will
soon be the dominating force in national life.   The
philosophies and politics of mere expediency are
crumbling into dust, and men are turning more and
more to the law of Christ as the true code of government for men and nations.   The new age will hate
cant more than heterodoxy, and will use very searching tests to sift the chaff from the wheat in
Christian profession.   If will be a real age, and will
demand reality ; it will be a morally courageous age,
and will demand courage in the followers of Christ.
You, young men, are the natural heirs of that great
age which is coming.   The twentieth century is yours.
You will march on when the flag has fallen from the
failing hands to-day ; you will be in the van of battle
when the dust lies thick upon the faces of those who

now front the music of the guns! Therefore I adjure you to be real, to be true, to be brave, to be honest men and unflinching witnesses, to quit you like men and be strong. And if I have seemed to set before you an impossible ideal of Christian courage—oh! if we look with yearning eyes towards that ideal, but with a sickening sense of our own impotence to reach it—then I bid you to remember also that we do not adore a Christ who simply tells us what we should do, but a Christ who lives in our hearts by faith, and helps us to do all that He has commanded us.

THE CHARACTER OF JUDAS.

" He then having received the sop went immediately out: and it was night."—JOHN xi.i. 30.

THIS history which lies behind these words is the saddest and most terrible in the annals of Christianity. We are most of us so constituted that we learn most quickly through the imagination; and that which the imagination has once bathed in its searching light the memory seldom loses. An ethical statement may be remembered by its epigrammatic force or clearness, but the history of a human life becomes woven into the very texture of our thought, and is never wholly obliterated. We best understand patriotism when we read the life of the hero, and faith when we study the martyr's farewell to life, and love when we recollect our mother's gentle ways, and self-forgetful toil, and nightly kisses. So, too, I think we shall best understand what is meant by deterioration of character culminating in crime and sorrow, not by any bare statements or appeals I might make, but by the living picture of a living man's downfall and despair. Just as Esau was the type of the fleshly man, waking up too late to the conviction of spiritual truth, so Judas

is the type of the *partially-spiritual* man, whose better
nature is gradually sapped by evils imperfectly resisted,
till the light of piety dies out, leaving the house of the
spirit desolate and dark. The whole tragic story is
summed up in this one dramatic touch of narrative,
" He went immediately out : and it was night."

I desire, therefore, to trace the main outlines of this
strange life, and to mark the moral issues it involves.
It is a difficult and delicate task, for while no personality is more pronounced than that of Judas, none is
more intricate and subtle. We have to grope in darkness or among half-lights to find the motives of the
man, and, when his character is revealed, it is suddenly
and for a moment only, in the vivid flash of some
solitary and significant word ; read, as it were, by
lightning, manifest only to be withdrawn. He himself,
like Esau, is one of the beacon-lights of history, casting
far over the troubled waters of Time a lurid gleam,
rising high above us on the solitary crag of this
immortal remorse in dreadful warning. He who would
approach the study of Judas therefore with bitterness,
or contempt, or hatred, does ill ; rather should he
approach it with infinite pity, such as men feel when
they see a great intellect warped, a splendid possibility
blighted, a noble mind overthrown. It is thus Christ
regards him when, with ineffable sadness, He dis-
misses him from the table of the passion, troubled in
spirit because He knows the devil has overmastered
one whom He had loved and trusted. It is thus
Peter speaks of him without bitterness, or passion, or

11

angry blame; the whole scene is too tragic for anger, too intensely sad for posthumous reproach—" he fell from his apostleship; he has gone to his own place." It is so we should speak of him : as a man and a brother, who suffered temptations which assail us, and fell, as the bravest might fall but for the grace and power of God.

First, then, let us glance at the *Apostolic Life of Judas.* It is obvious that Judas was once full of noble aspiration and pious thought. For what did it mean for a man to be an Apostle of Jesus Christ ? It meant following Him who had no place to lay His head, contentment with houseless wandering, resignation to perpetual privation. It meant the renunciation of all the ordinary avocations of human life which command fame or fortune, wealth or honour. It meant that a man should be prepared to leave father and mother, the calm of prosperous days, the prizes of successful toil, the strife of secular ambition ; or, to put the least evil last, that he should endure insult and ignominy, the proud man's contumely, the oppressor's scorn, the contempt of all cautious and sedate citizens, to whom the words and life of Christ were at best a sort of splendid madness. It was not, perhaps, the narrowing of life, but it was the concentration of life upon a single purpose ; and the effect of concentration is to intensify rather than to narrow life. And what bait had Christ to offer His followers ? What was the earthly reward for this great renunciation ? There was absolutely none, save His friendship ; and the friendship of a forlorn man, a

" Man of sorrows and acquainted with grief," is not usually attractive to shrewd and ambitious minds.

Let us put the case to ourselves, then, and let us measure Judas by it. Let us suppose there should appear in our streets a man of strange presence and stranger speech. He defies conventional ideas and out-rages conventional opinion. He has no visible means of support, no trade, profession, or occupation ; he is an itinerant prophet, professing to unfold a wholly original ideal of human conduct and duty. He has been an artisan, and is still dressed in the simple raiment of the humble toiler. His own brethren disown him, and the village of his birth yields him neither praise, attention, nor honour. Yet humble as he is by birth and train-ing, he has the audacity to attack the representatives of wealth, culture, religion, and social opinion. He is in the habit of using language of bitter sternness, almost one might say of bitter violence. Nothing is safe from the winged arrows of his daring words : the futile defences of custom and respect are shrivelled up, as though they were a spider's web, before the heat of his courageous speech. He stands utterly alone, in what some would call a ridiculous, and others a sublime, isolation from all sects and parties. His only following are women of the humbler class, and men like himself, artisans and fishermen. His one message is that he comes to found a kingdom of a new social and spiritual order, and that he holds his authority direct from the inscrutable Creator Himself. Do you see the scene ? Do you grasp the position ? Can you reason out its

probabilities? What should we do with such a phe-
nomenal man as this? Beyond doubt we should seize
him for the first indictable offence, and try him at the
nearest tribunal of justice. Who would follow him?
Who would believe in him? Should we? Should we
be eager to go after him in his lonely wanderings and
share his bitter bread of sorrow? Should we be
resolute to leave home, friends, comfort, and position
to follow one so despised, so strange, so lonely? Yet
that is just what Judas Iscariot did. He heard this .
Man's voice, and his heart was shaken by it. He left
all, and went out, and followed Jesus in the way. It
is needless, therefore, to repeat that Judas must once
have been a man full of noble enthusiasm, a rare soul,
an original nature, a man with great convictions and
courage enough to act upon them, a man noble enough,
and brave enough, and spiritual enough to do what
scarcely a hundred men in all London would dare to
do to-day, if the conditions were repeated!

It is always easy to be wise after the event, and
to say, as John says, when the tragedy is all acted
out, and he relates the episode of Judas' objection to
the waste of the ointment, "This he said because he
was a thief." Unquestionably a great act of crime
often does give a clue to many mysteries of past
conduct. It is the flashing of a signal which is caught
up and repeated along the whole line of the past, so
that many a trivial occurrence of that past leaps up
into new and startling significance. But, on the other
hand, the truly noble points in past character and

conduct are oftèn forgotten or obscured in such moments of tragic revelation. We are always ready to assume that the traitor was always a traitor, and the poor lost woman of the streets never anything but impure. It is a comfort to our own insecure virtues to assume that the vicious are certain special and unique monstrosities, exceptions to the common race of men, creatures built up from the ooze and ashes of hell, and dedicated to a preternatural wickedness from their earliest breath. But nothing can be more false or more unjust. It is the hypocrite's view of character; it is the Pharisee's attitude towards sin; and the human heart contradicts it. For ask, What is the root of murder? Oftener than not it is a sudden access of evil passion, and who has not been guilty of violence of temper? What is the root of treachery? It is insincerity, the unstable and double mind; and who has not sometimes acted below his convictions, and swerved somewhat from the strict integrity of his speech? What is the root of vicious excess and profligate error? Is it not unchastity of thought, and who has not entertained evil conceptions and dallied with the impure impulse? In the murderer, the traitor, and the outcast we simply see the consummation of our own evil tendencies, the dreadful exposition of our own privately rehearsed but mercifully unacted vices. " Let him that is without sin cast the first stone," said Jesus, and oh! how significant is the result—not one dared to smite the sinful woman at His feet, for each felt he might have

sinned even as she had! Until the seed of sin is
destroyed in our own natures, we have no right to
smite the fallen ; and when it is destroyed we shall
have no desire to do so.

No ; there is a picture in the far past of the life of
Judas very different to this closing down of despair-
ing darkness which St. John paints. We seem to see
the infant on his mother's breast, and hear the
innocent lips laugh loud with glee amid the flowers
of Kerioth. We see the serious child hushed in
evening prayer, or going up to the Temple, even as
Christ did, in some pilgrim band which fills the desert
solitudes with the song of solemn praise. We mark
the first Divine awakening of the spirit when the
voice of God reaches it, and the vision of truth is
revealed. He grows up strong in a Jew's faith and
nourished in a Jew's patriotism, a student of the
history of his people, an ardent youth burning for the
fulfilment of the great promises of sage and prophet.
And then somewhere, some time, there flashes on his
view the strange face of the Son of God ; he thrills
beneath the spell of His gentleness, and bows before
His Divine holiness, and is troubled by the searching
splendour and penetration of His speech. His admiration becomes love, his love becomes worship. He
is ever in the congregation, and for weeks together
leaves home and kindred that he may hear more of
the voice of this strange, sad, solitary Man. At last
the reward comes ; those keen eyes have marked his
presence, and that Divine hand is on his shoulder,

and that voice, only heard from afar before, speaks
to Him alone, "Judas Iscariot, lovest thou Me?"
And he stammers and is confused; he bows himself
hushed and lowly, as when a great, pure love dawns
upon a lonely soul, and says, "Yea, Lord, thou
knowest that I love Thee!" The spell draws him
and he follows on, and into his life, as truly as into
the life of John or Peter, there comes this new, Divine,
wonderful indwelling of the love of Christ. Oh, think
of that chapter in the life of Judas, for be very sure
some such unwritten chapter there was, some such
experience steeped in the tender lustre of love and
memory! Think of it, I say, and learn when you
meet the dishonest, the false, the wicked, the branded
felon, the poor shivering outcast of the streets, the
despised exile from the abodes of love and honour,
overwhelmed with contumely, only spoken of with
shame and shuddering, the swine and refuse of society
—oh! think then of the brightness and innocence of
earlier years, and remember you behold a spectacle
not to be shunned with loathing, but to be wept over
with tears of infinite compassion.

Remembering what Judas became, perhaps some of
you will ask, *Why did Christ choose him at all?* Christ
chose him for what he was, and what he might have
been, not for what he became. Christ chooses men
not for their attainments, but for their possibilities.
Do you suppose Christ chooses men for their ability
or their character? He chooses them that He may
give them character and inspire new capacities within

them. He chooses twelve men, and one was a traitor ; the average of treachery in human life is usually higher than that. Moreover, the election of Christ does not fetter the free-will of a man. In a certain high and almost inscrutable sense it is true that it all happens "that it may be fulfilled ;" for though the bad man may seem an accident he is not, but in some way fits into a Divine order. The wild wind roars through the troubled heaven, but somewhere there is a sail to catch it, so that all its fierceness is yoked to fairest uses, and transformed into a mysterious helpfulness. There are no accidents in the Divine order ; the harvest of to-day is the fruitful child of the storm-weat er of a century ago ; it was all that it might be fulfilled. But whatever may be the ultimate issue of events, the will of man works freely within their circumference. Christ has chosen every living soul, and called him ; yet few there are that shall be saved. You are as free to work evil in an apostleship as in a fisherman's boat. Nay, more, if this man was so cursed and burdened with evil aptitudes, was it not an act of divinest mercy to call him to an apostleship ? There are some men who never would be Christians at all unless they were Christian ministers. They need the constraint of solemn responsibilities ; the only chance of saving them is to set them to save others. And, looked at in this light of human experience, how Divine was that discernment which chose Judas, and gave him this unique oppor- tunity of making his calling and election sure beneath the very eyes of Jesus ! For the evils which destroyed

Judas had not ripened in him when Jesus called him. He came in the untainted freshness of faith, perhaps in the unbroken energy of youth. He had more than ordinary capacity, for at once he became the organiser of the little society, its steward, its financier, the custodian of its means. To paint him therefore in the light of the after event, as most painters have done, disfigured with the leer of low cunning, scowling with the meanness of baffled craft and delayed cupidity, is altogether false. He who paints Judas must put into his face the dying light of what was once noble enthusiasm—the shadowed eagerness of what was once heroic faith. He must paint a face full of the anguish of remembrance, the traces of perished nobility, the tragedy of overthrown ideals. He must paint no haggard miser—

> "I saw a Judas once,
> It was an old man's face. Greatly that artist erred.
> Judas had eyes of starry blue,
> And lips like thine that gave the traitor kiss."

In a word, we must remember Christ called him, and not in vain; Christ loved him, and not without cause; and, howsoever dreadful the end may be, there was once a bright, a brilliant, and a beautiful beginning.

We turn, then, to the *great error in the life of Judas.* It is impossible to tell where that deterioration in character began, but we know that it was not unobserved. Long before the end Jesus said, "One of you is a devil." Already He had marked the waning zeal, the growing worldliness, the encroaching greed.

But He did not cast this man out. He left Himself to be robbed and betrayed, knowing well that if the constraint of love will not keep a man, outlawry will not redeem him. It is the central point of God's thought about man; we are to be saved by love or no salvation is possible. The doors of His Church are wide open, and into them throng not only the meek and noble, but the ambitious, the sordid, the worldly; people touched by transient emotions of piety, and over-mastered by abiding instincts of wordliness, men desirous of power and covetous of publicity, they all come, and the sheep are not separated from the goats. It is difficult to find a pure breed of either sheep or goats; to our dull discernment the finer lines of demarcation are indistinct. There is no keen dividing line, no flash of revealing light, no angry roll of judgment thunder. Saint and pseudo-saint sing out of the same book, John and Judas bow in the same prayer. We do not see the difference; we even mistake fussiness for zeal, and thirst of power for ardour in work; and so the wheat and tares grow together "until the harvest." One only sees, and His face, full of solemn scrutiny, is never turned away, and His eye pierces all disguises. Strange words! "One of you is a devil." How they must have startled the disciples! In these early days when zeal was at its height, and no shadow of treachery had fallen, "One of you is a devil." "One!" —which? I do not know; I cannot tell. We look aghast into each other's faces. The words are like the flash of the thunderbolt out of the clear sky, like the voice of doom crashing in amid the happy singing. But He knows who He means, and already in some heart He perceives the first slow crumbling of decay, the beginning of irrevocable ruin, the signs which declare the denier, the apostate, the betrayer that shall be.

There were *two motives* which actuated Judas in the betrayal of his ·Lord : one is clear and certain; the other is probable, but perhaps not less real. The first was *cupidity.* Cupidity is the most mean and sordid of all human vices. It narrows the whole horizon of life to the rim of a piece of money, and discolours the whole world with the yellow blindness of gold. It distorts the intellect and hardens the heart, and, like all other vices, grows by what it feeds on. Into that vice Judas had fallen. His custody of the bag had led him to covet its contents, and a meaner sin—when we remember the poverty of the disciples, and the destitute, whose source of help was in the bag—it is impossible to conceive.

The second motive has strong probability upon its side. Perhaps Judas may have reasoned that the hour had come to force a declaration of Christ's kingdom on earth. Remember that it was an earthly kingdom, and no other sort of kingdom, which all the disciples anticipated. The two disciples on the road to Emmaus expressed precisely the sense of disappointment felt by all the disciples when they said, " We trusted that it should have been He that should have redeemed Israel." The very last question the disciples put to

Christ immediately before the cloud received Him out of their sight was, "Wilt Thou at this time restore again the kingdom to Israel?" What they all looked for was a great surge of patriotism, which should carry Jesus on its crest to the throne of David, and before which the invader and alien should be swept away. Three years had almost passed, and that kingdom had not come. To every word of warning wisdom as to the true nature of that kingdom they had been perversely deaf. It began to look as if that kingdom were never coming, as if they had followed a bright illusion, a fascinating but fatal phantom. What was the use of miracles, sermons, popularity, fame, if the kingdom did not come? Judas was astute enough to know that such things as fame end as rapidly as they begin, and he was ambitious enough to desire more tangible results than these. And now, as the days pass, and he seems no nearer to the goal,—always the crowd but never the army, always the homage of the crowd but never the fiery watchword nor the stroke for power—the hearts of men like Judas misgave them. If Christ did not move, then he, the prime minister of the little company, would move. To thrust Christ into the very hands of His enemies would be only to ensure one more stupendous miracle, and He who had trodden the angry seas into calm by the mastery of Omnipotence could defend Himself in such a case. It would bring matters to a crisis: either the kingdom on earth would be declared, or the whole bright dream would break up and vanish like an exhausted illusion.

And so for him there would be not only the reward of cupidity, but the pleasure of outwitting the high priests and gaining his own ambitious ends. I think, at least, that is a probable, as it certainly is a merciful, view of Judas, which we may permit ourselves to take.

Cupidity, vanity, worldliness, lust of power—all that is meant by the corroding influence of low ideals ever becoming lower, acting on the spiritual nature and wearing it down, that is the drama painted here, and it is being acted out in our midst every day. Is not that young man listening to me who, like Judas, has already been brought under the spiritual influence of Christ? Your life has thriven in the sheltered sunlight of a pious home, and across your youth has fallen the mysterious presence of the Christ ; your spirit has thrilled beneath His touch and responded to His voice. But that first freshness of faith has faded from your life, and now the blight of worldliness has fallen on you. You have not fallen into open vice, but you are estranged from Christ, and the spiritual is ceasing to affect your life. You are like a ship which still seems to hold the same course, but curious watchers on the shore perceive that the course is altered, and know that there are secret currents which are drifting you toward the rocks. The deterioration of character has begun. The integrity of your purpose is corrupted. The bright enthusiasm of boyhood is passing into the worldling's callous pessimism. Some secret sin is already festering in your life, and, like the slow worm toiling darkly and silently in the centre of the fair tree, is eating out your heart. And oh, what is half so terrible as this wreck of character? The loss of intellectual vigour, the slow decay of the body fashioned in strength and beauty, the crumbling of historic monuments, the downfall of great empires—all this is comedy beside the spectacle of the slow disintegration of character before the secret force of sin. What lips can utter the music of infinite lamentation which such a theme deserves? But this disintegration of character is going on even now in some of us, and as Christ passes through our midst He pierces all the clever shows of virtue with which we deceive others and half-deceive ourselves, and His word strikes like a lightning flash into the interior darkness of the most hidden life, "Verily I say unto you—one of you is a devil!"

But however we may interpret the motives of Judas, we cannot but reflect, *How inadequate the reward to the risk!* Take it on the nobler supposition,—was the possible result of compromising Christ worth the peril of the venture? Take it on the lower, and is it possible to conceive a more miserable reward for so stupendous a piece of wickedness? "Who sold his Lord for thirty pieces of silver!" You cannot utter these words without a sense of keen, sad, bitter irony. Between the act and the reward there seems an impassable gulf—the one is vast in Satanic wickedness, the other contemptible in Satanic meanness. But it is always so; the reward of evil is perpetually inadequate. Think, O traitor, in whom the spirit of falsehood has already begun to work—you will betray

your friend, your party, your country—think of what
it is you risk! What is that, do you reply? This:
the scorn of men, and the still more scathing scorn of
yourself—that all men will shun you as a moral leper,
that through all the years of your life you must
hide your shameful secret in solitary places, and cry,
"Unclean, unclean!" And this, also, that some man
may chance to take a pen and narrate your deed,
as the deed of Judas is narrated; and that little scrap
of printed paper will go fluttering down the centuries
and secure you the certain execrations of posterity;
and that all this will last as long as men can read
and there is a sun to read by, and a human heart
left to scorn the memory of your deed! Is it worth
the price? Think, O thief, pilfering only little sums
to-day perhaps, what it is you risk: the felon's
cell and the felon's brand, perpetual outlawry from
society, infamy for yourself, and heartbreak and
anguish for your friends; and for what reward? For
a few pieces of paltry silver, spent in shameful pleasure or hoarded in agonising terror; and tell me, is
it worth the price? Think, O youth, beguiled into
profligacy, what it is you sell, and for what a price;
a pure heart, an untainted imagination, a clean record,
and in exchange an infamous and transient pleasure
followed by guilty and degrading knowledge, an irreparable stain, growing like a spot of leprosy, till life
is loathsome, and death a rack of unspeakable anguish
and despair. Tell me, is it worth the price? Yet
such is the madness and folly of men, they are ready

to pay it.   They pay it, knowing well how vilely they
are cheated.   With a sort of insensate impulse men
do evil long after evil has ceased to gratify them, the
very power to do ill deeds making ill deeds done.
Call to me the great host of men who have taken the
price.   Is there one happy man among them ?   Was
there ever a joyful felon, a mirthful murderer, a merry
traitor ?   See them, as they shuffle forward in view,
the bondservants in iniquity !   All light save the
hateful light of cunning is burned out of their eyes ;
they laugh, but never smile ;   black fear is riding
at their back ; they flit phantomlike in desolate places
and have no rest, they hide themselves in the deepest
purlieus of great cities, they clothe themselves with
darkness as with a garment, for they ever feel the
strangling cord about their throats, and the dooms-
man's hand upon their shoulders—look at them with
their haggard brows, and silent lips, and stealthy,
crouching walk, and behold their faces are as the
faces of the lost, for already they dwell in the fiery
circles of a worse Inferno than any Dante painted !
These are the men *who have taken the price*, and,
like a low moan carried by a sad wind through the
lighted ways of life, the accumulated sorrow of their
wasted lives cries to those who stand in the first
happy sunlight of youth or strength or on the verge of
dark temptations: "The way of transgressors is hard !"

Mark, then, that *sin is a cumulative force*.   No one
ever expects to join that dreadful company of men
who have taken the price ; no one ever did.   No one

ever sees the ominous shadow of the prison or the lazar-house falling on him in his first act of sin, or believes he could betray Christ in the hour when he is first conscious of withdrawing from Him. On the contrary, each one is ready to say there are certain sins he could not do, and he honestly believes it. Probably no one was more indignant than Judas when Christ said, " One of you is a devil." But no man knows how far he may fall when the avalanche begins to move beneath his feet. The profligate always thinks he will be so cautious in his vices that their penalty will never fall on him, and the drunkard always says he knows just how much is good for him and is not likely to be the slave of drink. But see how rapidly the evil hidden in the heart of Judas is developed. A few months pass, and he is found at the Last Supper with the price of his Master's blood upon him. All are sad; he only is confident. All are touched with pity for the Divine sufferer; he only sits hard and resolute, with his guilty secret locked securely in his own bosom. And then Christ is troubled. It seems as if the sin of the whole world sits before Him incarnate in this one disciple. He cannot eat the sacred supper in that dreadful presence. He cannot speak the last words of ineffable love while such ears are listening. Christ knows that He will be betrayed, and says so. And then Judas, in a very consummation of effrontery, says, " Is it I ?" That sentence marks the last depth of guilt in Judas. Christ can only answer :

12

"Thou hast said." "And he . . . went immediately out, and it was night."

And then follows *the great Remorse.* " When he saw Jesus condemned—" So he did see it. He saw the trial before Caiaphas and Herod, the scourging and the mockery, and when he saw it, the whole horrible truth of his own crime broke upon him, and with one wild outcry of despair he threw up his hands, and fled through the thick darkness of Calvary, and went out and hanged himself. How terrible is that moment when a man sees himself as he is, and is able to measure the full consequences of his acts. After the darkness of evil deeds there always comes that clear, troubling, avenging light. In one of Frith's pictures, the culmination of the tragedy is reached when the day breaks, and shines through the uncurtained window on the ruined gambler. In the most tragic page of fiction our time has produced, the same truth is taught in that one intense ringing sentence, which tells us how when the murder was done the day broke, and the sun " shone upon the blood. It did." When Judas saw Christ condemned, the high priest scornfully flinging Him aside like the broken tool He was, the black cross lifted high against the lurid sky, the bowed head, the wasted blood-stained face of Him whom he had kissed, and heard the great cry of His parting anguish as He gave up the ghost, then the last veil of deception was rent in him, and he saw himself as Christ saw him. And the time comes when you will see your sin as God now sees it, and will measure it in its full irreparable consequences as God now measures it. When Judas saw that sight, he said, "I have betrayed innocent blood, and he went out and hanged himself."

Many and solemn are the lessons which crowd upon the mind as we close the record. Almost every phrase used about Judas is in itself a sermon, a tragedy, a revelation! "Is it I?" They all said it; for they were all shaken with fear, and felt themselves capable of the wickedness of Judas, even as we bow with a bitter knowledge of our weakness and pray, "Deliver us from evil." "He went out, and it was night." It is always night when a man turns his back on Christ; to leave Him is to enter the outer darkness. "He went to his own place"—that is precisely where each of us is going. There is a Voice which says, "I go to prepare a place for you;" but we cannot enter that place unless we are prepared for it. The final law of the universe is like to like; the closing voice of Time gives men the unrestrained heritage of their own free-will: "Let him that is unjust be unjust still." You will go to precisely the society you have fitted yourself for, and the place you have prepared to receive you. Where that place was for Judas, to what land of gloom and tears he went, we know not; but it was his own place. Beyond that word no other is given us. There the history closes on this side the veil, and it closes with the terror of suicide, the blasted tree with its grim burden hanging over the dreadful precipice, and the field of Aceldama, with its heap of bruised and battered clay, "the field of blood."

But if we cannot pierce that dreadful gloom and
follow the flight of that guilty spirit to the face of God,
or guess with what words the fallen Apostle and the
Divine Master may have met in that revealing light
beyond, one thing we do know, and are quite sure of :
we know that *Judas left Christ, Christ did not leave him.*
Oh, had he turned, even in that last moment when his
foot was on the threshold of the door, and he faced the
eternal blackness ; had he even then fallen on his knees
and cried, "Lord, be merciful, I am a sinful man,"
would not that great heart of Christ have taken him in ?
Would not He have rejoiced more over this one sinner
who was lost and found than over the ninety and nine
who need no such sore repentance ?   Ah ! can we not
picture how, while all the disciples shrink back in con-
sternation and dismay from such guilt as his, He alone,
the blessed Healer of men, puts His hand upon that
fallen head, and in the darkness Judas perceives above
him "the waving of the hands that blessed"?   And
can we not perceive further how, forgiven much, this
man might have loved much, and have been known to
us to-day by the splendour of his saintliness, and not
by the huge horror of his shame ?   It might have been
for Judas : it *may* be for you.   You are going out—
you are going out immediately ; are you going into the
night ? Oh, brother, I cannot let you go till Christ has
blessed you.   You stand on that threshold which is
the narrow verge between two lives.   Christ claims
your discipleship, and in Christ only is the secret of
true manhood.   Do you reply that this steadfast dis-

cipleship, this ideal manhood I have tried in these
addresses to point you to, is impossible for one so
weak as you? Then I reply once more, We go to
Christ not because we are strong, but because we are
weak, and all that Christ tells us to be He will help us
to become. Do you stand, weak, tempted, half-despair-
ing on the brink of that great darkness, that night of
nights into which Judas sank? Oh, listen, brothers!
He calls us; He bids us hope; He is saying, "Ye
shall receive power after that the Holy Ghost is come
upon you." That is what I want: power to do right
and love right; power to love Him and to suffer for
Him; power such as that which changed Peter, the
cowardly denier, into Peter the tongue of fire. As for
me, I obey that Voice. I turn my face from the darkness to the light. I come simply because He has called
me. That is all I can say as I fall contrite at His feet,
but it is enough.

> "Just as I am, without one plea,
> But that Thy blood was shed for me,
> And that Thou bidst me come to Thee,
> O Lamb of God, I come.'

X.

"Yet man is born unto trouble, as the sparks fly upward."—JOB
v. 7.

THE Book of Job is the grandest poem in the
literature of the world. The majesty of an
almost primeval world breathes in it. In all that constitutes the highest human genius—sublimity, devoutness, pathos, dignity of thought, largeness of touch
and view, it is unsurpassed. But it lives not merely
because it is the work of sublime genius, but because
the heart of the world beats in it. The deepest questionings and yearnings of the soul of man are embalmed
in it. The ages do not alter these : they do but intensify them. The Book of Job is being written anew
to-day in a thousand homes, where first the servant
sickens and then the child, first the treasure disappears
and then the house falls, till stripped and peeled, bare
and desolate, smitten but rebellious, men bow themselves in utter weakness and abasement, and cry with
an exceeding bitter cry, " My soul is weary of my life.
Would God that I were dead ! There the wicked
cease from troubling, and the weary are at rest !" Let

us look at Job's view of his troubles, as he stated it
in his darkest and most pessimistic moment.

First of all, then, we have an obvious truth, that
" man is born to trouble." That needs neither elucidation nor amplification. The life which has wholly
escaped the stroke of trouble has never yet been lived.
For there are at least two species of troubles, which
it is utterly out of the power of any man, however
prosperous, to checkmate or elude—viz., bereavement
and death; and neither can he escape the physical
ills which produce both. Long life, for instance, is
one of the blessings most coveted by men; but so
closely are blessing and curse interwoven, that the
longer the life, the more certain is the action of bereavement, and the more disastrous will its sorrows
become. Conceive to yourself the most perfect of
human lives—perfect in its health, in its vigour, in
unbroken intellectual activity, in capacity of enjoyment,
in its achievement of earthly successes. Watch such
a life, as it grows in power and breadth, as it wins
knowledge and experience, as it rises into public
honour and reverence. It is the life we all of us most
covet; and it is a healthy desire which prompts us to
covet it. But if you come to watch this life with any
closeness of scrutiny, you will see at once that one
grievous form of trouble is multiplied to it, though
many other forms are avoided— the trouble of bereavement is there. As it grows in years it becomes more
isolated and solitary. Friend after friend departs, and
shock after shock of sorrow must be endured. It is

the penalty of old age to be lonely. The old man is like a traveller who started long ago with a jocund company upon the mountain path; but as day wanes one by one his friends drop behind, and fall out of sight or hearing. One is lame and one is weary; the cloud rolls up and covers one, and the snowstorm blows and hides another: one sleeps beside some flowery hollow on the way, and one was smitten by the lightning or the avalanche : he alone is left, pressing on with failing heart to the solemn inn of death, which crowns the mountain summit, and where in awful solitude he lies down to die. He is born to trouble, and cannot escape trouble. Neither fame, nor honour, nor length of days can teach him any secret whereby he may elude that awful presence. The coin in which life pays itself to him may differ, as gold differs from silver or copper, but the mintage and superscription are the same.

Now if the most perfect human life which one can imagine is born to trouble, if hearts break in palaces as in cottages, and men bear the grief of a wounded spirit in the house of luxury as well as in the seclusion of penury, we need not pause to verify the words of Job from the more visible and open sorrows of the world. We need not enumerate the disappointments and disasters, the calamities and pains of a life which never knows good-fortune, or more than passing flashes of joyous sunshine. The poor, the broken-hearted, the unhappy, the unfortunate, are always with us. The invalid and the dying are in every street. No hour passes when Rachel is not weeping for her children, and when the cry of desolate hearts is not going up from the sick-chamber, which has become a death-chamber, while we laughed or while we slept.

But the great question that meets us is this : how do we interpret this unhappiness of human life ? We know how the pessimist interprets it. He tells us frankly that life is not worth living, and that no sane man would choose to live it, if power of choice were his. He tells us that the only way of getting through the bitter ways of life tolerably is to cultivate callousness of heart, and to wear the armour of a trained stoicism. He says that if any responsible Power did make the world, He blundered badly in His work ; so badly that we could make a better world ourselves, if the chance were given us. And finally he tells us that the best hope of man is to be done with life as soon as possible, the best power of man is power to terminate it at once, and the best wisdom of the race is universal suicide. This is a philosophy of hopelessness which is being preached to-day. Its effect is to fill the world with—

> "Infections of unutterable sadness
> Infections of incalculable madness,
> Infections of incurable despair."

Its gospel is —

> "O brothers of sad lives! they are so brief,
> A few short years must bring us all relief;
>   Can we not bear these years of labouring breath ?
> But if you would not this poor life fulfil,
> Lo, you are free to end it when you will
>   Without the fear of waking after death."

Let us examine this view of life then, and see how far its pretensions can be sustained.

I. First, then, *What is trouble?*

Now trouble is a wide word, and may be said to include three ideas at least; viz., labour, pain, and dissatisfaction. Trouble and labour in the Old Testament writings are often used synonymously, as you will see by a glance at the marginal reference of this very verse. Pain and dissatisfaction are constant sources of trouble, in the conventional acceptation of the word. If then we take these three facts of life as constituting what men assume to make the bitterness of existence, we shall not be far off a right understanding of the text. It is these three facts of labour, pain, and dissatisfaction in human life which fill the pessimist with despair, and on which he founds his railing accusation against the Governor and the government of the universe. First of all then, let, us examine the meaning and effect of labour on human life.

Well, what is it the pessimist has to say against labour? It is that it is a curse, and nothing but a curse. In a well-constituted world labour would not be a necessity. In such a world all mouths would be amply fed without toil for bread, and all lives freely lived without the grinding yoke of toil. Labour prevents the free development of human life. It makes men for the larger part of their time slaves and drudges. It is like toiling at a dyke—keeping its frail barrier up with infinite effort against an encroaching sea, because we know that if labour is relaxed, the waters of desolation and misery would rush in upon us, and overpower us. The ideal world is an idle world— a paradise of loungers, a land where it is always afternoon, a lotus-eating realm of drowsy ease, where ring of hammer or roll of wheel is never heard, because the fruits of Eden drop unbidden into sensual mouths, and food and raiment are provided with the same bountiful precision as light and air. That is the pessimistic ideal of perfect life, and a perfect world.

But now ask, Is labour a curse? Something of truth there is in the pessimist wail, because the incidence of labour oftentimes is unjust. The frantic effort of the world from the beginning has been to escape work. It seems as though every man had asked himself, " Can I set some one else to work for me, and steal the fruit of his labour?" or, "Can I live without work?" or, "Can I, by labouring at express speed for a given number of years, at last manage to live without work?" I do not pause to examine these questions fully, but I remark about them all, that the escape from labour which men covet, and do often gain in part, so far from blessing them, generally ends in cursing them. To modify the drudgeries of human life is, and should be, the aim of any Christian civilisation. Labour *is* a curse when it allows man no leisure for books, or for recreation, or quiet thought. But the escape from labour by setting another to toil for you, or by toiling at double speed yourself for half a lifetime, to idle through the other half, is a worse curse than honest drudgery. Indolence leads men

not to paradise, but to hell. It debauches and it sen-
sualises; it depraves and it debases; it poisons the
blood and fans the passions into perilous activity; it is
the destruction of a man, not his elevation or emancipa-
tion. Let the lives of the idle and effeminate rich be my
witness in this! And how can it be otherwise? Such
lives are lived in direct defiance of the just law of life,
that "if a man work not, neither shall he eat;" and the
outraged law is avenged upon them in *ennui* and misery,
in the disintegration of the moral nature, and the
effeminacy of the physical; and therefore I say human
experience condemns the pessimistic ideal of paradise
as wicked and absurd. It is the conception of a mean
mind and grovelling nature. It springs from an utterly
base and paltry view of human nature and its capacities,
and were such a paradise gained to-morrow, it would
soon prove a field of Aceldama, or garden of Gehenna.

"As the sparks fly upward"—yes, *upward!* says
Job. That is the true tendency of labour—upward!
Labour is the safeguard of human manhood. It is the
source of human civilisation. What is it but the
necessity of labour that has drawn man from his cave-
dwellings and mud wigwams, and taught him to build
palaces and temples; and in order that he might build
them, has set him to pierce the barriers of nature, and
wrest from the stubborn mother the secrets of her
wealth? Is it not labour which has disciplined his
powers, and by the development of those powers has
lifted him from the ranks of the savage to a place but
little lower than the angels? Is it not in the school

of labour that his hand has gained deftness and flexi-
bility, his eye has learnt precision and discernment, his
brain has broadened into a supreme engine of thought,
before which the secret of the heavens has stood revealed, and the mystery of nature has been laid bare
and naked ? All that man is, all that man has, he
owes to labour. It has lifted him up, not cast him
down. It has become the music of life, the secret of
health, the minister of peace, the impulse to development. Is it then to be deplored as a disaster ? Is
the best dream of man an idle world ? Is this the sort
of paradise to which he aspires ? The man who has
no higher aspiration than desire for ease has already
abdicated his royalty, and ranged himself with the
monkey and the ape rather than with the man. But
the man who toils, and rejoices in his labour, has
already drawn the sting of the primal curse, and finds
how true is the word of Job, that as sparks fly upward,
when the smith's hammer rings upon the anvil, so a
man rises when he works, and sinks when he disdains
work, and chooses rather sensual ease and indolence
and self-indulgence.

II. Take again the *idea of pain.* What has the pessimist to say to that ? His reply is, Pain is nothing
but a curse, a malady, a disaster ; something that no
God who was good could ever have permitted in the
constitution of His world. Any able pessimist could
have made a better world, and in the pessimistic world
pain would have had no place. Now perhaps that
seems to some of you a just criticism. There is a

plausible benevolence in the idea that is seductive.
You will recollect that this power and presence of
pain in the world, was one of the difficulties of my
unknown correspondent, referred to in an earlier
address. But ask again, would a world without pain
be an improvement? We are born to it; would it
make better men of us to cheat our fate? Is it a
right assumption that a world without pain would be
a better world than the world as it is? You have but
to think to see how false is the assumption. For, to
begin with, pain is the operation of law, and is one
safeguard against peril. Look at it in regard to our
own daily well-being. Suppose nothing warned you
when you did a wrong to your body. Suppose you
could eat or drink without any sensation of fulness,
or any pain to teach you the error of gluttony. What
would happen? We know that very soon death would
be upon us. Pain is the sense which interprets our
peril, and warns us against errors which end in death.
It seizes us roughly, and touches us with its flaming
sword; but the sharp twinge of agony prevents a
worse thing happening to us. It is the voice of law,
which says, " Thus far shalt thou go, but no farther:
for beyond this lies physical extinction." And so true
is this, that in many sicknesses, when pain ceases, it
is the sign that hope of life is over. Pain is the sign
that life still struggles against its foes, and strains
every nerve for victory. But when a sudden blissful
ease shoots through the wearied frame, and the sick
man says, " I no longer suffer," the wise physician turns

away with downcast eyes: he knows mortification has
set in, and death is near.

Or look at it in regard to the outer world. Suppose
no torture warned us that fire burned, how could we
guard against it? Now we are warned, and therefore
we are safe. Pain stands like a wise sentinel at all
the points of danger in the path we take, and will not
let us pass with impunity. It warns the drunkard of
his folly, the profligate of his fatal recklessness, the
mountain-climber of the line of peril which he may
not cross, and the miner of the danger which lies in
wait for him. It clutches the throat of the miner and
the athlete, and pushes them back from the jaws of
death; and it touches the heart, the head, the limb, and
nerve of the drunkard, and reminds him that a worse
thing may yet befall him. Dismiss that sentinel; then
what happens? The man is doomed. The red flag
of peril is removed, and he goes on to his fate un-
warned. There is no one to warn him back from the
pit of destruction, on whose brink he stands defenceless. In other words, pain is the armour of safety in
which God has clothed mankind, and when that is
removed, man stands without shelter in the presence
of inevitable death. And here again Job's words confront us: "As the sparks fly upward!" In the
development of character pain is one of the greatest
of all teachers. It does not crush: it elevates. It
teaches sympathy, tenderness, compassion. It refines
the heart, and sends the thoughts of men flying upwards, like the bright sparks of the smith's fire, in

which the shapeless is fashioned into youth and beauty, and the useless into grace and service. On beds of pain the spirit of man has gained its clearest visions of God, and uttered its noblest thoughts about Him. Beside the bed of pain the hands of man have been trained to their wisest tasks, and the heart has been touched with the great purgation of a Divine compassion. How much poorer the world would be without the ministry of pain, let the man answer who can conceive what the world would be without the patience and resignation of the sick-room, the Christ-like service of the hospital, the sedulous and self-sacrificing tenderness of the nurse. Pain is a fire indeed, not penal, but cleansing; not diabolical, but Divine; and through it human spirits rise into the vision of that God, whose only-begotten Son was also " the Man of sorrows, and acquainted with grief."

III. Or take the *idea of dissatisfaction*, and here again the same truth is taught. Dissatisfaction, as the pessimist interprets it, is one of the worst curses of life. The ideal life is the satisfied life. The ideal life should know no passionate craving or restless yearning. It should move calmly, and with invariable pulses, in meek obedience to the law of its own limitations. Now man is tortured with the restlessness of visionary aims, and impossible hopes. He

> " looks before and after,
> And sighs for what is not.
> His sincerest laughter
> With some grief is fraught,
> His sweetest songs are those that tell of saddest thought."

He cannot be content : he has stolen the Promethean fire, and it burns in him with a devouring energy. Or so he says : inventing, and then believing idle myths, to justify his revolt against his environment and his incurable ur happiness.

In the ideal world of pessimism all this will have entirely disappeared. And with it, what else ? For dissatisfaction is the secret of human progress. It is dissatisfaction with filth which produces cleanliness, dissatisfaction with savagery which leads to civilisation, dissatisfaction with ignorance which kindles the thirst for knowledge. It is the master-stop of the great organ on which the noblest music of the world has been sounded. It breathes alike in the invocations of the saint and the passion of the poet. It is the ceaseless impulse pushing man on to be more and better, greater and wiser, than he is. It will not let him rest in ignoble ease. It passes like a spirit of fire through his stagnation, makes him leap up into action. It lures him on and on, to ever greater heights of achievement, and deeds of nobler victory. It quickens his spirit with infinite longings, and then it is that he becomes the seer, the saint, the prophet, and the poet, whose eye sweeps the universe, and whose thoughts find no resting-place but in God. Withdraw that sense of dissatisfaction, and what have you left ? You have left the life and habitudes of the beast. The beasts rise no higher, because they have not this impulse of dissatisfaction ; and man, without it, would become even as the cattle. Born to dissatisfaction indeed we are ;

13

bu. see, the sparks fly upward! Man's discontent is
the wing of his spirit, the impulse which gives him
power to soar. His thoughts then become prayers, his
desires great purposes, his yearnings Divine achievements. He is dissatisfied with his environment, because
he is greater than his environment, and his dissatisfaction is the evidence of his greatness. Withdraw
that, and his soul has passed out of him, and he is
but an animal. Foster it, and the spirit grows within
him till he cries, " God is my refuge and my strength.
Whom have I in heaven but Thee, and who upon the
earth is like unto Thee ?   I shall awake in Thine image,
and be satisfied ! "

And so in relation to those anxieties and conflicts of
life, which we often speak of as trouble, it will be found
that out of them we emerge stronger and better, and
the tendency is upward. Take, for instance, the cares
and burdens of motherhood. At the gates of motherhood Death stands on guard, yet not the less motherhood is desired by every woman's heart, and is counted
an unspeakable bless'ng. And why is this? It is
because motherhood is the broadening and fruition of
the woman's nature, and is the cleansing and consecration of her affections. But it implies heavy, and almost
endless burdens, beyond this peril of death and anguish
of birth. The mother's hands are never still, her task
is never done, her vigilance never asleep. Her days
pass in the perpetual round of small recurrent duties,
and for years the true mother, whose means are small
and family large, must needs be the willing drudge of

her children. But what is the effect of such sacred drudgery? Does it deprave and narrow the heart? Does it take the sunlight out of life? No, the sparks fly upward. The woman's nature fulfils its highest possibilities in faithful motherhood. She finds a sunlight in her children's smiles, and a music in their laughter, which sun could never shed, nor the skill of harp and dulcimer produce upon the ear. The children, with all their querulous demands upon her patience, are nevertheless to her as messengers from God, who call the thought up higher; and every night, as she bends over the little cot, and kisses the tumbled gold upon the pillow, she counts herself blessed among women for the joy that God has sent her. Yes; let us grant that motherhood is toil and care, and is purchased at the price of pain and peril, nevertheless it works out the purification of human nature, and is the consecration and coveted goal of human love. It does not depress, but elevates, human nature: the sparks fly upward."

Let us hear then the conclusion of the whole matter. Trouble "does not spring out of the ground," says Job. That is to say, we are not the victims of blind chance, though in our darker hours we are apt to think so. A Power is fashioning us, we know not how. See how yonder mountain is made. First of all, if we have strength of imagination to look back far enough, we see the rolling back of some abysmal sea, and the emergence of the rude shapes which the ebb and flow of mighty waters have beaten into isolation and consistency. Then come long ages during which the ice reigns, and the darkness and sterility of death and desolation is over all. Then at last a new movement is begun, and the great ploughshare of the glacier begins to work, and to drive its way onward to the plains that lie below, splintering the solid granite as it goes, and rounding it into a thousand strange and shattered shapes of fantastic novelty. Every year now the mountain changes shape : the tempests beat upon it, and wash away its soil ; the fiery bolts of the lightning burn along its grim serrated front ; the hurricane drives across its brow, and the frost chips and fashions it, as with the untiring strokes of an incessant chisel. At last there comes an hour when the process is complete, and upon some summer's evening we stand and look upon it, and see the sunset clothe it with a purple magic, and watch the waning light transforming and transfiguring it, till at last the glorious enchantment is complete, and the cressets of the stars shine over it like watchfires signalling the triumph of some mighty cause: and we say, " Now we know what a mountain is, and understand what the Psalmist meant when he talked of looking to the everlasting hills, from whence came his strength !" What Power has shaped that mountain ? The Power of law. What Power is shaping us ? The Power of love. There is no malice in its work, no mercilessness ; every stroke of the chisel is needed in the process, if the shape of beauty may emerge at last. The whole process is for us an upward process, and the glory of its consummation justifies the sorrow and the patience. Out of the

ground? Trouble the mere caprice and spite of blind
unseeing chance? No; a Mind is there; a Heart
is there!

> "Let us be patient! These severe afflictions
> Not from the ground arise,
> But oftentimes celestial benedictions
> Assume this dark disguise."

Finally, then, we should embrace any and every
agency likely to make us better men and women.
That is a final test, and a complete one.

Would absence of labour, or pain, or dissatisfaction
be good or ill for us? If ill, the theory of the pessimist
stands utterly condemned. But if labour gives patience,
and sorrow teaches faith, and dissatisfaction breeds
Divine aspiration, hard and sharp as the tools that
shape us are, let us welcome them. The one thing we
have to do is to become like God. The one ambition
worth fulfilling is that. In a few years it will matter
very little whether we laboured or rested, rejoiced or
sorrowed; but it will matter everything whether our
life on earth lifted us to the life of heaven or no.

Keep the thought fixed on that. Put that supreme
aim before you, and then welcome any discipline that
will help you to become "perfect, even as your Father
which is in heaven is perfect."

XI.

THE literature of the world probably contains no more pitiably human story than the story of David's great sin. The man who can gloat over it with heated passion is an animal; the man who can laugh at it with malicious cynicism is a fiend. It is one of those sad and lamentable stories which make us ashamed of our passions, which make us feel a sort of degradation in the possession of desires which can be potent with such infernal mischief, and can lead to such foul and tragic consequences. As we read the story we are ashamed of human nature, and it is not difficult to despair of it. " If," we say, " the sweet singer of Israel, a man so true, so valiant, so heroically manly, could fall so deeply, who is safe in the presence of temptation?" One can readily understand how such a story as this might fascinate and terrify a sensitive nature, till the only way of escape seemed celibacy, and the only true method of life a monastic isolation from temptation.

But presently sturdier and calmer thoughts return to us, and then we instinctively perceive that isolation is no remedy. It is the retreat of the coward, not the victory of a brave man. The mischief is within us : it is simply the accident of circumstance which develops it. It is at once futile and foolish to quarrel with the elementary facts of our nature : the passions are as truly a part of ourselves as the intellect and spirit. It was no deficiency of intellectual perception which made passion triumphant for a single damning moment over the nature of David. There are cases where the intellectual faculties are so much less than the physical, that men commit the grossest sins of the flesh without any adequate realisation of the degradation they incur. But the sin of David was the sin of a savage committed by a saint. It was a terrible and sudden outbreak of the lower nature in a man who had for years sedulously cultivated the spiritual nature, and it is that which makes it so tragically significant. It was in fact one of those sins of surprise by which really noble natures are suddenly swept away, and to which the noblest are liable. I am not speaking to men in whom savage and passionate instincts are dominant, with whom gross desire is the law of life, and the gratification of desire the joy of life. I am speaking to men accustomed to the restraints of civilisation, acknowledging the royalty of goodness, conscious of the crown of honour which chastity confers on human nature ; and it is for you this story is so full of warning. So full of warning : why ? Because David acknowledged these very truths and forces, and yet committed one of the cowardliest and foulest sins on record. It fills us with astonishment and horror. We ask, How could he do it? What made it possible for him suddenly to fall into such horrible sensuality and crime? It is that question which is answered in the touching parable of Nathan. With the sure analysis of spiritual insight the whole drama of the fall of David is here laid bare. Let us mark the story: God help us to learn its lessons.

The first fact revealed by Nathan is, then, that such a sin as David's *springs from selfishness;* for the man who spares to take of his own flock, and steals the poor man's one ewe lamb, is the type of the basest selfishness. Now by common consent the highest ideal of manhood is unselfish. Why is it that we enthrone in the highest immortality of fame the patriot and martyr, the man who toils for men and the man who dies for men? It is because we reverence their sublime unselfishness. They quietly put down the lower forces of their nature and obeyed the higher. They reached a noble altitude of spiritual development which to us seems miraculous and unattainable. There is no real hero who has survived in the reverence of mankind of whom it is not true that his sublime unselfishness made him supreme. Any stain upon a character like this is like a blow which falls upon our own hearts. Imperfect as we are, we are conscious of what perfection is; and impotent as we are, we still struggle to achieve it. We may stand at the foot of the mountain among the common crowd who never get beyond its lower slopes, but at least our eyes can yearn toward the sunlit crags we do not climb; and we can perceive the dignity of those who stand upon the summit, and discern how it was they triumphed, and how it is we fail.

Now just as unselfishness is the true triumph of life, so selfishness is the degradation of life, and is the secret of its failure. Reduce sin to its primal elements, the last result is always selfishness. Begin where you will among those common and well-known sins and defects of habit, whose nature is perfectly ascertainable by sad experience and bitter knowledge, and see if this be not true. Take, for instance, temper. That is a common sin enough. There are thousands of households wrecked by the ungovernable irritability of an individual. He cannot restrain his tongue. The slightest provocation produces an explosion. Then follows a torrent of bitter, biting, sarcastic words, which fill the air like a cloud of poisoned arrows, and rankle in the wounded heart long after the careless archer has gone upon his way and forgotten them. You may explain that phenomenon by euphemistic talk about a hasty nature, or the irritability of genius, or what you will; but the real root of it lies in the unregenerate selfishness of the man's nature. Because passionate sarcasm is a momentary relief to his nervous irritation, he indulges in it. The essence of unselfishness is to realise what another feels, to interpret his needs, to share his thoughts by the revealing power of sympathy, to be able instinctively to understand what will wound or grieve, and to exercise a severe selfrepression to avoid it. But the angry man has no such realisation of the nature of others, and cannot understand the havoc which his hasty words produce. He is simply conscious of himself, of his own wrongs and discomforts, and just as one man flies to drink, or another to dissipation, to relieve his misery, so he flies to the undiscerning wrath of hasty words. If you are a violent-tempered man, learn to be unselfish, and that will teach you to restrain yourself, and to be pitiful one with another, forgiving one another, even as God for Christ's sake hath forgiven you.

Now if this be a correct analysis of mere hasty temper, which seems far removed from the region of vice, how much truer is it of indulgence in carnal passions! "The one ewe lamb"—most pathetic, most powerful image! Here is a man blest with all human blessings—riches, fame, honour, provision for all the natural desires of the flesh, for whom no healthy wish goes unsatisfied, no want unmet; a great captain, a great king, with intellectual resources such as few kings have ever known; loved, powerful, idolised·; but but there is a poor man at his gate with one ewe lamb, and the king covets it. The madness and delirium of desire begin to riot in his blood, and he must have it! To the thick vision of his lust adultery is no sin, and killing no murder. When did the man in whom the brute was master ever stop to count consequences? What is it to him that the one ewe lamb is all the poor man has? What cares he that the poor man has nourished it, and round it the tendrils of his heart are bound, and in that deep affection all his peace of

mind and all his pride of life are centred ? " The
one ewe lamb," the one daughter of the house, the one
hope and pride of some honest man's heart, the one
light and joy of his hard existence, innocent, helpless,
defenceless, at the mercy of a rich man who desires to

> " Dower her with shame,
> With a sort of infamous fame."

Alas ! it is a picture which needs no elucidation. There
is no mercy in the profligate ; there is nothing which
so sears and deadens a man's heart as lust. There is
nothing in this spectacle of cottage peace, this pure and
contented innocence, to move the profligate when once
his eye has shot its evil fire of impure coveting towards
this unpolluted dwelling which love has made a home.
" The one ewe lamb ; " and, says Nathan, with grim
emphasis, it is to be *slain* to feed the rich man's
appetite, for that is what it means. There is no death
but sin, and this fair innocence is to be slain, this pure
life is to be blasted, to gratify the covetous appetite
of a tyrannous rich man. Does not some lurid light of
revelation begin to break upon the mind of David as
the prophet speaks ? Does he not begin to perceive
what he means—that the lamb means innocence, and
that it is innocence, the modesty and chastity of an
uncorrupted nature, modesty once gone and gone
for ever, that he has sacrificed to his guilty passion ?
" The one ewe lamb ! " Does not our imagination, and
perhaps our guilty conscience, interpret all it means ?
Do we not see, as in some dream of horror and amazement, in some happy British home the fair bright face

of the one ewe lamb, the destined victim of the spoiler,
for whom shame and anguish wait, and whom the darkness and corruption of wicked cities shall swallow up,
and hide away in obscure and voiceless infamy? Oh,
do I speak to one who has committed such a wrong as
this? Let him tremble. Do I speak to one who has
stood upon the verge of such a sin? Let him loathe,
and hate, and despise himself. Let the vision of that
one ewe lamb rise before him, as the vision of the slain
Lamb of God, all pallid, dust-smeared, bleeding, shall
rise in the Judgment Day before the eyes of them who
slew Him, in the hour when all nations of the earth
shall wail because of Him! The Lamb of God—the
poor man's one ewe lamb—shall not Christ com-
passionate this poor slain innocence, and avenge His
own elect who cry unto Him day and night? Yes,
His own elect, elected to a purity man has made
impossible; to a love man has forbidden; to the
honour of a wholesome life man has devastated and
destroyed—oh! do not their wasted faces float upward, pale and ghastly, on the bitter sea of tears, and
their dying voices moan into the ears of Him who
made the heavens? This is the work of selfishness.
This is the most terrific exposition of what selfishness
can do in human life. Reduce the diamond to its
elements, it is soot; reduce such sin as this to its elements, and, brilliant and alluring as it may look to the
fevered fancy—see, it is blackness at the core, the most
diabolical and damnable of all sins which a man can
commit! And again I say, if you would be proof

against such crime as this, there is but one way—by overcoming self, by rising into that Christlike purity of manhood which is infinite in sympathy, in tendeiness, in thought for others, to which the thought of another's pain is intolerable, and another's shame an agony worse than death.

But it is not merely the selfishness, it is the *deceitfulness of sin* which is illustrated here. We can picture David listening to Nathan's story, with a keen sense of its artistic truth, its imaginative force, its dramatic power, and thrilling with sympathetic admiration as he listens. And the most striking moral lesson in the whole narrative, perhaps, is that David does not appear to have realised what his own sin was like till it was interpreted to him by the lesser sin of another man. There is a dreadful power in unresisted evil to stupefy the moral sense. Thrust your hand rapidly first into hot water and then into cold, and do so many times, and presently you are unable to detect which is hot and which is cold. The sensitive nerve grows callous, and its discernment is destroyed. So a man may experiment with sin till he feels no instinctive recoil from its abiding horror. The moral sense is like some delicate and sensitive instrument, which indicates with perfec* accuracy the tendencies of conduct so long as it is untampered with ; but once wronged its power is gone. It is like putting the clock back because we do not wish to know the hour ; the clock goes on working, but henceforth all its results are wrong. So the moral sense still works, but it strikes the wrong hour. It tells us what we want to hear, not what we need to hear, and what we know is true. Who has not been made conscious of this pliant perversion of the moral sense? You have not desired to believe a thing wrong, and you have soon succeeded in believing it almost right. You have first shaped your conduct, and then invented theories to justify your conduct. The justification of conduct rarely precedes the sin; men first sin, and then seek to justify their sin. Look back, young man, to that dark and well-remembered hour which has wrought such havoc in your life, and tell me if I do not chronicle your life aright when I sketch it thus. First came the divine shock of shame, the keen consciousness of wrong, the perfect truth told upon the clock of conscience; then, when the deed was done, followed the justification of the sin, and that process has gone on till some of you are now ready to argue that sins such as yours are venial and not to be avoided, and indeed are excused, and ought to be excused, by all reasonable men of the world. You have put the clock back, and that is why you cannot tell me the hour. That is precisely what David did. There was doubtless no trace of remorse or shame in David's face when Nathan began his parable. He had justified his sin, and the drugged conscience was fast asleep. It was not until the stern hand of the prophet put the clock right, and it struck with a tone that rang like the bell of judgment through the whole nature of the guilty king, that he saw the abasing vision of his own vileness, and cried, in the bitter horror of that revealing moment, "I have sinned against the Lord."

How true and striking this aspect of our subject is our own experience testifies. Watch how angry David grows as Nathan's story is told. He is the very incarnation of indignant justice. He is absolutely eager to punish the selfish scoundrel who has injured the poor man. The spoiler eager to punish the spoliator ? The villain burning with a fine sense of angry justice against the lesser villain ? It is even so. We can pluck out the mote from our brother's eye, and be utterly regardless of the beam in our own. We can pass sentence and applaud judgment on the cruelty of another, but our own cruelty we do not even perceive. It is not until some prophet focuses the light of judgment on our act, and puts before us what such sins as ours work in other spheres and other lives; it is not until we see our ungovernable temper reflected in the awful spectacle of the man upon the gallows, whose passion has carried him just a point beyond our own ; till we see our self-indulgence vividly illustrated in some broken drunkard shambling down to his obscure and shameful grave; till our solitary carnality takes a living, leprous shape and form in the corroding vice which poisons all the world with its reek of horror ; till our individual impurity stands typified in the wasted face of some wronged and shameful woman, lifted towards ours in dumb reproach beneath the city gaslight ;—it is not until this happens that the real truth about ourselves flashes on us, and the cry of Nathan,

"Thou art the man!" terrifies us with its heart-search-
ing accusation. And the accusation is true—you cannot
deny it. That infinite hell of human corruption into
which thousands of poor wretches drop off every hour,
pushed out of the ways of human honour, overwhelmed
with the black waves of infamy and anguish,—that
is your doing, O young man, sinning against purity
to-day! Thou art the man! The wave of shame
recoils on you, and covers you with its darkness. The
vast agony and horror of that shameful side of human
life we dare hardly name accuses you, and a million
fingers of the wronged and lost through all the ages
point against you, and their lips wail out your name.
No man liveth to himself, none dieth to himself, and
in the death of your purity the innocence of others
has perished. Numbers will not conceal you, solitude
cannot cover you, exile cannot hide you ; the blackness
of the night is as the light about you ; and like that
avenging finger which pointed from the heavens to
the spilt blood of Abel, the finger of Him to whom the
darkness is as the light points you out, and His voice,
pealing from the chambers of eternity, cries, "Thou art
the man!" God forgive the man who has doomed any
human soul to the long searing agony of a slain innocence. But to be forgiven the conscience must first be
roused. A man must perceive what he has done. He
must realise that his solitary sin has added something
to the weight of that intolerable load which crushes
down as in a living grave the blighted lives of multitudes. He must perceive that the cruelty of him who

takes the one ewe lamb, "and has no pity," is akin to the cruelty in his own heart; that by whatever dazzling name he has called his sin, it was nothing but base, devilish, hideous cruelty, such as a man might well be content to die in atonement for, if by his death he could restore what he has taken. Oh, terrible yet healing hour, when a man sees himself as he is, in all his unrecognised baseness and unremembered vileness, and cries, with breaking heart, "I am indeed the man: God be merciful to me a sinner!"

And once more we are taught the *Divine supremacy of conscience.* What was it made Nathan so fearless? Why was it the king quailed before his subject, whose life was altogether in his hand? We know well why it was. It is the ancient spectacle, repeated in precise form when Elijah stops the chariot of Ahab, and John denounces Herod to his face, and John Knox thunders in the court of Mary Stuart. We know that "conscience doth make cowards of us all." We know that a man standing on the right is mightier than kings, and that kinghood is impotent before such a man when kinghood is defiled. It was a pure conscience animated Nathan with dignity, and clothed him with a Divine royalty; it was an evil conscience which made David cower and tremble before his servant like a beaten hound. Some of you may perhaps smile at this talk of conscience. The hour of your awakening has not yet come—my voice does not penetrate your heart. But there is an hour when a voice mightier than mine will speak; when in the solitude of sickness strange

14

thoughts and memories will perplex the mind ; when in the embittered loneliness of an unloved life, the sun going down while it is yet day perchance, strange footsteps will seem to move about the house, and "in the dead unhappy night, when the rain is on the roof," strange yet remembered voices will fill the ears ; when, in the hour of death, from the grave of the unforgiven past strange shapes will rise, and throng about the dying bed, and wring their hands, and shriek their curses on you, and cry, "Despair and die!" And then you will *know what conscience is.* You. will know what a tremendous power of life there is in it, and how it can suddenly subdue and defy us, like a spring held back by force for years, which at last mocks our failing strength, and leaps up in derisive mastery. And there is an hour beyond that, when "we must all appear before the judgment-seat of Christ," and the Voice before which heaven and earth shall flee away shall cry, "Thou art the man!" And then conscience will become a terrific force, a companion who cannot be shaken off, a living terror which we cannot annihilate, while the *Thou art the man* of God rolls like thunder through the vast darkness which closes over us, and shuts us out from the vision and companionship of our Father who is in heaven. "Blessed are the pure in heart, for they shall see God ;" the impure shall not see life, "but the wrath of God abideth on them."

Finally, we have lessons of *retribution* and *reparation* here. There is forgiveness, but it is not possible without retribution and reparation. God's curse is

to fall on the house of David, and he who has slain
the innocence of the mother is to witness that saddest
of all sights, the dying of his own innocent little child.
And in some way—in bitter memory if not in public
shame ; in lifelong humiliation before God if not in
physical results of disease and sorrow—we must be
punished for sin. There is no salvation which promises
escape from that. It is for God to measure that
punishment, and appoint its methods ; let us be glad
that it is not man who judges us and afflicts us. If
we are sincerely penitent we shall not seek to escape
punishment. Nor shall we forget that it is for us to
do what we can in reparation of our error. Do not
pray to be forgiven and reinstated till you have done
that. Let him who has stolen not merely steal no
more, but restore fourfold. Let the cruel and passionate man humble himself before his victim. Let
the man who once fell into impurity give up his life
to rescuing the impure. God will not destroy while
fulfilment is possible ; let us seek to fulfil in sacrifice
for the world what we nearly destroyed in our wrong
done against the world. Are you penitent ? Do you
see as you never saw before the hideousness of your
sin ? Is your heart broken at the vision ? Listen
then to the words of the kingly penitent, written probably in those bitter hours when he mourned over his
dying child, and bowed before God : " The sacrifices
of God are a broken spirit, a broken and contrite heart
Thou wilt not despise. Hide Thy face from my sins,
and blot out my iniquities. Create in me a clean heart,

O God, and renew a right spirit within me. Restore
unto me the joy of Thy salvation. Then will I teach
transgressors the way, and sinners shall be converted
unto Thee."

Young men, I have specially addressed you because
I know that the temptations to unchastity in a great
city are numerous and incessant. I bid you remember
that an impure man is as shameful as an impure
woman, and should receive the same treatment; nor
will he find any difference of treatment with that God
who is no respecter of persons. The woman receives
her punishment here : the man will receive his hereafter. You are and will be daily tempted to unchastity
of thought and imagination, if not of act, and therefore
I pray you keep the mind pure. Do not listen to the
voice of unholy seduction. Learn to hate impurity
in thought, in speech, in gesture, in suggestion, in
literature, in life, with an invincible abhorrence. The
crown of manhood as of womanhood is chastity.
Respect and guard it in yourself and others with a
sacred vigilance. And to those who have fallen into
the snare, as to those who have resisted it, I preach
Jesus Christ: Christ in His purity, His tenderness,
His self-sacrifice, as the type of perfect manhood, and
I bid you follow Him. In Him is forgiveness for the
fallen, and strength for the tempted. In the abiding
sense of our love and devotion to Him is the best safeguard against sensual surprises, and the best impulse
toward the service of humanity. It was the vision of
the Holy Grail that lifted Sir Galahad into supreme

purity and steadfastness of manhood ; it is the vision of the living Christ Himself that inspires us ; and when that blessed Presence is an abiding presence with and in us, then, and then alone, our

> " Strength is as the strength of ten,
> Because our hearts are pure."

XII

"For we can do nothing against the truth, but for the truth."—
2 COR. xiii. 8.

ST. PAUL is writing to a Church in which grave
disorders have arisen, and he says he comes with
the mandate of God, and will not spare. He views the
office of the Christian minister as not only persuasive
but judicial. It is at once the most solemn, the most
awful, and the most responsible, which any human
creature can assume; none should dare to assume
it except upon the irresistible call of God, and none
who understand its privilege and burden rightly will
attempt to do so on any other call. The issues of life
and death for multitudes are in the lips of the Christian
minister, and none can tell how far his lightest word
may travel, or how much his invisible influence may
accomplish. Words are like the feather-seed, carried
afar on the wings of the wind over busy cities and
void valleys, but sure to fall at last and spring up in
prolific harvest. Influence is like the air that girds us,
—invisible, but stirred by the slightest sound or movement, and multiplying that movement. To all men
the power of speech and influence belongs, but to none

in more solemn degree than to the minister of Christ. Recreancy on his part is disaster to the whole army of God. If he dares not smite the wicked, if he is dumb when he should speak, or forgives where he should judge, or judges hastily where he should forgive, his defection weakens the whole Church of God, and what is sin in another becomes crime in him. He is specially set for the defence of the Gospel, and should be so completely under the guidance of the constraining love of Christ that he has the right to say: "I can do nothing against the truth, but for the truth." He is the vassal of the truth, and the measure of his consecration is the measure of his power.

But these words obviously command larger issues than any which are personal to Paul: they involve great facts which concern all men. What are those facts? Briefly these: that *revolt against the truth is wholly futile*; but that submission to the truth is the secret of peace and of service.

I. *The futility of revolt against the truth.*—Now there are two great truths against which the world has been in perpetual revolt: the one is the moral truth of God's government, the other is the spiritual truth of God's government by Jesus Christ.

(i) *The moral truth of God's government.*—That seems a vague and frigid phrase: let us try to translate it into living fact. What does it mean? What does it imply? It means that there is a living and a righteous God; that God's righteousness governs the world, and that all the strength of God is against evil. It means that He will reward righteousness wherever it is found, and that He will pursue with unfailing retribution the unjust, the unholy, and the wicked. That is the sublime belief uttered in every page of the Bible; it is announced at the threshold of the world as man crosses it into the life of action; it is elaborated at Sinai; it is glorified in the beatitudes of Jesus; it is the last note of the Bible, as it was the first, enforced in the words of John that there is a second death, and that without the gates of life are thrust the adulterer, the unclean, and whosoever maketh a lie. By that belief the noblest nations have lived, and the noblest periods of history have been the periods when that belief was most vigorously held. It has transformed slaves into peoples, peoples into heroes, heroes into saints. It regenerated Europe through the voice of Calvin, as afterward it regenerated Scotland by the energy and faith of Knox, and England by the voice and deeds of Cromwell. It vibrates in every word of the old Hebrew prophets, and is the foundation of the teaching of Christ. There is a God, and He is just; His sword is sharpened against iniquity. He rides upon the wings of the wind, and the thunder and the lightning go before Him; He maketh wars and desolations in the earth, and the hills shake at His presence; He is " angry with the wicked every day;" He is "glorious in holiness, fearful in praises, doing wonders." So sang Moses beside the Red Sea, when he had looked on the great deliverance God had wrought; so have sung the innumerable choir of just men ever since; so sing the spirits made perfect who are before the throne, for even there, there is a Song of Moses as well as a Song of the Lamb, the song of judgment as truly as the song of love, and both make one music in the ear of God.

Brother, do you accept or do you deny that truth ? Denying that truth, the world becomes an unintelligible riddle, a bitter mystery, a fathomless and maddening problem. Its sun is put out, its meaning gone, and it swings on through the wide spaces of the firmament like a lost star, a blind, wandering fragment of wreck and chaos. It becomes what Carlyle said the materialists made it—"a mill without a miller," whose wheels turn endlessly in the tide of the ages, but without purpose or result. There are those who have no better explanation of the universe than this. They are in revolt against the truth of the moral government of God. They deny what the wisest ages have believed, and deride the faith which made the greatest peoples great. And it is as though a child mocked the sun for shining, or lifted a finger to stay the passage of the hurricane, or bade the tide rise no farther on the shore; for such revolt is the madness of an empty pride, and is as futile as it is wicked. "We can do nothing against the truth : but for the truth."

(ii) The second great truth against which the world is in revolt is *the spiritual truth of God's government by Jesus Christ.* Christ stands before men as the embodied holiness of God, and His law of life is the law by which human holiness is attained. He proclaims His law of unworldliness, self-sacrifice, and self-abnegation, submission to God and service to man. Against that Divine Presence the world has been in perpetual revolt. The past sign of that revolt is Calvary; its present sign is the selfishness and un-Christliness of human life. Just as the one seemed triumphant long ago, so the other seems triumphant now. That blood-stained Cross, lifted against the lurid light of the darkened heaven, is the symbol of its ancient triumph, and the selfishness of human life is its symbol to-day. But long since the Cross has been answered by the sepulchre, and on the steep stairs of sacrifice Christ has ascended into universal supremacy. Do you remember what happened immediately after the entombment of Jesus ? The Pharisees had hated Him living, and they feared Him dead. And so they come to Pilate, and ask him to give them a watch to set around the tomb where the Wonderful lies silent. And what is his reply ? " Ye have a watch "—set it ; seal the tomb ; " make it as sure as ye can." How sure was that ? Was it prophecy or irony which animated Pilate's speech ? If the nations could be set in watch around that tomb, or the vast round of the firmament itself be the seal upon its doorways, how shall they restrain the Lord of Life —the Lord before whom Death had evermore receded, and who at last was destined to confront the dread destroyer, and

> *"—quell him with a breath,*
> *And lead him where He will*
> *With a whisper in the ear"?*

The revolt against Him was futile then, and it is futile now. The Cross *has* become the meeting-place of the nations, and He, being " lifted up," *is* drawing all men unto Him. There are those who resist that infin'te attraction, for whom the law of Christ is a law of folly, and the supremacy of Christ a phrase for laughter. They live only to get and gain, not to help and serve ; they rejoice in unrighteous laws, and oppose the law of sacrifice. They suck the poisoned honey-flower of vice, and drink the red wine of voluptuous pleasure, and hasten after the fatal fruit of Mammon, and " crucify the Son of God afresh." They crown Him with the thorn-crown of derisive malice, and offer Him the gall and vinegar of agnostic mockery. Some of you have done it. But again the voice of Paul speaks, and eighteen centuries have only added victorious confirmation to his words : it is a vain conflict, a futile and pitiful rebellion, a mutiny born in folly and ending in despair. Christ does reign, and is King already, and all power is given unto Him. " We can do nothing against the truth."

But it may be said, After all this is mere affirmation : where is the proof? what *is truth*? By what signs can we discern it ? One proof of truth, at least, is found in the *eternity of its life* : it is immortal. I do not say that error does not possess life, and long life ; but error carries the seeds of its own death with it, and its life at best is transient and intermittent. The truth is known by the indestructibility of its life. It is error that changes : truth abides.

Ask, for instance, what has been the history of

civilisation? It has been a history of the slow but certain conquests of truth. There have been periods when the world has seemed to have fallen asleep, and the centuries have passed by dark and silent with noiseless feet, or have been as a heavy tide whose slow and sluggish waves, with their mechanical rise and fall, have only lulled men into deeper slumber. No great voice has spoken, no heroic act has flashed an ennobling fire through the evil darkness, no Divine purpose has called the nations to its victorious crusade. Years have passed; years of languor, impotence, and sloth. Then from that vast slumbering host one head has lifted itself, and one man has seen a new light kindling in the far firmament. He has risen and announced his great discovery, and called on men to believe in it. Sometimes he has been a prophet with a new spiritual message for his age; sometimes a thinker, with a new and living word of wisdom; sometimes a student, who has kept his ear close to the beating heart of nature, and has at last perceived the rhythmic working of some great natural law, which for him has altered the aspects of the universe; sometimes a statesman, with daring schemes of government, which promise a new era of hope for subjugated peoples. What has been the history of such men and their discoveries? They have been disbelieved, ignored, persecuted; thrust into the dungeon or gibbeted for the scorn of fools. Their words have been fiercely debated; flung hither and thither as firebrands of contention and division, and the conclusions they set forth have been attacked by the enmity of ignorance, derided by the flippancy of folly, asserted with the enthusiasm of faith. But one thing has always happened : time has tried them. The error has proved itself error by perishing ; the truth has proved itself truth by living and triumphing. Astrology has perished, but astronomy survives ; alchemy has been dismissed as a cheating fantasy, but chemistry has grown into a mighty science. The scientific heresies of one age have become the ccmmonplaces of the next. Time, hoary and mighty, has stood like a gigantic thresher, and on the threshing-floor of the centuries has threshed out the wheat from the chaff, annihilating that which is false, and keeping only the eternal truths of things. Against the chaff he has been victorious, but he has been able to " do nothing against the truth, but for the truth."

"Thus it is that through the ages an increasing purpose runs,
And the thoughts of men are widened with the process of the suns."

The untrue thing proves its untruth by perishing, but the truth vindicates itself by living. Inch by inch the darkness has been driven back, and wedge after wedge of light has pierced its solid bulk, until the hour of its uttermost disintegration seems at hand. And so men have advanced from height to height of knowledge, and the dust of the centuries upon their feet is the crumbled *débris* of error, and the light upon their path is the broadening day of wisdom, and the banner which waves before their innumerable host bears this great inscription : " We can do nothing against the truth but for the truth ; great is truth, and it must prevail."

In like manner we say that one proof of the moral government of God is that the centuries assert it ; and of the spiritual kingdom of Christ, that the centuries have been unable to destroy it. No righteous government of the world ! The world a mere drifting chaos of anarchy and tumult ! Not thus does the wise man read history. Is there nothing in the history of nations significant of retribution ? Think how many great monarchies have arisen and covered the world with empire, and where are they now ? " Where are the snows of yester-year ? " Did ever empire seem more likely to endure to the crack of doom than the Roman ? Was there ever a people more splendid in resource, more victorious in achievement, more world-wide in ambition ? But they are gone ; how, and why ? They perished of excess of vice, they became loathsome with impurity, and then the invisible vengeance which had long tarried fell upon them, and all that mighty empire of the Cæsars fell like a house of cards, and crumbled like a pillar of dust in the desert. On all nations which become corrupt the same fate falls sooner or later, and on all men.

"The mills of God grind slowly, but they grind exceeding small;
  Though with patience He stands waiting, with exactness He
    grinds all."

Have we not before our eyes to-day the spectacle of a great nation shrinking into narrower and yet narrower bounds, forfeiting year by year the pre-eminence of the past, worshipping the " goddess of Lubricity," and careless of the God of Purity ; and what does the philosophic historian say about France? "France slit her own veins and let her own life-blood out on the day of St. Bartholomew, and has been perishing of exhaustion ever since." And what does all this mean, but that there is an avenging Holiness in the world mightier than man, which rules the nations with a rod of iron?

Or ask how is it that the spiritual empire of Jesus Christ has survived? The world has been leagued against it from the beginning. Rome, which tolerated all local religions, instinctively realised that this religion was more than local, and for three centuries did her best to crush it. She perceived that in the forlorn and famished missionaries of the Cross she had to deal with the agents and heralds of spiritual revolution. Against them, and their kingdom, men have done their worst. The key-note of revolt and hatred struck on Calvary has echoed through the ages. Kings have summoned their armies to destroy this kingdom; hell has loosed its flaming seas to overwhelm it. The world has blazed with stakes as the battle-field with watch-fires, and has rung with cries of anguish as the battle-field with death-cries. Yet the kingdom survives, and the fiery waves have fallen back quenched and impotent, and the wrath of man has passed like a waft of smoke, and the sun has shone out again in ever-brightening glory. The Christ survives. The wrath of man praises Him, and only serves to reveal and enhance His majesty. Scourged, crucified, dying, slain and sepulchred, Christ has still triumphed, and is the moral Emperor of the universe to-day. What does it all mean? It means that the kingdom of God in Christ is a fact, and cannot be destroyed : it is true, and men "can do nothing against the truth." Their fury is impotent. " Why do the heathen rage, and the people imagine a vain thing ? . . . He that sitteth in the heavens shall laugh : the Lord shall have them in derision." Oh, think of it !—the derision of Omnipotence, the dreadful laughter of Him who inhabiteth eternity, to whom this great world itself is but one dust-mote floating in the rays of His terrible and glorious light ! Who shall stand before that consuming fire of Holiness and Power? Let a man wrestle with the " live lightnings " and crush them in his grasp, let him chain the sun down that he shall not rise— then shall he also upset the chariots of God with the cords of pride he weaves across their path, and dethrone the Christ by the words of fury he utters at His feet! The whole rebellion of man against God is one wild spasm of despair : it is pathetic in its hopelessness, pitiable in its folly, sad in its very futility ; for the word which rings through the ages is : " We can do nothing against the truth, but for the truth."

Here, then, is that *aspect of terror* with which Jesus Christ confronts the world, and which is too generally forgotten. Meek as a lamb, gentle as a mother ; yes, but His is "the glory and the majesty and the power;" He is "the Wonderful, the Counsellor, the mighty God ;" " King of kings, the Lord of lords," the Judge of quick and dead. Are those dread ascriptions the poetic exaggerations of devout souls, or are they truth ? Do we modern Christians use them with any awe-struck sense of their sublime significance ? If we do, we shall not appeal only by the pathos of Christ's love, but by the greatness of His power. " Knowing the *terror* of the Lord, we persuade men." He is not a Presence meekly soliciting the suffrage of our pity; He demands the loyalty of our obedience. We have something more to preach than Calvary, something more to see than the Man of Love; who for love of the world had no place to lay His head ; we see the grave shattered at His word, and the heavens opened before the majesty of His voice. Is there nothing terrible in all that ? Dare we trifle with Him before whose face heaven and earth flee away ? Dare we treat Him with indolent disdain, before whom we must appear to answer for the deeds done in the body ? Dare we fulfil His demands with languor, or run upon His errands with reluctance ? Is there nothing in the thought of this sovereignty of Christ which gives pause to our foolish laughter, and fills us with a solemn fear ? And some of you come to sing His praise, and then go out to shape your life of pride and pleasure, and forget that His doom has gone out against such a life as yours. You defy Him before whom the keepers of the tomb were as dead men, and all the enmity of the ages but the foam upon the wave, which ebbs even while it rages ! O fools and slow of heart, know ye not *ye can do nothing*

15

against Him who is the Way, the *Truth*, and the Life ?

You can, of course, deny the truth, and defy it : in the ruined greatness of man made in God's image there is still power enough left to do that. So, too, you may deny the law of gravitation, but if you defy it, and leap from yonder steeple to illustrate your defiance, there is one sure result—the law triumphs and the man is slain. You can deny the penalties of vice, but if you defy them the slow poison will eat the heart out notwithstanding, and in premature old age, and broken health, and crippled intellect, they will vindicate themselves and be avenged on you. You may deny the movement of the earth, but the earth will go on moving, and the stars will go on shining in their calm and perfect strength, as though you had never spoken, and such an one as you had never been. There are certain things which have long since been lifted out of the realm of speculation into certitude. It is no brilliant conjecture which calculates the hour of the eclipse, or the track of the tornado. Why is it no one doubts these prophecies of science ? It is because we have discovered certain laws of the universe which are subject to no caprice, open to no revisal. They are not hindered by our malice, nor disturbed by our indifference or insolence. And so in the spiritual universe, when we see the same cause producing the same effect through the long course of various centuries, we know we have found a truth which is untouched by human transience, and unchangeable by human opinion.

When we see, through all the faded past of human history, Christ's love inspiring love, and Christ's light bestowing light, and Christ's life imparting life, we know that we are dealing with an unchangeable Force, and can forecast the spiritual future of the world with unerring accuracy. There is my warrant for preaching : the unchangeableness of the Christ I preach, and the absolute certainty that His power over men is unchanged too : " Jesus Christ, the same yesterday, to-day, and for ever." With Him we are omnipotent, for we " can do all things through Christ that strengtheneth " us : against Him we are impotent, " for we can do nothing against the truth."

II. And now take the second clause : " But for the *Truth.*"—The truth even prospers on our opposition. It has always been so in the day of persecution. The hurricane has carried the seed of truth afar ; the fire has purged the hearts of men ; the storm has destroyed the old building, only that it shall be replaced by a nobler and more stable structure. It is the very mockery of triumph : the very irony of victory ! God indeed holds His enemies in derision, when their best-planned revolt crowns His arms with new glory, and the very ingenuity of their hatred helps on His sovereign purpose.

But impotent as we are to assail the truth, we are all able to assist it. Do you say, how can that be ? How is it possible that the creature who can offer only futile resistance should yet be capable of effectual aid ? Can he who is impotent to thwart be strong to assist ? It is no empty paradox to reply that he can. You cannot hinder the truths of astronomy ; but think of it,—those high miracles of starry wonder shone unrecognised for ages, the mere street-lamps of the city of night, waiting for the man whose divine curiosity should pierce the curtains of their chambers ; and how much did that man do for the truths of astronomy who levelled the first telescope against the blue vastness of the midnight firmament ? You cannot hinder the truths of medicine; they are one and indivisible ; but the secret waits for the patient and splendid research of man ; and how much does that man do for the truths of medicine who, like Pasteur or Jenner, finds a new remedy for some hitherto incurable disease ? You cannot revoke the laws of science, they are the same to-day as when the dawn of the world broke ; but they lurk in silence, and wait the approach of the intellect of man, and the demand of his noble curiosity. You can destroy none of these forces ; but how much you can do *for* them ! It is even so with the kingdom of Jesus Christ. You cannot destroy it, but you can aid it ; you cannot overcome it, but you can spread it : the mightiest cannot hinder its certain victory, but the meanest can hasten it by his devotion, his valour, and his love.

Let our hearts rejoice, then : Christ's kingdom cannot be shaken. Think of the continuity of faith which has run through all the ages. Think of a Paul, an Augustine, a Tertullian ; think of Christian painters like Raphael and Angelica, Christian historians like Neander, Christian scientists like Newton, Christian musicians like Bach and Handel, Christian poets like Milton and Wordsworth, Christian martyrs in a hundred generations, and Christian saints in every century, and then ask : Is it possible that all these believed in vain ? Was the spring of all this heroism, the well of all this faith, the source of all this inspiration, a mere idle myth, a noble phantasy ? We are face to face with an age of doubt and denial. To-morrow the shrewd sceptic will propose his question to you. I give you a question to propose to him. Ask him—put it on no higher ground—simply, Is it *probable* that all the ages have been wrong, that at last Herbert Spencer alone of all living men should be right ? Is it probable—I put it on no higher ground—that this great galaxy of genius and goodness, this innumerable company of human spirits made perfect, who have found their joy and life in Jesus, —is it probable that they have all believed in vain, and that the nineteenth century agnostic alone is right ? Well, an *agnostic* is *one who does not know,* and the man who does not know we usually call an *ignoramus.* For my part, I decline to follow one who tells me he does not know ; and I prefer to believe that vast anthem of certitude which rolls upward from the saintliest and noblest hearts of all the world's great past : "I know whom I have believed, and am persuaded that He is able to keep that which I have committed unto Him against that day."

I call you, then, to loyal submission and noble service. Cease from a revolt which is impotent, enter into that allegiance with God from which shall issue peace and victory. Submission to God is the first step towards peace, and then comes love, which, turning its face toward God, becomes piety, and turning its face toward man becomes morality and service. Love has its rules, its restrictions, its bondage; but it is a golden fetter, and the lowliest service of love is better than the wildest liberty of revolt. Christ's "yoke is easy," His "burden is light;" for we have come unto Him and found rest unto our souls. Put yourself on the side of His truth, and then you will be clothed with an irresistible moral force, which will make you true helpers of the race, and invincible soldiers of the right. Then you will have a serene and unsubduable faith in the victory of the kingdom of Christ. Remember it has triumphed over greater odds than any now arrayed against it. Picture to yourselves, if you can, the young convert of Paul's day as he enters some great pagan city. On every side he sees the pomp of martial power, the luxury of sensuous life. There vast temples rise, and altars smoke to Jupiter; there philosophers dispute, and yonder go bright garlanded processions, with the sound of flutes and dancing, to unhallowed festival. Soldiers march with steady tramp, and everywhere the silver eagles of the empire gleam. But to him, poor youth, fresh from fast and vigil, lonely prayer and spiritual ecstasy, deep and humble pondering on

the lessons of the Crucified, all this seems strange,
sad, hateful:

> "He looks upon the city every side,
>   Far and wide,
> All the mountains topped with temples, all the glades,
>   Colonnades,
> All the causeys, bridges, aqueducts, and then,
>   All the men;"

and he turns away saddened and disheartened. Is it
possible all this can be changed; changed too by the
gospel of One called a felon? And then he turns
aside into some lowly street, and amid the humblest
people begins to preach that strange Gospel of Jesus
Christ. And what happens? In three centuries not
a heathen temple is left in Rome; the Cross has
everywhere triumphed over the eagle as love must
always conquer strength. The truth as it is in Jesus
was but as a little leaven, but it was sufficient to
leaven the whole lump of that corrupt pagan world.

> "And centuries came, and ran their course,
>   And unspent all the time
> Still, still went forth that Child's dear force,
>   And still was at its prime."

I call you to new and nobler enthusiasm for this
kingdom. Enthusiasm is the true fire of manhood,
the pulse of action, the soul of heroism; and when
that leaves a man, a church, a nation, its true glory
is departed. Empires are not won without self-
forgetting valour and devotion. "Paradise lies under
the shadow of the swords," cried the mighty Omar,
when he urged his armies to the death-grip; and we

want something of that magnificent frenzy which counts life worth having only for the accomplishment of great deeds. We are the children of a King; let the royal note of confidence fill our preaching, our praises, our life. We want the enthusiasm of that young minister who refused a hard and poor station, but that same night heard Bishop Simpson preach, and as he heard sprang to his feet, and cried: "Bishop, I will go anywhere for Christ now!" We want the enthusiasm which shames men of their niggard gifts, and counts no box of frankincense too precious for that Head which bowed in death for us. To be half-hearted in worldly things is folly, but to be irresolute in heavenly things is treachery and infamy. Oh, if that sacred tide of love of truth, and over-mastering love for Him who is the Truth, now rises in the heart, sweeping away all barriers of selfish prudence like films of shattered gossamer, do not restrain it, do not be ashamed of it; thank God for it! There is little enough of enthusiasm for the truth of Jesus in an England which saves annually two hundred and thirty millions of money, and gives a million and a half for missions; which spends one hundred and thirty millions in drink, and squanders thousands daily on the trifles of an unregarded luxury. And if this kingdom of Christ's truth is to change the world, to whom can I appeal more reasonably than the young men who for good or evil must shape the future? We shall not think we have done too much, or given too much, when Christ's trumpet peals. All the holy recklessness of generous deeds will be well rewarded then. The night is far spent, the day is at hand; already the heavens signal His approach, and His chariot-wheels are heard afar.

"O that each in the day of His coming may say,
I have fought my way through,
I have finished the work Thou didst give me to do!
O that each from his Lord may receive the glad word
Well and faithfully done;
Enter into My joy, and sit down on My throne!"

Fix this then in your minds; *you* can help the truth. The humblest life may be inspired and animated by spiritual honesty, by resolute sincerity, by dutiful allegiance to that which it recognises to be best and highest. The service of the truth is a bond whose catholicity includes all earnest souls through all the ages, and it utterly ignores all differences of social state or intellectual culture. The truth is served by the meekness of the saint and the boldness of the true reformer; by the audacities of genius and the patience of mediocrity; by the resignation of suffering and the valours of action; by the master spirits of humanity, whose voices rouse the world with trumpet-music; and the insignificant toilers, whose names are never known beyond the humble limits of the street wherein they have lived, and the church in which they prayed. One of the things most difficult for us to learn, and therefore most slowly learned, is that mere narrowness of circumstance can set no bound to our power of doing good, and that men of humble powers can serve the world not less efficiently than men of magnificent endowments. To the man of one talent the rate of usury is just the same as to the man of five; and he can make his life as noble as the lives of those who began with the larger capital of opportunity. A new Augustine may not read this page, but an undiscovered John Howard may; and who shall say which has served the world the better, the genius of Augustine or the sympathy of Howard? Do not plead then the disqualification of narrow powers or opportunities: you must serve the truth where you are, or nowhere; with the powers you have or not at all.

If you have ever gazed upon the Matterhorn, that lone and dreadful peak, thrust up like a huge black wedge into the everlasting blue, so steep the snow can scarce do more than powder it, so terrific in its grandeur, all other mountains seem huddled at its feet in terror, you will have thought that if ever there was a type of majestic strength it is the Matterhorn, standing there immutable since the beginning, and you will have pictured its mighty spire catching the first splendour of that first dawn when God said: "Let there be light!" But ask science to tell you how the Matterhorn was made, and it will tell you how, ages upon ages since, there were drifting mica-flakes floating in an abysmal sea, and one by one they came together, and were beaten into hardness and consistence, and grew in bulk and steadfastness, until at last the waters rolled back, and there was uncovered that vast Alpine tower against whose "imperishable spire" "the wild north winds should rage in vain, and the great war of the firmament should burst, yet stir it not." *   And even so Christ's kingdom is built up. Little by little, life by life, the kingdom grows. Out of weakness God brings strength, and humble things confound the mighty, and at last become the mightiest of all. It is built up inch by inch, until at last it rises mighty, impregnable, "and the gates of hell shall not prevail against it."

Shall our lives be added, as living stones, to this growing grandeur ? Shall they be fretted out in blind rebellion against this Rock on which men are broken, and which when it falls crushes men to powder ? For, or against ? But before we answer, the decree is fixed and is irrevocable : we may know the Truth, and the Truth will make us free ; but *we can do nothing against the Truth, but for the Truth.*

---

* Ruskin's "Modern Painters

XIII.

THE FATHERHOOD OF GOD.

"Philip saith unto Him, Lord, shew us the Father, and it sufficeth us. Jesus saith unto him, Have I been so long time with you, and yet hast thou not known Me, Philip? he that hath seen Me hath seen the Father; and how sayest thou then, Shew us the Father?"—JOHN xiv. 8, 9.

OUR subject of thought is Christ's conception of God; and to arrive at what we mean by that, I ask you to consider this question which Philip put to Christ, and Christ's reply. And as we turn it over the first thing we feel about it is, that it is extremely difficult to determine the spirit and temper in which it was uttered. It is at once acute and foolish: it may be the extravagant demand of an unbounded but mis-guided faith, or the vain demand of mischievous igno-rance. Perhaps we should not be far wrong if we assume that it was one of those foolish and blundering questions which the disciples often put to Christ, through their entire misconception of His person and His teaching. John, when he wanted Christ to call down fire upon his enemies; Peter, when he lectured Christ on the folly of the speech in which He anticipated crucifixion, both manifest precisely the same spirit as Philip does in reference to this question. They did not comprehend the majesty of Christ. They wanted to apply the test of a blind and brutal criticism to His most transcendent utterances of faith, of insight, and of imagination. Peter patronises Him; John is disappointed in Him; Philip controverts Him. They are perpetually reducing His poetry to prose, and punctuating His speech with the narrow ideas of a provincial intelligence. To His Divine height of thought they cannot rise, and therefore they try to drag Jesus down to their own miserable level. The picture is very human, and we can understand it, because it is just what men are doing still with the words and the teaching of Jesus Christ. They fail to see their infinite suggestion, their illuminating meta-phor; they invent a theory of theology which was never Christ's, and, by the wresting of solitary and isolated verses, try to make us believe that Christ taught what He could never even have conceived. When the words of Jesus suit their tastes, they recommend them to us with a patron's commendation; and when they do not, they either ignore them, or say that Christ was no doubt misreported in this or in that respect; and so Peter and John and Philip still give to us their muti-lated and imperfect Christianity, and the Christianity of Christ is recklessly forgotten, or wickedly obscured.

Now, for me at least, this much is clear, that I must take Jesus Christ for all in all, or not at all. It is nothing less than intellectual dishonesty to play fast and loose with the words of Christ, choosing what suits me, and rejecting as unauthentic what I do not care to hear or believe. Supposing I took up some book of

astronomical science, and calmly marked out all the
passages which I did not approve, not because I had
any wider astronomical knowledge than the writer of
the book, but simply because his conclusions upset
my preconceived conceptions of astronomy. Or suppose I re-edited Plato, or Xenophon, on the principle
of eliminating all passages that I personally disliked,
on the ground that no doubt they were unauthentic,
mere interpolations of some other and later mind.
What an outcry there would be! How the Press
would jeer at my supreme ignorance and egotism!
Why, they would say, on that principle no book is
safe. Milton may be re-edited on the plea that so
great a poet could not possibly have written such
poor theology ; and Bunyan, because no great English
writer ought to teach such a material theory of
heaven as he teaches. But if I said Milton's daughter
misrepresented Milton when she took down the mighty
lines from the lips of the blind old scholar, or that
Bunyan's fellow-Baptists had no doubt written portions of his works, especially the portions that I dislike, and therefore I eliminate such portions from his
works—if I did so, you would call me a blundering
egotist. You would be eloquent about the intellectual
dishonesty of a process which re-edited great authors
on the principle of leaving out what we disliked, and
retaining only that which we approved. Yet that is
the new criticism which men to-day apply to the
Gospel of Jesus Christ ; and I say that it is unfair, it
·is dishonest, and it is intellectually contemptible. We

must take Jesus Christ for all in all, or reject Him. But if we accept Him, we must accept the difficulties of the position, and be content to accept them. When Jesus Christ utters hard truths we must neither rebuke, nor correct, nor controvert them ; our duty is simply to take up the intellectual cross and follow Him.

Whatever may be said about the spirit of Philip's question, it is obvious, however, that it touches one of the deepest needs in human nature. Man desires to worship, if he can find an object worthy of his worship, and he cannot worship that which is unknown and unconditioned. If there be any power in the universe other than ourselves, we want to know that power, and we must know it. Professor Huxley has recently told us in *The Nineteenth Century* that he invented the familiar and popular term, "Agnostic," and he invented it because very early in life he found he could know nothing about that Divine Power which was said to govern the universe. And while he admits that religion has done much to elevate human conduct, he thinks that human conduct may now be safely trusted to go on by itself in moral evolution without any further interference of the idea of God at all. Do you think it can ? I do not. The ship does not go on when the fires are put out in the engine-room, and human conduct will not go on when the noble impulse of divine and personal relationship to God is quenched. When the fires in the engine-room are put out, the ship swings hither and thither in the trough of the sea, and it is drifted by the tide, or it founders in the tempest ;

and human conduct founders when the soul of man is bereft of God. I grant that there are men—who owe, however, much more to the influence of Christianity than they are conscious of or admit—I grant that there are men who still retain irreproachable character amid the decay of faith. But try your experiment on any large and general scale, and you will find that the loss of God means ruin to character and conduct. Occasionally the doomed ship can set a sail when the engines are silent, and may find some port and escape shipwreck ; but taking it as a rule, we know that the ship in which the engine fires are put out has no chance of any sail being spread or port being gained, and is pretty sure to founder in the darkness of the night. No ; the knowledge of God is the foundation of all noble human life, and to know God is the insatiable thirst of the human heart. We want to know what God is ; we want to know what God demands ; we want to know what God is to us, and what we are to Him ; and therefore it is one of the deepest cries of the soul of man which pierces through the strange speech of Philip when he says, " Show us the Father, and it sufficeth us."

Such, then, is Philip's question to Jesus Christ. Now let us look at Christ's answer to that question, and let us note : *The completeness with which Jesus Christ reveals to Philip this idea of the Fatherhood of God.* Now, when we speak of Christ as revealing the Fatherhood, what is it that we mean ? We have before us to-day a Bible—not one book but many books, ranging over vast periods of time, summing up the history of vast numbers of the human race, and in this series of books the Gospel of Jesus Christ is but a part, and it is a small part. In all the books known as the Old Testament there is comparatively little trace of this idea of the Fatherhood of God. God is strength, God is power, God is wisdom and purity, but not Fatherhood. His purity is the flame before which even the angels shrink dismayed,it is the essential light which no man can look upon and live. His wisdom is manifested in the governing of human destiny, His power in the up-rearing of the starry pavilion of the firmament, His strength in the mountains, which are His handiwork, and the sea, which is held in the hollow of His hand. A thousand images, sublime, terrible, majestic, bring home to us the conception of the supreme purity, wisdom, and majesty of God : it is a glorious conception, before which we quail with terror and bow in abject humiliation. One idea only there is running through the Old Testament which recalls us to a spirit of solemn content, that is, that God is at least manifested in the particular care He has for individuals of the human race. He talks with Enoch ; He comforts Jacob ; He counsels Moses, but it can hardly be said that love enters into these various relationships. He is Jah, Jehovah, terrible in strength ; He is easily offended, hard to be conciliated ; not a man that he should lie, nor the son of man that He should repent ; a Being to be served with awe, with trembling, with contrition, but not with free and filial affection. To

16

the mind of Moses I suppose that the idea of affection towards God would have seemed almost blasphemy; something little short of sacrilege and profanity. There are, no doubt, tender moods and moments in the Old Testament when the heart gushes out in lovely longings after God, and uses sweet and tender words of yearning. But take the Old Testament through and through, and the general impression given us of God is of purity, not pity; of majesty, not compassion ; of supreme, ineffable righteousness, and power, and wisdom —the God of the roaring sea, and the live lightning, and the tremendous thunder, not the Parent of little children who can claim His love and render in return their filial service. The Old Testament pictures God as a King, not God as a Parent.

And let me say that this idea of God still dominates theology and fills the thoughts of men. And I think it will not be difficult for us to understand why it is so. Before the Reformation, amid all the pollutions of Catholicism, there was one thing true and noble which it preserved, that was the idea of tenderness in God. When it paid homage to the Virgin Mother, when its poets sang lauds and chants in honour of the Nativity, when its painters painted with perpetual zeal the holy Mother bearing in her arms the infant Christ; when its priests placed upon the throne of heaven the Mother and weaved in her hair the seven stars of government, and placed in her hand the golden rods of empire, they at least did this—they preserved the idea of Divine pity, and tenderness, and compassion. That

is the great lesson that comes to us to-day from the
glorious pictures of Raphael and Murillo, and which
gives to them their ineffable grace and pathos. But
when the Reformation came, in its righteous indignation against the pollutions of Rome, it swept away this
idea of Divine tenderness; and the old Hebrew idea
of God, as infinite strength and majesty, was rehabili-
tated. The Parent disappeared, the King again became
visible. Calvinism built up its iron logic, and struck
the fear of God into the hearts of men. The fiercest
Psalms of David became the popular lyrics of the day,
and it was the God of battles who was again invoked
and worshipped. The God Cromwell worshipped was
the God of the Hebrews who was clothed with thunder;
the God Milton believed in was the Great Taskmaster
in whose eye he sought to live. The age demanded a
stern ideal of God to inspire the valour of the battle-
field, and the strenuous agonies of renunciation unto
death, and it found it in the ancient Scriptures of the
Hebrews. And that is the idea of God which still
prevails in every land where the Reformation was
triumphant—God is still worshipped with fear and
served with trembling. It is from the Hebrew Scriptures
preachers take their texts, and it is the Hebrew idea
of God which is set before the people. And what is
the result? At its highest, life is elevated by a stern
ideal of duty; at its lowest, life is crushed into a slavish
and joyless round of formality. But the ideal Christ
l as given us in the parable of the Prodigal Son, or that
of Paul when he says, "We have not received the

spirit of fear, but the spirit of adoption, whereby we
cry, Abba, Father"—this is forgotten; and so the joy
is taken out of piety and the sunshine out of life, and
instead of being Christians we are really Jews, permeated with Jewish ideas of God, and forgetting, if
not repudiating, the very different ideal of God which
is set before us by Him we call Master.

Do you say, then, What are we to do with the
Hebrew Scriptures? Are they not inspired? Yes;
they are inspired, in that they give us the history of
inspiration; they are the gradual unfolding of the idea
of God as man was able to bear it. It is no irreverence
for me to say that the God of Jacob is not my God,
because I am not Jacob, and Christ has taught me
infinitely higher views of God than ever Jacob had.
Jacob's God was a Being with whom he made bargains,
and Jacob's prayers are bargains made with God. My
God is the Father with whom I talk in friendly and
loving intercourse. It is no irreverence for me to say
that David's God is not my God: David's God was a
mighty King who blessed him but cursed his enemies,
and who would continue to do both one and the other
as long as His law was obeyed. David's God is not
my God, because Christ has taught me that the Father
makes His sun to shine upon the good and the evil, and
His rain to fall upon the just and the unjust, and that
He is no respecter of persons. Do not shrink from
admitting these statements: they are the statements of
Jesus Christ Himself. Christ took up the law of Moses
and rent it into shreds when He calmly said, " They

of old time said, An eye for an eye and a tooth for a tooth ; I SAY, Bless them that hate you, and pray for those that curse you " ; and One is our Master, even Christ. His ideal of God we accept, and not the ideal of any Hebrew patriarch or lawgiver, however eminent. That, at least, is Christ's claim. He does not destroy : He does something far nobler—He fulfils. He gathers up all that is true in the Old Testament, and interprets it and confirms it. Against all the voices of the past He opposes His majestic " I SAY," and closes all controversy. If I want to know, then, what God is, I must not ask Moses, but Jesus ; for Moses has resigned all authority unto Him to whom every knee shall bow, and of whom every tongue shall confess that He is God, to the glory of the Father. The revelation of God proceeds along one continually broadening line, from the imperfect to perfection, from the crude and the incomplete to the final and complete, till at last we hear the universal litany from the million-peopled earth rising upward in one continuous cry of trust and exaltation, " Our Father, who art in heaven." That is the revelation Christ gives us of God, and it is something more than a coincidence,—it is the seal of the perfect authority and knowledge of Jesus, that His first recorded word in this world was, " I must be about My Father's business," and His last recorded word was " Father," when He bowed His head in the agony of Calvary and said, " Father, into Thy hands I commend My spirit."

What is there then that is new in this revelation that

Christ makes to us of God?   Briefly put, it is this—
that He perceived that the ruling power of the universe
is not force, but love.   And what is love ?   We all
know what it is better than we can define it.   We
have had parents, and we know how our father
and our mother interpreted love to us ; we have
children, and we know how we think of them, and
what we do for them.   Let our mothers lift up their
work-worn hands and tell us how many stitches they
have put in little garments when the house was quiet
at night, and how many distasteful tasks they have
done for little feet, never finding them distasteful,
because of the power of love which animated and
inspired them.   Let our fathers stand up and tell us
how they have pinched themselves to purchase pleasure or education for their children, and how light
they have thought the sacrifice when they have seen
them growing up into vigorous and honoured life.
Let those who have children who have wronged them
—the father of the prodigal and the mother of the
outcast—stand up and say whether the latch of the
heart is not always lifted for the wanderer's return, and
what they would give if only they could fold their
lost child to their hearts again.   Let us know why it
is you keep that tress of faded hair in the secret
drawer, and why it is that distant grave is so perpetually in your memory.   Let the poets tell us of the
passion of love which many waters cannot quench, and
fill our ears with their unearthly wailing of distress for
vanished love, and their rapturous rejoicing in love that

finds its consummation in united lives. Whatever other forces there are that shape our lives in this world, love is everywhere the master-spring, and the deepest impulse of life.

> "All thoughts, all feelings, all delights,
> Whatever stirs this mortal frame,
> Are but the ministers of love,
> And feed his sacred flame."

Is that true of man ? Christ says it is infinitely truer of God. It is not that God is not just, for love can be just ; it is not that God is not strong, for love can be strong ; it is not that God is not pure, for love is purity ; it is not that God is not wisdom, for love is wisdom ; but it is that every attribute of God feeds the attribute of love, and love is the sacred flame which burns in the heart of the universe and illumines all the worlds. God is love, and, because God is love, God is light, and in Him there is no darkness at all. Every act of earthly love is but a gleam of light fallen from His nature, and is a hint of His unutterable love. What my mother was to me, God is to me, but with a wiser and tenderer affection than ever any earthly mother knew, or could know. Take parentage at its very noblest among men ; that is the type of God's parentage to us, and that is the truth that Christ came to reveal. That is the idea of God which He perpetually enforced ; and how divinely new and original it was you may judge by comparing His words with the words of Moses ; and you may judge also by the fact that, though 1,900 years have nearly passed away, the world is still startled by this thought of the Fatherhood of God, and still hesitates to accept it.

And the corresponding truth is that Fatherhood in God means childhood in man, and carries with it brotherhood among men. It is upon the basis of the Fatherhood of God that Christ founds all His doctrine, and if you take that away it will all collapse. When He tells me to become a little child, and to be born again, the truth that lies behind His words is that God is my Father, and loves me; when He tells me to love my neighbour as myself, He puts a new interpretation upon the word " neighbour ;" and it is only the common Fatherhood of God that can interpret it and justify it. If God be my Father, I have claims upon Him for protection and sympathy and pity, and He has claims upon me for love and obedience and service. God meets my claim when He tells me that the hairs of my head are numbered. He bids me meet His claim by " loving the Lord my God with all my heart and mind, and soul and strength." Force disappears and love reigns. Force is there still, just as force is the prerogative of the father, in the vigour of whose arm there is ten thousandfold greater strength than there is in the child's arm ; but love commands the force that is in the father, so that the arm that could crush defends, and the hand that could smite caresses. Prayer is no longer a bargain; it is the free intercourse of love. I do not ask certain gifts of God, and promise Him in return certain duties. The merchandise of love knows no

tariff. The child does not love the father because he
ought to love, but because he cannot help it. I love
God because He has first loved me. And so life
moves out of the shadow of fear into the atmosphere
of perfect sunshine. I love, and the world is all
sunshine to love. Why should I trouble about the
disposition of my life ? The Father knows what things
I have need of. Why should I fear sorrow or death ?
Whether I live or die it is nothing to me ; I am the
Lord's. " Who shall separate me from the love of
Christ ? Shall tribulation, or distress, or persecution,
or famine, or nakedness, or peril, or sword ? I am
persuaded that neither death, nor life, nor things
present, nor things to come, nor height, nor depth,
nor any other creature shall be able to separate me
from the love of God which is in Christ Jesus, my
Lord." So the great Litany ends in one long chorus
of rejoicing, and the hallelujahs of that chorus shall
reign for ever and ever.

" Show us the Father then," says Philip, " and it
sufficeth us." *What was it that Philip expected ?* Is
it some sudden unsealing of the heavens, some tremendous vision of the Omnipotent and Eternal ? Jew
as he is, with all the sublime words of the Hebrew
Scriptures ringing in his memory, words that set forth
the unapproachableness of God, the flame of His awful
purity which angels cannot look upon, the intense ineffable glory before which all the light of all the worlds
pales its ineffectual splendour,—can he suppose that
he is able to look upon such a vision ? Is it the

sublime defiance of despair which cries, "Let me see it, though I perish, so, at least, I perish sufficed and satisfied, and every doubt set at rest"? That, at least, has been the cry of noble human spirits who have sought by fast and penance, and arduous purification, to fit themselves for the vision of God, and who would have been content to die if they could but have seen for a single moment the vision of the infinite God revealed and made manifest to them. But it is not thus that God reveals Himself. The reply of Christ is : "He that hath seen Me hath seen the Father." That is to say, all that you can see or know of God is manifest in Jesus Christ. And what God is you may measure by what Christ was. Think of the hands that healed and the heart that loved ; think of the purity of Him in whom even His worst foes could find no sin or reproach ; think of the compassion which never tired of toiling for the ungrateful ; think of the patience which tolerated and taught the ignorance of men like Peter and Philip ; think of the tenderness for all weakness and the sympathy with all suffering ; and remember also the hatred of all injustice and tyranny and wrong that was in Jesus Christ. Picture that, and you see God. Perfect light we cannot see : "Light untempered would be annihilation. Light is only beautiful, only available for life, when it is tempered with shadow. Pure light is fearful and unendurable by humanity." And it is in the humanity of Christ we find that shadow through which the pure light of God is tempered to our vision. Happy he who sees that vision, to whom the shadow is a help to vision and not a hindrance, an interpreter of light and not an enemy, to whom Christ has no need to address the pathetic reproach of this text : "Have I been so long time with you, and hast thou not known Me, Philip ? "

"Show us the Father." It may be the cry of despair in the presence of the grim facts of nature. Men have said, "Where is there any sign of the mercy of God in nature ?" One of our greatest naturalists*—or perhaps I should be more correct if I said our greatest writer upon nature—has told us that nature cares nothing for man; she is blind and deaf; she does nothing for him, and she can do nothing for him; man must do everything for himself. The most trivial observer sees nature "red in tooth and claw with rapine," and is appalled at the ruthless cruelties of life; and Paul acknowledges that "all creation travails together in pain until now ;" and the anguish of the world is never-ending. Do you say, "Where is the Father in all this ? Is not the law of life sorrow, and is not life full of everlasting cruelties ?" Do you cry in despair, "Show us the Father caring for His creatures, and it suffices " ? Christ asks you, was *He* cruel ? Did ever any living thing suffer at His Hands ? Was not He a Beneficent Presence bringing light and healing everywhere ? Laws there may be, and must be ; but though the leper is in the highway, the paralytic in the temple, and the dead child in the home, Christ was a power higher than law ; and wherever He came there

* Richard Jeffries.

was healing for the stripes that law had made; and
wherever he came He asserted the supremacy of love.
That, then, is the nature of God. He overrules sorrow
and pain. He causes all things to work together
for good to those that love Him. He knows every
sparrow that falls to the ground, and perhaps in His
love there is compensation even for the sparrow's pain.
He shows us in Jesus Christ His living Fatherhood,
and it sufficeth us.

"Show us the Father, and it sufficeth us." Perhaps
it is with you the cry of vain curiosity. You want
a completer demonstration of God than I can give
you. You want to prove His existence with the
logical certainty of mathematics; you want to certify
it as you would certify a chemical experiment. The
answer is, that if you will but **try to understand** Christ
you will begin to comprehend God, and not otherwise, because He is the supreme demonstration of
Deity; He is the express image of God's person, and
the fulness of the Godhead bodily. You sweep the
firmament with piercing scrutiny, but the true star
shines over the manger in Bethlehem; you look for a
burst of splendour in the heavens, but the revelation
comes to you in a little Babe; you ask for a terrible attestation of power, God replies to you with the tender
attestation of love. It is not with the intellect that we
know God, and it is not to the intellect that God reveals
Himself, but to the heart; and when we love Christ,
through Christ the infinite God is revealed to us, and
we know Him whom to know is life eternal.

Or it may be the cry of the man who is overwhelmed with the sense of his own personal insignificance in the great sum of things, and who cries, " Show me the Father, and it sufficeth me." You realise the infinite multitude of men, and it seems altogether unthinkable that God can care for each one. So you might argue that it would be impossible that one sun could lighten every man that cometh into the world ; and yet it is done, and every day there are millions of eyes that rejoice in the same sunbeams. Because God is the Father, this sense of personal insignificance is destroyed for me. I am no longer a mere atom of life driven and drifted along the great vortex of time and death. I am an individual with a birthright and with a destiny. The father cannot help knowing his child, and the child the father. We move in the cognisance of the Father's eye, and the embrace of heaven is upon us. To mere power we might be mere atoms, unconsidered dust-motes, floating in the cold light of eternity ; but to love we are individuals to be loved with discriminating tenderness, and in the love of God we are sufficed and satisfied. Oh the sense of infinite peace that falls upon us when we realise for the first time that we are brought into personal relation as sons with the blessed Father ! And that you may realise now and here. This is the Gospel I preach to you, my brothers, that you may know the Father. That is the Gospel that Jesus Christ preached. There is no other gospel ; it is the Gospel that sufficeth men.

In the life of Henry Ward Beecher there is a very

striking passage. A young man wrote to the great
preacher and said to him : "I am sinking down into
the depths of shame : preach the terrors of hell to
me—anything to me—I shall be at the church next
Sabbath—anything that will save me." The preacher
said, "That night I preached about the Fatherhood
of God : I felt, if that would not save him, nothing
would." That is the Gospel of Jesus Christ to you,
my brother. Is it clear? Do we now understand
what it was that Christ wanted us to know about
God? Have we now grasped the great conception
of God that Jesus Christ would flash home upon
our spiritual intelligence? If you are not quite
clear about it, listen ! Listen to the words of Jesus
Christ Himself ; and they shall close my sermon for
me. This is His word about a wayward and dis-
obedient child : " But when he was yet a great way off,
his father saw him, and had compassion, and ran, and
fell on his neck, and kissed him. And the son said
unto him, Father, I have sinned against heaven, and in
thy sight, and am no more worthy to be called thy son.
But the father said to his servants, Bring forth the
best robe, and put it on him ; and put a ring on his
hand, and shoes on his feet : and bring hither the
fatted calf, and kill it ; and let us eat, and be merry :
for this my son was dead, and is alive again ; he was
lost, and is found. And they began to be merry."
There is the complete picture of Fatherhood, both in
its severity and goodness. Behold the severity which
will not allow men to fall without being hurt, and

ordains for prodigals who spend their substance in riotous living, the bitter pains and penalties of disobedience. Behold the goodness, which has compassion on them when they are yet a great way off, because they are still children dear to the parent's heart. They began to be merry, and the universe resounds with that Divine merriment, with that infinite and unspeakable joy still, when son and father meet. Do you wish to know what Christ wanted you to know about God? Turn to the fifteenth chapter of St. Luke's Gospel, and read the parable of the prodigal, and see there the conception of God that Jesus Christ carried in His own heart, and expressed in His own life, and preached to all who heard Him, and preaches to the world to-day, if we will but listen, if we will put aside the fears and darkness of a distorted theology, if we will but accept Him and find rest and satisfaction in Him. May we say: "Lord, it sufficeth us." "I will arise, and go to my Father."

XIV.

THE USE OF MYSTERY.

"And Jesus answering saith unto them, Have faith in God."—
MARK xi. 22.

THE incident of the cursing of the fig-tree is one
of the most remarkable and mysterious in the
career of Jesus. The impression which the occurrence
produced on the minds of the disciples we can readily
understand. There was something in this display of
power over nature which awed them more than the
healing of the sick or the cleansing of the leper.
Alone among the miracles this is a miracle of cursing;
but it is a curse upon inanimate nature, and for a
reason which seems sufficient. When Christ would
show the retributive aspect of His power, the bolt falls
not on a man, but on a tree; not on an enemy, but on
that which cannot feel loss, and yet may teach the
unspeakable lessons of what such loss means. For the
first thing we have to recollect about the miracles of
Christ is that they were never purposeless, and never
appealed to the mere terror or admiration of men.
Let there pass before the mind's eye the long array of
miracles, the great crowd of lame who leap, of dumb

who speak, of lepers who are cleansed, the mighty
pageant of stormy seas hushed into silence, and the
forces of a hitherto unfettered nature bound into
obedience,—and then ask, Did Christ work these signs
and marvels only to excite the curious wonder of
men ? It is because men have risen no higher in their
conception of what a miracle is than this, that they
have found it difficult to believe in miracles. But the
true signification of a miracle is that there was a new,
a supernatural, power in Christ to undo the results of
evil, to restore lost good, to set up a more beneficent
order among men, and at the same time to judge and
condemn men. The miracle is always more than a
marvel, it is a sign.

You will notice that Christ does not make the fig-
tree barren ; He simply seals its barrenness with the
curse of death. As it rises before the tired eyes of the
tráveller, with its tender green and promise of fruit, it
is a living deceit, and its punishment is a judgment on
deceit. In fact the only possible signification of such a
miracle as this, is that it is an object-lesson and index
of certain aspects of Christ's power which are generally
overlooked. The tree is stricken because its profession
is false, because it stands like a bold hypocrite chal-
lenging the praise of men, but mocking their expecta-
tions. Its true use was to bear fruit, and the life that
has no fruit is a life on which the doom of death must
fall, and ought to fall. Thus, then, the cursing of the
fig-tree is the exposition of the retributive power of
Jesus Christ, the Divine vision which discerns deceit,

17

the Divine power which punishes it, the Divine anger which consumes it.

But to the disciples there was another and more awful thought ; the miracle seemed to oppress them with a sense of mysterious judgment which they could not explain nor understand. It seemed to open to them a vision of those hidden processes of law which underlie the smooth surface of life, and only now and again startle us with their tragic force and swift display. Explain it how they would, the act of Christ was mysterious. And what do we mean by a mystery ? We mean something which we cannot explain by any process of reasoning or by any facts of knowledge, som.thing that baffles, that puzzles, that dismays us. For instance, we meet from time to time certain curious legends of ghostly lore—warnings conveyed in dreams, coincidences which se.m more than accidental, premonitions which stir the blood with terror, wailing voices in the air before the dea h of heroes ; as though some unseen mechanism in nature had suddenly acted, and along some hidden chords of sense there had flashed the subtle and supernatural presage. For such occurrences we have but one word—they are mysterious. Reason them away as we will, according to the knowledge of the laws of illusion which we possess, yet there is a point where no explanation is vouchsafed, and the mind can produce no satisfactory solution of the problem. Even so Christ seems to acknowledge that there are certain things in His actions, certain processes in God's providence and government, which must remain for ever insoluble to man. He does not explain the moral lessons of His miracle. He does not justify His act. To the curiosity of the disciples He replies with—a sublime silence. And yet it is not a complete silence. While He does not answer the query of the intellect, He addresses Himself to the question of the heart, and solemnly says, as though admitting all the spiritual difficulties of the disciples and sympathising with them,—" *Have faith in God.*"

Now let us mark how these words apply themselves to our modern needs. I use the word " modern," but in truth all human needs through all the ages are alike ; God and the soul of man alone abide. We often speak of an age of faith and an age of unbelief, as though at certain periods every one believed and at others no one did, and as though such periods were separated by distinct and arbitrary demarcations. But than this no assumption can be falser. The " thoughts of men are widened with the process of the suns," but the root-thoughts of men are always the same, and suffer little change. We tell ourselves that " had we lived in that great day" when Christ moved among men, belief in Him had been easy ; but I think that belief would have been certainly not less difficult, but more difficult, in the presence of the human than the Risen Christ. If we believe not Moses and the Prophets, neither should we believe though one rose from the dead. To have been born two thousand years earlier would not have helped us in the least degree towards belief. What these disciples saw is what we see : a sublime, unearthly

Figure, calling Himself the Son of God, moving with calm majesty and mastery through the crowded world, at once terrible and tender; doing things which make the unbidden tears fill our eyes, and things which make the heart stop with terror, and thus representing in Himself the "goodness and severity of God." What they saw is what we see: a world that is evermore a problem, conditions of society which shock and startle us, goodness interwoven with evil as clouds are mixed with sunlight, or the grey and crimson threads of silk in some strange and lovely fabric; a world where so much is unexplained and inexplicable that there is a perpetual call for faith, and a perpetual rebuke to the mere vain-glorious pride of knowledge. In so far the world has not altered one jot since Peter looked upon the fig-tree in curious and half-terrified amazement. We too have our fig-trees, our mysteries of law and judgment, our apparent anomalies in the Divine order. We too are often full of pained surprise, nay, more, of doubt and dread. And to us also Christ speaks, and it is no perfect explanation of the mystery He vouch-safes; it is indeed no explanation at all: it is simply the quiet voice of One who looks up through the opened heaven, and sees behind the rolling thunder-cloud and angry lightning the face of the Father in heaven, and, pointing to that vision of a throned and mighty Love, says, " Have faith in God."

Let the words be applied to *mysteries of nature* : for obviously this fig-tree, thus withered at a word, was a miracle of nature, appalling, startling, inexplicable. In

like manner we are face to face to-day with a vision of
nature which appals and thrills us. It is no arbitrary
or isolated miracle we behold : it is the vision of a
gigantic miracle slowly evolving itself through uncounted ages, the stairs of life widening as they rise
higher, the forms of life rising out of one another in
vast phantom-like procession, all life linked with life
from the lowest to the highest, and betraying its
relationship in a veracity of likeness beyond dispute;
and, above all, this gigantic process going on, as if of
its own will, with a pitiless, unerring precision, kind
only to the strong, pitiless to the strong and weak
alike. That is the vision of the mystery of nature
which confronts us to-day. Age by age the curiosity
of man has questioned nature, and the patience of man
has wrested her secrets from her. Like one who
penetrates into the vast silence of the mountain ice-
world, and brings back stories of what is there, so
marvellous that he who dwells in the valleys cannot
comprehend them, so a long line of great scientists
have returned from the secret places of nature, and have
startled us with the strangeness of their .revelations.
Little by little the great chain of evidence has been
welded together, and the inherited ideas of men have
perished before its force. But how have men received
such evidence ? What have they said ? What did
the world say to Galileo when he pierced the secret of
the stars, or Columbus when he calculated the secret
of the waters ? What did the Puritans say to the
revelations of astronomy ? What did our fathers say

when geology began to reveal the age of the earth, and
to lift the veil from a world not six thousand years old,
but six thousand times six thousand ? These revelations were to them little short of blasphemies, and
were resisted with intolerant disdain. They assumed
that all that could be known of God they knew, and
that any fresh knowledge was a delusion and a lie.
The little transcript of nature which they had prepared
was to them the charter of the universe, and to deny it
was to deny God. In a word, they had not faith in
God. They found it hard to learn the lesson of the
use of mystery. · They could not trust God to survive
the revelation of the scientist, and therefore they
treated science as necessarily opposed to God. Has
that temper quite departed ? Are not men's hearts
still full of fear, foolish fear, futile fear, because science
is revealing new mysteries in nature ? Do they not
act as though they were afraid God could not take care
of Himself ? And because they are afraid therefore
they are unjust and intolerant, for there is nothing so
unjust and intolerant as fear. What if our inherited
ideas of natural law do perish ? Truth must stand
whatever perishes. The God who has survived astronomy and geology will also survive biology and
evolution. "Have faith in God," says Jesus. There
are unexplored remainders of knowledge, and ever will
be : there are mysteries of nature which dazzle and
confound us ; and this is so, simply because the law
of progress, which applies neither to God nor to the
beast, does apply to man, and the discovery of igno-

rance is the condition of progress. And there are revelations of law and judgment which will some day come to light and will explain the things that are now mysterious, just as the lost line of some ancient poem, when we find it, gives us the clue and meaning long concealed. But whatever happens, " Have faith in God ! " Before the mountains were brought forth, or ever the earth and the world were formed, from ever-lasting to everlasting He is God. The word that opens the book of history is " In the beginning God,"—God creating, God thinking, God governing ; and in the end the last word will still be, GOD. And so our fear passes into faith, our confused darkness into light, as we hear from the great abyss of Time the breathing of a mighty Voice which says, " Why art thou disquieted in vain ? Be still, and know that I am God."

So, also, the counsel of Christ applies itself to the *mysteries of judgment in human life*, with which we are confronted. It was the mysterious judgment which had fallen on the fig-tree which perplexed the disciples. Suddenly and invisibly the blow had fallen, and there before them in the morning light stood the ruined tree, its foliage withered as with the fires of shame, its life and beauty brought to an ignominious end. And even so we look upon terrible dramas of human life which confound and perplex us. We see them among men. Here is a man at the very height of earthly prosperity and success. Suddenly he is withered. A mysterious judgment has fallen on him. In a moment his wealth has vanished, on the point of public triumph he becomes

a gibbering paralytic, in the full heyday of fame some
damning secret of his past life is ripped open, and his
career is ended. We pass him by and see in him a
monument of ruin. There is something pathetic in
his disaster which appeals to us, just as we can readily
conceive that the passer-by would find that there was
something pathetic in this* blasted tree, standing bare
and scorched, like a leper among its fellows, which
far and wide lifted their green boughs in the tossing
breeze and happy sunshine. What has the man done
that this appalling fate should overtake him ? Why
has this happened to him ? There are thousands as
bad as he, just as every hillside of Palestine had its
barren fig-trees which made a specious show of fruit.
Why was he selected for this overwhelming vengeance?
As we pass in the morning light, there stands this
ruined man, a tragic figure, an embodied mystery
of judgment, haunting our imagination with strange
thoughts, and suggesting painful reminiscences for
many a day. Who can explain it ? Christ does not.
He says, " Have faith in God," because it needs faith to
interpret judgment. Men sometimes question me about
the origin of evil, and ask me how I can satisfactorily
explain *that?* I cannot explain it, and I will not argue
with them. It is a baffling circle in which the mind
travels evermore, unresting and unrested, till at last
darkness closes down, and the fierce tension of the
brain ends in death or madness. Christ gives me a
wiser counsel when He says, Do not seek to know it.
Be content with such knowledge as is given, and have

faith in God, that He who has made the world, and in the beginning said it was "very good," will do all things well, and in the end will finish His work with a new heaven and a new earth, wherein dwelleth righteousness.

Or we see such mysteries of judgment on a larger scale among nations. Suddenly, as though smitten by a secret disease, nations wither away. Sometimes by the shock of unexpected battle, sometimes by the swift outburst of hidden and destructive forces, a nation is blotted out, and the morning light rises on a gigantic ruin, a smoking plain where Sodom stood, a wilderness of sand and lava where yesterday was Pompeii. Who can reflect on such a spectacle unmoved? Who has not had solemn and searching thoughts, which he has scarce dared to utter to himself, in picturing such a tragedy? Who does not say, It may be the nation was corrupt and deserved to perish, but see, the innocent suffer with the guilty, the babe perishes with the mother, the only son of the widow is trampled down on the bloody field, from which the man who made the war escapes; the bullet strikes the bravest and spares the guiltiest. Is this fair? Is this just? Is this the discrimination we expect of Deity, or is it the mere madness of wild chance, which sweeps like a storm, irresponsible and ruinous, across a land? And again the one reply is, "Have faith in God." Who are we to measure the methods of the Divine judgment, we whose judgments are so faulty, whose keenest discriminations are so full of error ? How do we know what recompense God has hereafter for those who suffer innocently in the overthrow of guilt ? How can we judge or foresee the Divine reconstruction which will presently arise out of the calamity which appals us ? He who knows nothing of surgery might denounce the inhuman butchery of the surgeon's knife : but science knows nothing of butchery,—it calls such work by another name, and says that though the knife be called severity the hand that holds the knife is mercy. National putrefaction is a worse thing for the world than national extirpation, and when God's judgments are written in flaming ruin across a land, there is at least driven home to the heart of nations the truth of an eternal Righteousness which cannot be mocked with impunity. In such hours of national crisis the greatest spirits learn to say as Emerson said of the American civil war, "I shall always respect war hereafter. The waste of life, the dreary havoc of comfort and time, are overpaid by the vistas it opens of eternal life, eternal law, reconstructing and upholding society." The sun rose upon Sodom as Lot entered into Zoar. There lay the blackened plain indeed ; but high above the drifting smoke-cloud which rolled upward from that glut of death, there rose the serene unsullied sun, the fair new day ; and so, once more, a quiet Voice calls us from the regions where the new day is being born and new nations are always being trained into greatness, " Be not afraid. Have faith in God ! "

The same counsel applies to all the social problems

which distract our times. Civilisation is the history of systems which have seemed perfect in their day, but which at last have borne no fruit of use or beauty, and therefore have withered away. We too stand amid the decay of social systems. The England of the knight has given place to the England of the worker, the wealth of inheritance to the wealth of commerce, the England of villages to an England of cities, and the time is full of the death-cries of the old and the birth-throes of the new. Do we despair? Does the future seem to us big with terror? Is there the stir of revolution in the air? No true Christian dare despair. The temper of Christianity is a wise optimism founded on moral certitude and faith. "The old changes, giving place to new," but nevertheless God does "fulfil Himself in many ways." He still sits above the Time-flood, and if we do believe in Him with all our hearts, fear will not afflict us with its shuddering and dismay: for amid the wreck of all human systems and kingdoms, we shall see that kingdom which cannot be shaken rising into everlasting domination. There is no sterner or diviner lesson which we need to learn than this, that throughout God's universe the one title to life is use, and when use ends the quick judgments of God destroy that which has already become a mockery and a fraud. But it is the misfortune of our ignorance not always to know, indeed seldom to detect, when the period of use is past in systems and institutions. To us they appear as the fig-tree appeared to the disciples,— still sturdy, still vigorous, lifting themselves up in pride and beauty, and we are unconscious that the spreading foliage covers no fruit, and that, measured by the only true test, the test of use, they are already worse than worthless. Oh, be sure of it, no institution, no system of society, no code of social order, has ever existed that was not in the first place justified by its uses ; and none has ever perished till its period of use was past, and already corruption had eaten out its heart. Amid the dissolution of old forms of society in which we stand to-day, this then is our hope,—God still rules, and He is just. He will destroy nothing that is worth keeping. He whose power guided and controlled the monastic age and the feudal age, will not forsake us in the vast democratic age which has now burst upon us. Let the old perish : let us embrace the new and salute without fear that strange dawn which grows upon us. For, as men hear out of the gray heights when the light is just breaking the chimes of some great cathedral tower, uttering silver voices, sacred music, holy anthems, carillons of hope, above the waking city and the sleeping earth, so we hear above all the movements of human society, in the hush of prayer, the voice of Christ speaking, and saying, " Have faith in God."

Or apply the counsel again to the judgments of a *Future world.* The very idea of faith implies that which is unseen, that which eludes the senses, and hence is full of mystery. If the judgments we see below be mysterious, how much more mysterious those that are beyond. How dreadful and overwhelming, almost too terrible for contemplation, is the idea of the final adjudication on all human affairs, the summing-up and completion of all human life ! How appalling that vision of barrenness confirmed in barrenness, and deceit fixed in unalterable revelation of its own nature, when God separates the sterile from the fruitful, the sheep from the goats ! What wonder that the eager eyes of men strain into the great darkness, and that we long to read the mystery. What wonder that the idea of individual life going on through endless æons some-times seems unthinkable, and the idea of age-long pain unbearable. What wonder, too, that a hundred instances of human lives—bad, but not wholly bad ; vitiated, but not quite vile ; failures, yet touched with some possibilities of success never ripened into activity on earth—suggest themselves to us, and we ask with tremulous hope what judgment shall the God of the whole earth pass on these ? What shall be said of those cursed by heredity,—the drunkard's son who became a drunkard, the harlot's daughter who is a cast-away ? What shall be said to those nurtured in crime, with but the faintest chances of good or know-ledge, and those chances snatched from them by the cruel irony of life and the uncharitable callousness of man ? How about those who wither and bear no fruit because no kind hand nurtured them when the sap of life began to flow, or trained them when the hour of leafage came ? It is thus our thought pierces into the unrevealed future, and flutters back again, like a bird that meets an icy air and is afraid and faint. We should not be human if we did not have such thoughts, if we did not sometimes feel what Wordsworth called the burden of this "unintelligible world."

These obstinate questionings are as old as human thought, and what answer is there to them? Simply this, " Have faith in God." There are many things God has not revealed, and they are hidden that we may learn to trust Him. The use of mystery is that it is the school of faith. We have to trust God's wisdom as well as His love, and accept the unrevealed in meekness as well as the revealed in thankfulness. We must submit our intellect not less than our heart to God, and serve Him with our ignorance as well as with our wisdom. Knowing God is Love, we must have faith in God that Love will not fail to do the uttermost of which Love is capable for every creature it has made, and to our murmurs and our tears the voice of Him who inhabiteth eternity replies, "What thou knowest not now, thou shalt know hereafter, for thou shalt know even as thou art known."

There are two or three lessons that remain ; and first we must grasp as the great vital truth of all religion, that God is good, God is wise, God is over all. There are nations which have cast out the idea of God, and have done it boldly. Greece, in her decline, denied her gods and brake their carven images. France in the fury of the Revolution spat upon the name of God, and would not retain God in her knowledge. We English-speaking peoples have never done that, but we have done that which is worse. We have said, " There is indeed a God, but His government is defective ; there are flaws in His order and errors in the process of His law; He orders, but He does not govern; He commands, but it does not stand fast; we praise His mercy and His justice, but we do really believe in neither of these things, and therefore, though we honour His name with public reverence, He has no place in our hearts, and no real rule in our lives;" and that is worse than saying boldly and defiantly, "There is no God." It is atheism set to hymn-tunes; it is atheism with the rags of worship left to cover its deformity and nakedness. This mere outward worship of a God who does not rule our hearts or inspire our lives, has no power either to bless or purify, to teach us courage in the conflicts of time or humility before the mystery of eternity. There is but one way of believing in God which brings us peace, and that is to believe in Him with all our hearts. If God is, we must needs believe He does all things well; if He does things ill, it is better for us that God should not be. To believe that God is over all, over all judgment, retribution, and calamity, and that He rules wisely, is the main article of any true and vital piety. Have you that faith in God? If you have it not, in very truth you have no God; you are without God, and without hope in the world.

And then, too, we have to learn that part of the discipline of life is faith. If all were known there would be no room for trust: for trust is the eye which sees Him who is invisible, the hand that pushes itself out into the unknown.

> " You must mix some uncertainty
> With faith, if you would have faith be.

The use of mystery is seen in the training of those facu l.ies of the soul which, like some of the fairest flow ers, thrive best in shadow, and, indeed, can thrive well nowhere else. We might desire a world without shadow, as men often desire a sky without cloud; but presently we should complain of the monotonous rigidity of the landscape, as men have often complained of the "cerulean vacancy" of Italian skies. Mystery is the shadow of God, in which the flower of faith prospers, and attains its utmost purity and fragrance. We have to recollect always that there is a larger life to come, and be content to wait its larger revelations. The man who lives in that spirit will find that the mysteries of life purify and elevate him, and teach him how to walk in childlike humility of soul, ever waiting for that hour when the day breaks and the shadows pass away. Such a man will be strong for duty because he is serene in spirit, and amid all the shocks and buffetings of earthly life, will learn to feel the spirit of those lines of Browning's, often on the lips of General Gordon, and so applicable to his steadfast and heroic manhood :

> " I go to prove my soul!
> I see my way, as birds their trackless way.
> I shall arrive! what time, what circuit first,
> I ask not : but unless God sends His hail,
> Or blinding fire-balls, sleet, or stifling snow,
> In some time, His good time, I shall arrive!
> He guides me, and the bird."

Lastly, Christ teaches us that *Faith solves all diffi-culties.* "Say to this mountain, Be thou removed, and be thou cast into the sea," and if thou shalt not doubt in thine heart, it shall be done! Inscrutable words! They sound like a splendid paradox, a brilliant exaggeration. What do they mean? Not that the mountain ceases to be a mountain, or that it is removed bodily into the sea; but that it ceases to be an obstacle, its grim menace is forgotten, its power to depress us is removed. This is the true work of faith. We cease to torture ourselves with questions impossible of answer, and are content to be numbered with the simple. We know not how, but we do know that all things work together for good to those who love God, and that it "shall be for ever and for ever well with them." We see the vast chaos of human society, but know there is a Divine Spirit who broods above it: we hear all the clamour and turbulence of men, but we feel the presence of One who holds the winds in His fist, and hushes the tumult of the people. Like little Pippa, in the famous poem, we walk through a world where base and bitter things abound, but we have become little children in our faith, and we sing:

> " The lark's on the wing,
> The morning's at seven,
> The hillside's dew-pearled,
> *God's in His heaven,*
> *All's right with the world.*"

THE END.

The Clerical Library.

THIS SERIES of volumes is specially intended for the CLERGY, STU-DENTS AND SUNDAY SCHOOL TEACHERS OF ALL DENOMINATIONS, and is meant to furnish them with stimulus and suggestion in the various departments of their work. Amongst the pulpit thinkers from whom these sermon outlines have been drawn are leading men of almost *every* denomination in Great Britain and America, the subjects treated of being of course practical rather than controversial. The best thoughts of the best religious writers of the day are here furnished in a condensed form and at a moderate price.

Eight volumes in crown 8vo are now ready (*each volume complete in itself*). Price, $1.50.

NOW READY—FOURTH EDITION.
300 OUTLINES OF SERMONS ON THE NEW TESTAMENT.

By **72** Eminent ENGLISH and AMERICAN CLERGYMEN, including

Archbishop TAIT.	Canon LIDDON.	Rev. Dr. H. CROSBY.
Bishop ALEXANDER.	Canon WESTCOTT.	Rev. Dr. Pres. McCOSH.
Bishop BROWNE.	Rev. Prin. CAIRNS.	Rev. Dr. M. R. VINCENT.
Bishop LIGHTFOOT.	Rev. Dr. M. PUNSHON	Rev. Dr. JNO. HALL.
Bishop MAGEE.	Rev. Dr. W. M. TAYLOR.	Rev. Dr. C. T. DEEMS.
Bishop RYLE.	Rev. PHILLIPS BROOKS.	Rev. C. H. SPURGEON
Dean CHURCH.	Rev. Dr. R. S. STORRS.	Rev. Dean STANLEY.
Dean VAUGHAN.	Rev. Dr. W. G. T. SHEDD.	Rev. Dr. A. RALEIGH
Canon FARRAR.	Rev. Dr. T. L. CUYLER.	*And many others*
Canon KNOX-LITTLE.	Rev. Dr. J. T. DURYEA.	

OUTLINES OF SERMONS ON THE OLD TESTAMENT.

AUTHORS OF SERMONS.

G. S. BARRETT, B.A.	J. OSWALD DYKES, D.D.	Canon LIDDON.
Dean E. BICKERSTETH.	E. HERBER EVANS.	J. A. MACFAYDEN, D.D.
Bishop E. H. BROWNE.	Canon F. W. FARRAR.	ALEX. MACLAREN, D.D.
J. BALD. BROWN, B.A.	DONALD FRASER, D.D.	Bishop W. C. MAGEE.
T. P. BOULTBEE, LL.D.	J. G. GREENHOUGH, B.A	THEODORE MONOD.
J. P. CHOWN.	W. F. HOOK, D.D.	ARTHUR MURSELL.
Dean R. W. CHURCH.	Bishop W. BASIL JONES.	JOSEPH PARKER, D.D.
E. R. COUDER, D.D.	JOHN KERR, D.D.	Dean E. H. PLUMPTRE
T. L. CUYLER, D.D.	Canon EDWARD KING.	JOHN PULSFORD. [D.D.
A. B. DAVIDSON, D.D.	Bp. J. B. LIGHTFOOT.	W. MORLEY PUNSHON.
ROBERT RAINY, D.D.	WM. M. TAYLOR, D.D.	M. R. VINCENT, D.D.
ALEX'R RALEIGH, D.D.	S. A. TIPPLE, B.A.	W. J. WOODS, B.A.
C. P. REICHEL, D.D.	H. J. VANDYKE, D.D.	C. WADSWORTH, D.D
CHAS. STANFORD, D.D.	Dean C. J. VAUGHAN.	G. H. WILKINSON.
Dean A. P. STANLEY.	JAMES VAUGHAN, B.A.	Bp. C. WORDSWORTH
W. M. STRATHAM, B.A.		

Copies sent by mail, postpaid, on receipt of price.

OUTLINES OF SERMONS TO CHILDREN.

With numerous Anecdotes. Crown 8vo. Cloth, $1.50. (Being the 3d vol. of the CLERICAL LIBRARY.)

"*These sermons are by men of acknowledged eminence in possessing the happy faculty of preaching interestingly to the young. As an evidence of this, as well as of the character of the teaching, it is only necessary to mention such names as those of* WILLIAM ARNOT, THE BONARS, PRINCIPAL CAIRNS, JOHN EDMOND, D.D., Drs. OSWALD DYKES *and* J. MARSHALL LANG, *besides many others."—Canada Presbyterian.*

"This book contains a very high grade of thinking, with enough illustrations and anecdotes to stock the average preacher for many years of children's sermons."—*Episcopal Register.*

"They are full of suggestions which will be found exceedingly helpful; the habit of using apt and simple illustrations, and of repeating good anecdotes, begets a faculty and power which are of value. This volume is a treasure which a hundred pastors will find exceedingly convenient to draw upon."—*N. Y. Evangelist.*

PULPIT PRAYERS BY EMINENT PREACHERS.

Crown 8vo. Cloth, $1.50. (Being the 4th vol. of the CLERICAL LIBRARY.)

The British Quarterly says: "*These prayers are fresh and strong: the ordinary ruts of conventional forms are left and the fresh thoughts of living hearts are uttered. The excitement of devotional thought and sympathy must be great in the offering of such prayers, especially when, as here, spiritual intensity and devoutness are as marked as freshness and strength. Such prayers have their characteristic advantages.*"

London Literary World : "Used aright, this volume is likely to be of great service to ministers. It will show them how to put variety, freshness and literary beauty, as well as spirituality of tone, into their extemporaneous prayers."

Anecdotes Illustrative of New Testament Texts.

With 600 Anecdotes. Crown 8vo, 400 pages. Cloth, $1.50. (Being the 5th vol. of the CLERICAL LIBRARY.)

London Christian Leader says: "*This is one of the most valuable books of anecdote that we have ever seen. There is hardly one anecdote that is not of first-rate quality. They have been selected by one who has breadth and vigor of mind as well as keen spiritual insight, and some of the most effective illustrations of Scripture texts have a rich vein of humor of exquisite quality.*"

The London Church Bells : "The anecdotes are given in the order of the texts which they illustrate. There is an ample index. The book is one which those who have to prepare sermons and addresses will do well to have at their elbow."

N. Y. Christian at Work : "AS AN APT ILLUSTRATION OFTEN DRIVES THE NAIL WHICH FASTENS THE TRUTH IN THE MIND, THIS VOLUME WILL PROVE AN ADMIRABLE AND VALUABLE AID, NOT ONLY TO CLERGYMEN, BUT TO SUNDAY-SCHOOL TEACHERS AND CHRISTIAN WORKERS GENERALLY."

N.Y. Observer : "A book replete with incident and suggestion applicable to every occasion."

Copies sent by mail, postpaid, on receipt of price.

EXPOSITORY SERMONS AND OUTLINES ON THE OLD TESTAMENT.

Crown 8vo, cloth. $1.50. Being the 6th vol. of the *Clerical Library.*

Containing Sermons by

W. ALEXANDER, D.D., BISHOP OF DERRY.
A. BARRY, D.D., PRIMATE OF AUSTRALIA.
DEAN BRADLEY, OF WEST-MINSTER.
STOPFORD A. BROOKE.

PROF. A. B. DAVIDSON, D.D., LL.D.
VEN.ARCHDEACON FARRAR.
CANON W. J. KNOX-LITTLE.
CANON H. P. LIDDON, D.D.
ALEXANDER MACLAREN, D.D.

GEORGE MATHESON, D.D.
JOSEPH PARKER, D.D.
DEAN J. J. S. PEROWNE.
C. STANFORD, D.D.
LORD BISHOP OF CHESTER.
DEAN VAUGHAN.

"*Rich in practical application, these Sermons will be an education and an inspiration to many.*"—N. Y. CHRISTIAN ADVOCATE AND JOURNAL.

PLATFORM AND PULPIT AIDS.

CONSISTING OF STRIKING SPEECHES, HOME WORK, FOREIGN MISSIONS, THE BIBLE, SUNDAY SCHOOL, TEMPERANCE, AND KINDRED SUB-JECTS, WITH ILLUSTRATIVE ANECDOTES FROM ADDRESSES. Crown 8vo, cloth. $1.50. Being the 7th vol. of the *Clerical Library.*

By

PREBENDARY AINSLIE.
W. ARTHUR.
BISHOP OF BEDFORD.
DEAN OF CANTERBURY.
BISHOP OF CARLISLE.
BISHOP BOYD CARPENTER.
DEAN OF CHESTER.
DEAN CLOSE.
R. W. DALE, D.D.

J. C. EDGHILL, D.D.
DEAN OF BANGOR.
BISHOP ELLICOTT, D.D.
ARCHDEACON FARRAR.
CANON FLEMING.
NEWMAN HALL.
DR. LIVINGSTONE.
BISHOP OF LONDON.
J. A. MACFADYEN, D.D.

R MOFFAT, D.D.
SIR W. MUIR, K.C.S.I.
J. PARKER, D.D.
W. M. PUNSHON, D.D.
PRINCIPAL RAINY, D.D.
C. H. SPURGEON.
A. MOODY STUART, D.D.
ARCHBISHOP TAIT.
CANON TRISTRAM.
And others.

"*Just the book to give to some overworked pastor who has many speeches to make, with little time for study, and less money to spare for new books. We have here a collection of some of the best speeches of many of the great platform speakers of our time.*"—CHRISTIAN.

ANECDOTES ILLUSTRATIVE OF OLD TESTA-MENT TEXTS.

With over 500 Illustrations and Index of Texts. Crown 8vo, cloth. $1.50. Being the 8th vol. of the *Clerical Library.*

"*It will be found invaluable to all preachers, teachers, and public speakers, as placing at their command a vast storehouse of incidents with which to enforce and fasten an idea or point a moral.*"—N. Y. CHRISTIAN AT WORK.

Copies sent by mail, postpaid, on receipt of price.